THESE DEADLY DREAMS

FATES

BOOK TWO

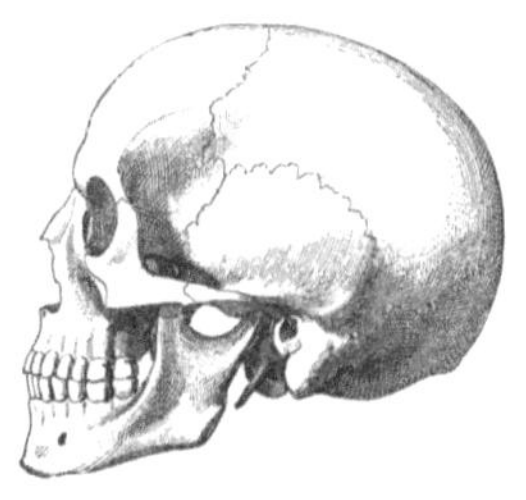

WHITNEY L. SPRADLING

Midnight Tide
PUBLISHING

These Deadly Dreams

Copyright © 2023 by Whitney L. Spradling

First Edition

ISBN 978-1-958673-55-3 (paperback)

Published by Midnight Tide Publishing | Midnight Tide Publishing

Edited by Sara Coombes | Sara Coombes

Cover by The Cobs | The Cobs

Midnight Tide
PUBLISHING

To my family...

Once again, I beg you, if you are in any way related to me, please put the book down. I really hate awkward encounters, and that is exactly what will happen the next time we see each other if you read this book.

I appreciate the support, but DO NOT READ THIS BOOK!

Thank you.

Content Warning

This book contains adult themes that may not be appropriate for all audiences. These themes include: violence, graphic sexual scenes, CNC, language, drug/alcohol use, torture, blood play, and mention of past non-consent encounters and sexual assault.

This is a why choose romance, meaning the main character will end up with at least three guys by the end of the series. If you enjoy tattooed bad guys who'd do anything for their girl, MM relationships, and plenty of heat, then join the fates in These Deadly Dreams.

National Domestic Violence Hotline

If you or someone you know needs help, please call the National Domestic Violence Hotline at 800-799-7233. You are not alone. Help is available.

To the beaten, broken hearted, and downtrodden...
To the misunderstood, marginalized, and unloved...

Find your wings and fly.

1. Ellis

There are moments in your life that don't quite seem real. I felt that after every interaction with Sam, my abusive, rapist ex-fiancé. I also felt that upon learning I had a beloved, a mate, and was soul-bonded. Now, I'm having that feeling again.

I'm not sure my limbs are connected to my body. It's possible I'm floating, untethered to the ground under my feet. Or perhaps I'm dreaming and everything that has happened in the past few weeks was just part of my imagination. Maybe my subconscious hopes and desires have manifested this crazy dream world as a way to escape the nightmare of my life.

I mean, that would make more sense than it being reality.

If I were to sit down with someone and tell them my story, they would probably have me committed, and I wouldn't blame them. It's hard for me to believe, and I've lived it.

"Harpy?" Kai echoes.

I look to my left, to my beloved. My dark and dangerous vampire. His gray eyes are trained on me, his usually pale skin even paler. The black strands of hair falling across his forehead stand out in stark relief against the white.

I look to my right, to my soul-bonded. My sweet and caring

mage. His violet eyes are wide with disbelief. His hand squeezing mine almost painfully.

I turn and look behind me, to my mate. My reserved and secretive wolf. His icy blue eyes bore into me, like he can peel back the layers of my skin to see what makes up my insides.

The disbelief and uncertainty are palpable in the air. The silence stretches on, each second making it heavier and heavier. My bestie is staring at me like she doesn't know who I am. Her great aunt is shaking her head, like she can't believe she's looking at something known to be dark, deadly, and horrendous.

"Bullshit," Sterling spits from behind the couch, breaking the silence. "Harpies are myths. And even if they were real, there is *no way* Ellis is one."

"I have to agree," Cade said slowly. "Ellis is the opposite of what a harpy is. She is light and peace. Joy and love. She is nothing like a harpy."

Harpy. A creature of fairytales. A bringer of death and destruction on wings of wind.

Aunt Madge shakes her head at the guys, but she looks at me when she speaks. "The portrayal of harpies in history morphed from the truth. It happened long before any of our times, and the truth has since been lost to history. A harpy's job is to keep the balance between good and evil, but the means by which they do so is sometimes violent and horrendous."

"Hold up," Kai says. "You are seriously suggesting harpies are real?"

The look Aunt Madge gives Kai could freeze the blood of a demon. "Harpies are very real, boy. You'd do well to listen and learn." Only once Kai nods his head in apology, does Aunt Madge continue. "Not much is known about the truth of them. Throughout our history, the majority of times harpies have had to get involved, have been to stop an evil force from gaining too much ground. The one time it was the opposite, where the force of good had to be stopped, is the reason harpies are so feared."

Aunt Madge glances at her niece and without speaking, Allie

knows to get her grandmother a glass of water. While Allie is in the kitchen, Aunt Madge continues. "The story is that the Star Elves were only years away from attaining true peace in the world. It had been a long and difficult fight, but the forces of evil at that time were on the verge of extinction. Unfortunately, a world without evil cannot exist. There must be a balance, or the world will fall to stagnation. Without something to struggle against, our world would collapse from within."

Allie returns with a glass of water and Aunt Madge takes a drink. "A harpy named Maeryrea, was sent to stop the Star Elves from obtaining their victory. Unfortunately, the balance had been so far skewed in the favor of good by this point, the only way to bring it all back to equal, was to destroy the Star Elves. The entire race."

"That's why Star Elves are a myth. They used to exist, but no longer do." Cade sounds amazed as he works through the logistics. "So, Maeryrea restored the balance, but got a bad rap because she destroyed an entire race of beings who dedicated their lives to good."

"It wasn't just Maeryrea that got the bad rap," Aunt Madge clarifies. "That was the catalyst that turned all harpies into horrible creatures. But, they aren't. They do what they have to to preserve the balance."

"And you think Ellis is a harpy? A being meant to keep the balance?" Kai asks.

"I don't think so," Madge sharply. "I know so. Without a doubt, Ellis is a harpy."

"I'm supposed to be the balance between good and evil?" I breathe. "How is that possible?"

"That is a good question, and one I do not have the answer to," Aunt Madge replies. "What I can tell you, is that you were brought into this world to bring balance. A harpy only exists if there is a need."

"But what need?" I ask, my voice taking on a shrill tone. "Shouldn't I know these things if I'm a harpy?"

"Think about it, Ellis," Aunt Madge says calmly. "You can't look at your life and tell me there isn't a need?"

I'm silent for a moment while I process her words. I mean, yeah. My life has been a living hell up until recently. But that is just my life. No one else was impacted, so how is there a need to balance good and evil?

"I've been saying something bigger is going on," Cade says. "There's more to Kennedy and Sam's desires to get their hands on you than just to cause you pain."

"Is it possible they know she's a harpy?" Sterling asks quietly.

I rest my elbows on my knees and let my head fall forward into my hands. "I don't see how, seeing as I had no idea I was one." My words are muffled by my palms. This is all too much.

I'm shutting down. A coping mechanism my body hasn't needed to use since I met my guys. My heart rate slows and my breathing matches it. Numbness forms in my hands and feet, slowly spreading up my arms and legs. I'm burying my consciousness beneath layers and layers of fog. All so I don't have to deal with what's happening to me.

Kai must pick up on my rapidly shifting emotions because he turns to face me and grabs my hand. "I think we have heard about all she can handle right now. Her heart is sluggish, like she's shutting down."

He uses his fingers to turn my head so I'm looking at him, only I'm not looking at him. I'm looking through him. Not registering anything around me.

"Shit," he curses. "Her skin is like ice. We need to get her home."

I'm barely aware of Cade and Kai standing, pulling me up with them. Someone's arm is around my waist, but I'm not sure whose it is. They lead me through the house and to the front door. Before we pull the door shut behind us, Aunt Madge says one last thing.

"It's not a warehouse you're looking for. Search for the sale of a building that caused a lot of discontent in the community about ten years ago."

Cade mumbles his thanks, and the guys shuffle me to the car.

———

I DON'T REMEMBER the drive home or the walk to Kai's room. Everything is blurry and muffled around me. Almost like I'm existing underwater and the rest of the world isn't. It's like I'm moving in slow motion as Kai leads me to the bathroom and sits me on the counter.

"Hey," he says quietly, gently taking my face in his hands.

His gray eyes swim in my vision, but they register through the fog. My beloved.

"It's okay, baby girl." His voice sounds strange, echoing inside my head. "We're still here and we're not going anywhere. We'll figure this out together, okay? You're not alone."

I don't really comprehend his words, but his voice is soothing. It's like a melody that sings to my heart. Vaguely I hear water running, and soon the bathroom is filled with billowing steam. It's like whatever in my brain is leaking out into the world.

Kai lifts my arms over my head and Cade steps into my narrow field of vision. His violet eyes hold mine as he pulls my shirt over my head. Something slithers down my arms and I look to see my bra fall to the floor. Cade lifts me from the counter and helps me keep my balance while Kai slides my leggings and panties down my legs.

It doesn't click in my head that I'm now naked in Kai's bathroom. I hear the rustle of clothing and the sound of lapping water, but I'm too stuck in my own head to care about what's happening. Cade leads me to the edge of the sunken bath and Kai, who is already naked and in the water, lifts me up and slowly sinks into the heat with me tucked against his chest.

Instinct has me cuddling closer to him. He holds me tightly which I'm thankful for. I think if he let go, my body would float away. The hot water seeps under my skin and into my muscles. It feels good, and it starts to draw me out of the fog. Slowly...very slowly.

A naked Cade slides into my vision, sitting next to Kai, taking my legs and placing them in his lap. His violet eyes pierce deep into my soul, offering me a ladder to climb back to the surface. I'm not quite ready yet, though. His hands rub up and down my legs, a tether to the real world I hold on to so I don't get lost.

After seconds, minutes, hours, days—I'm not really sure—I realize my fingers are grazing the skin of Kai's chest. It's smooth under my finger tips. Warmer than usual in the heat from the tub. I press my palm flat and his heart thumps steadily. In my own chest, my heart echoes his. The two beat together, twin drums forever fated to beat as one.

I raise my gaze to catch his. His gray eyes are shining as he watches me. So much emotion in that look, it makes my breath catch. I cut my gaze to Cade, and his violet eyes hold the same. Love, adoration, wonder, amazement. It's all there. Laid out in their eyes and the way they hold me, like I'm something to be cherished and protected. Like I'm not some mythological monster sent to cause chaos and destruction.

Cade's hands rub a little higher on my thighs, curving inward as they do so. My breath hitches, and by the smile gracing his lips, he knows exactly what he's doing to me. He's pulling me out of the fog. Bringing me back to the present.

"Come back to us, baby girl," Kai whispers in my ear.

I shiver despite the heat of the water and my back arches involuntarily. Kai's hand travels up my back to my neck where his fingers trace over his mark. Heat courses through my blood, a need only they can satisfy. Kai tangles his fingers in the strands of hair falling out of my messy bun, and he forces my head back. My eyes flutter shut. Anticipation grows as I wait for his lips to brush against mine. He doesn't make me wait long.

The kiss is slow and gentle. It's a reminder of everything waiting for me in the present. More of the fog dissipates as the kiss deepens and his lips pry mine open. I eagerly brush my tongue along his, tasting him, a flavor that is distinctly Kai.

Cade's hands continue their exploration of my inner thighs. Each touch pulls me further away from the claws of my subconscious. I break away from Kai to look at Cade. His gaze is heated as his fingers dance perilously close to my center. In the water, I'm almost weightless and it is no effort at all to let my legs fall apart, inviting him in. He doesn't take the invitation though. Instead, he moves his hands away, and I pout.

His chuckle washes over me as his hands trail up my hips and over my sides. Desire burns through me. My body craves more of him. More of both of them. He cups my breasts and rubs his thumb over my nipples, gently at first then increasingly harder until I'm gasping and arching into his touch. Kai's fangs drag along the side of my neck and I let my head fall to the side, eager for the rush of euphoria his bite gives me.

He places a gentle kiss on my pulse point before his fangs sink deep into my skin. I cry out as the pain turns to pleasure and burns straight to my core. The pleasant ache of Cade's thumbs on my nipples is magnified, the touch almost so good it hurts. He bends down to suck a nipple into his mouth and he grazes his teeth along the sensitive flesh. I grasp his hair in my hands, unsure if I want to push him away or pull him closer.

My core clenches with each pull Kai makes on my vein, and it's still not enough.

"Please," I beg. "I need more. I'm so empty."

Cade pinches my other nipple before sliding his hand down my abdomen and slowly slipping his fingers through my folds. I arch off Kai's lap but he brings his arm around my middle to hold me in place. When Cade finally slips a finger inside, I'm panting and needy. I clench around him as Kai pulls more of my life force into himself.

"You want more?" Cade asks in a deep, gravelly voice that makes me shiver.

"More, please, Cade. Give me more."

"Anything for you," he whispers, gaze burning as much as the fire in my veins.

He pulls his finger out and I make a sound of protest that is quickly cut off as he adds two more fingers. He thrusts in and out, while Kai continues to feed from me in long, slow, pulls. Everything is intensified with Kai's fangs buried deep in my neck, I know it isn't going to take much more for me to tip over the edge.

Cade curls his fingers, rubbing that magic spot that makes me see stars. With nothing but Cade's fingers and Kai's fangs, I tumble over the cliff of ecstasy with my head thrown back and a scream on my lips. They slowly draw me through my pleasure while Kai licks away any excess blood, shivers running over my skin at the contact.

Hands rub up and down my arms and legs. I'm too blissed out to notice what hands belong to whom. My head rests on Kai's chest, and I close my eyes, exhaling a huge breath as my limbs go lax.

Kai kisses the top of my head. "Are you back with us?"

Unable to form words, I nod my head and attempt to burrow deeper into Kai's chest.

"Glad to have you back, love." Cade leans forward and kisses my forehead before standing.

I can't help it. I peek an eye open to catch the sight of his naked body dripping water. His cock stands proudly at attention and his eyes appear to smolder when he notices me looking.

"I'm not sure she's had enough, Kai. She's looking at me like she wants to eat me." He glances at Kai and smirks. "Then again, so are you."

It takes monumental effort to tear my gaze from Cade's body, but I manage to lift my head and glance at Kai, who is indeed looking at Cade like he wants to eat him. And shit, I'm all for that.

"Okay, fuck. This is happening." Kai stands and throws me over his shoulder in one movement.

I squeal and his hands lands on my ass with a stinging slap that makes me clench my legs together. From this angle, I have the best view of his tight ass as he climbs out of the tub and walks into his room. I can't help myself. I drop my hand down and give that tasty ass a squeeze. His step falters before he brings his hand down in another stinging slap.

I don't have time to react. He tosses me onto the bed without any warning. I shriek as I fall, my stomach swooping. Landing in a naked, wet heap on the soft mattress, I swipe a few curls from my eyes and my gaze snags on the boys standing shoulder to shoulder at the foot of the bed. Damn. I really got lucky when I was fated to these beautiful creatures.

Kai is leaner than Cade, but his muscles are no less impressive. His lithe frame speaks to how fast and flexible he is when completing impressive feats, like scaling buildings and jumping from roof to roof. And those tattoos. Mouthwatering doesn't begin to describe all that black ink covering his chest and arms and creeping up his neck.

Cade, on the other hand, looks like he was carved of marble with his cut muscles and tan skin. I feel so protected in his strong arms, safe from every danger in the world. His ink is colorful, compared to Kai's black and gray. His left arm is covered in swirling cosmos that I could get lost in.

When my gaze finally tracks up their beautiful bodies to their faces, they're both grinning at me.

"I think she likes what she sees," Cade says. He crawls up the bed, his gaze traveling over my naked body as he does so. "I like what I see, too," he whispers against my mouth.

He kisses me. It's almost enough to pull me from the thought that pops in my head. Almost. But it's not enough. The thought grows until it's all I can think about. How can they possibly like what they see? I'm a fucking harpy. A monster. They should be running in the opposite direction.

Kai settles next to me on the bed and tugs me away from

Cade's mouth with a firm grip on my chin. "What's with the melancholy? Is Cade that bad at kissing?"

A smile tugs at my lips briefly at his words. He knows as well as I do how absurd that question is. The smile doesn't last though.

"Ellis, baby girl, what are you thinking right now?" His gray eyes search mine, like he is trying to read through the emotions to the cause.

My lower lip wobbles, and I press my lips together to hide it. They see it though, and shadows float through their eyes. I take a deep breath, swallow the lump in my throat, and prepare myself.

"How can you guys still want me?" I ask. My eyes burn, and I know I'm seconds away from crying.

"How the fuck can we not want you?" Kai asks, blunt as ever.

"I'm a monster," I whisper, unable to say the words aloud. It's like if I voice them, it will make them true.

Cade's eyes flash with anger before he blinks and it disappears. His thumb traces my trembling lower lip. "I never want to hear you say that again. There are real monsters in this world, and you are not one of them," he says firmly. " Despite everything that has been done to you and everything you have been through, you never once let them turn you into what they are. There is no one more pure and beautiful in this world than you."

The tears threatening to fall, spill over at his words. Kai brushes one from my temple with his knuckle. "You see past our darkness and accept us for what we are," he says quietly. "How could we not do the same for you? Ellis, you could be the biggest, baddest monster in Lustros and we would still burn the fucking world to the ground to be with you."

I slap a hand over my mouth to contain the sob that climbs up my throat. Their words. Their acceptance. Their support. *Their love.* That's what this is. That's what this flutter in my chest is. *Love.* I love these guys. In this short amount of time of knowing them, I have fallen in love with each of them. I think I would have fallen for them even without the bonds that fate placed on us.

Kai's eyes shine as he reads my emotions and the truth of the words that I just admitted to myself. He smiles and nods. "I love you, too. And if you're a monster, Ellis, then you're our monster."

Cade brushes more of my tears away and kisses me gently. "I love you, too, Ellis. Nothing will ever change that."

The guys settle down on either side of me, tucking me close to their chests, tangling their legs with mine. The sense of safety calms my racing heart. Nothing can hurt me if they're here.

Kai pulls the sheet up over us before kissing my forehead. "Get some rest, baby girl. We'll be here."

I fall asleep to their hands brushing over my skin, cocooned in their warmth, and wrapped up in their strength and love.

2. Malakai

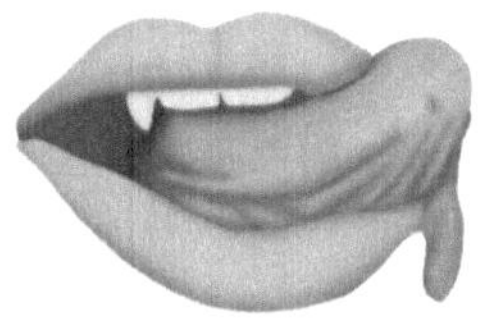

Waking up in a pile of tangled limbs with warm bodies pressed together is how I want to wake up every morning. Nothing beats it. Except waking up in a pile of tangled limbs, warm bodies pressed together, and a hand slowly working my cock.

I groan softly and thrust my hips a little, pressing into the hand. It's Cade. I can tell by the size. Ellis's hand barely wraps all the way around. I keep my eyes closed and let him draw forth my pleasure. It's hard to keep silent, but I don't want to wake Ellis, so I force down any moan that tries to escape.

I never imagined my life would lead to this. Yeah, Cade and I have fucked in the past. A lot. But it was always just a way for me to get my emotions under control, to let out the anger and frustration that builds in me until I feel like I'll explode. Maybe there has always been a secret part of me that wanted it to be more, but it wasn't until recently that I started noticing Cade in a different way.

When Ellis came into our lives, and she made it clear she enjoyed watching us together, it was a natural decision to give her what she wanted. I had never let myself read his emotions, especially when we fucked. Maybe that was the first sign I felt something more for him. That little bit of fear of what I would find if I let myself read him.

Now, I open myself up to his emotions. I let them wash over me, and holy shit. The force of his longing hits me like a ton of bricks. Under that initial layer of desire, I detect faint traces of emotions I've only ever felt directed toward me from Ellis. Caring. Love.

My hands fist in the silken sheets on my bed—sheets that smell like Ellis and Cade—and I groan out loud this time. Cade's thumb rubs over the tip of my cock and I curse.

"Fuck." I open my eyes and find Cade staring at me with a sleepy smile and hooded violet eyes. Sexy motherfucker. "Fuck," I curse again.

Gently, I untangle myself from Ellis and climb over her to lean over Cade. One of my hands goes to his throat while the other grabs his hip. Our mouths crash together in a bruising kiss. Tongues battle for dominance and our hips thrust against each other, looking for friction.

He grabs the back of my head and pulls the strands of my hair and I almost lose it. His body is rock hard under mine, his skin warmer and so enticing. I break the kiss and move to his neck, grazing my fangs along his throat. I want so badly to bite him. I always have. He groans and his cock twitches against mine. Interesting. Maybe he wants it too.

I move lower, licking and nibbling my way over his chest, down his abs, lower. His hand in my hair tightens and he closes his eyes and exhales as I lick up the length of his cock. I lap up the bead of precum at the tip and swirl my tongue, making his hips lift off the bed. When I take the head of his dick in my mouth and suck hard, he groans again and his jaw clenches tightly.

I get to work, sucking and licking, scraping my fangs gently which drives him wild. He is panting and sweating when I finally notice Ellis is awake. We were so lost in each other we didn't notice. I glance at her and find her watching us with lust filled eyes while her hand moves between her legs. A beautiful rosy blush covers her body and her chest rises and falls almost as rapidly as mine and Cade's.

Cade still hasn't noticed, so I slide his cock out of my mouth and say, "We have an audience."

Cade's eyes pop open and he grins shamelessly at Ellis.

"Don't stop on my account," she says, mimicking what I said the first time I walked in on her and Cade.

I slap her hand away and replace it with my own. Whoever said men can't multitask have never seen a man presented with a dripping wet pussy and rock hard cock both begging for attention.

Ellis moans at the same time Cade does as I slip my fingers inside her and swallow down his cock again. The chorus of their groans and breathing, complimented by the wet sounds of fingering and sucking, is erotic as hell and my own cock is aching for attention.

I can't take it anymore. Watching both of them receive pleasure from my hand, my mouth, has me coming undone. I pull back and grin at both of their expressions. Pouty and disappointed. I chuckle darkly as I get up and walk to the bar, grabbing the bottle of lube I keep there. When I turn back to the bed, both of them are staring at me.

"What are you waiting for, Cade?" I ask darkly. "Show our girl how you can take care of her."

He grins before climbing atop Ellis and kissing her passionately. She wraps her legs around his waist and pulls him close. Idly, I stroke myself as I watch them for a few minutes. It's sexy as fuck, and does something to me. Watching my beloved and my best friend together brings me a joy I never thought possible. When Cade pulls back and lines himself up with her entrance, I walk to the side of the bed and run my hand over her collarbone and down her breast.

I pinch her nipple right as Cade slides inside. His hard length disappears into her, and she makes a noise somewhere between a sigh and a moan. Bending down, I kiss her while Cade slowly pumps in and out. Watching them is almost as enjoyable as joining them. Almost.

I trail my hand over Cade's shoulder and down his back as I climb on the bed behind him. With a hand on the back of his neck, I push him lower onto Ellis to give myself better access to his ass. He starts when I slide a lubed up finger between his cheeks and circle his hole before pushing a finger inside. I tease him, making him grunt while I stretch him for my dick.

"Damnit, Kai. Just fuck me already," he growls.

Well, how can I say no to that? I grab Cade's hips with one hand and my cock with the other. He slows his thrusting long enough for me to push inside him. We both exhale slowly as I slide in. My eyes are shut tight, heightening my other senses. Heavy breathing, hearts racing, scents of sweat and arousal in the air, Cade's ring of muscles squeezing me tightly. It's all perfect. I slowly pull out and push back in, making sure Cade is ready. When he is, he begins thrusting into Ellis again, sliding off my cock, before taking it again as he pulls out of Ellis.

Cade rocks back and forth between us, and I lock gazes with her. She's flushed and sweaty, eyes heavy lidded and a smile spreading across her face. Her breathing quickens and my heartrate kicks up, matching hers. I know she's close just by that alone.

The sounds of flesh slapping and moans of pleasure fill the air. I can smell all three of us, sweat and arousal, our scents mixing and twining, drawing us even closer together. The very thought causes my movements to falter. How I could have something so incredible with both of them is unbelievable. It's powerful, exciting, and terrifying all at once.

Acting on instinct alone, I let my fangs lengthen further before I grab a fistful of Cade's hair and yank his head to the side. Without warning, I sink my fangs into his neck and latch on, sucking his blood into my mouth. He curses and as the pain morphs into intense pleasure, his thrusting falters. His blood tastes good. Not as amazing as Ellis's, but dark and rich, like spiced wine.

Ellis's eyes are wide and trained on the point where my lips are sealed around Cade's neck. Each pull on his vein causes him to jerk. His breathing increases rapidly and his muscles start to tremble. I use my own hips, thrusting hard into his ass, to make him move again.

He snaps and begins fucking Ellis with enough force and speed to push her up the bed until her head hits the headboard. Her fingers curl around the top of the wood and squeeze hard enough I swear I can hear the wood groaning. The sight of her coming undone, with her head thrown back into the mattress and her throaty screams as she orgasms, sends me over the edge. I suck hard on Cade's neck and slam into his ass until we both come as hard as she did.

Somehow, Cade and I manage to collapse to the side so we don't crush Ellis. All three of us lay in my bed while our breathing and heart rates settle and the sweat cools on our skin. When I'm sure I can stand and walk to the bathroom, I grab a washcloth and a towel to gently clean up both of them before collapsing back into the bed with Ellis between Cade and me once more.

Their breathing evens out and I glance over to see them sound asleep. I smile and close my eyes. Guess we wore ourselves out.

―――――

"WHERE'S STERLING?" Ellis asks later that day as we lounge in the library-turned-man-cave.

Cade is back to researching property sales after the tip Aunt Madge dropped before we left. Ellis is sprawled on the couch with a book laying on her chest, more interested in watching me than reading. I'm in the corner of the library where our workout equipment is set up. From the mirror, I have been able to watch Ellis as I lift, and she didn't turn one page of that book before she eventually gave up pretending.

"Probably out for a run," Cade replies without looking up from his laptop. "He does that when he has a lot on his mind."

I set my weights down and grab a bottle of water from the mini fridge. "You haven't talked to him yet, have you?"

She shakes her head. "There hasn't been any time."

She worries her bottom lip between her teeth, and I walk over and tug it out with my thumb. I bend down to kiss her but she puts a hand on my chest and wrinkles her nose.

"You stink. Go away."

She gives me a slight shove and I chuckle darkly before tackling her into the couch cushions, rubbing my sweaty body all over her. She squeals in disgust and tries to squirm out from under me, but I'm so much bigger than her and she gives up with huff. Mission accomplished. I got that dark look to fade from her eyes and I distracted her from her worries.

I stand and study her with a random thought floating through my head. "Hey, can we test something?"

"Test what?" She narrows her eyes at me and doesn't move from her spot on the couch.

"Just humor me." I grab her hand and pull her up before dragging her over to the mats on the floor. "I want you to hit me," I say when I turn to face her.

She looks at me like I've lost my mind. "Hit you? Why would I do that?"

Cade finally looks up from his laptop and gives me a look. "Did you notice that, too?"

"Notice what?" Ellis asks.

"I thought I was imagining things, but I'm not so sure." I ignore Ellis and reply to Cade. "Especially if you heard it as well."

"Heard what? Hello? I'm standing right here." Ellis waves her arms around and dances on her feet in front of me "What the fuck are you guys talking about?"

"I think you might be showing some supernatural abilities, besides being able to use Cade's magic," I say.

"What do you mean?" She studies her hands like she can see the supernatural strength flowing through them.

"This morning, while we were fucking, you grabbed the headboard and I swore I heard the wood cracking. I just assumed I was imagining things, but if Cade heard it too, I'm starting to wonder if it really happened." When she just stares at me with her hands palm up in front of her, I wink at her. "Come on, hit me. How often do you get a free shot at me? Take it while you can."

She rolls her eyes and releases a breath. Half-heartedly she throws the sloppiest punch I've ever seen. She hits my stomach with barely any force.

"Really?" I ask, raising one brow. "Do I need to get Sterling in here so you can break his nose again? I know you can hit harder than that."

With a flat stare, she squares up and throws a punch at my middle. I tense my abs on instinct and exhale when she hits me. Still, she didn't hit as hard as she could.

"Do I need to do something to piss you off? Maybe I shouldn't be surprised." I give her an evil grin. "You are only human after all."

That did it. I see the fire light in her amber eyes. She clenches her jaw and sets her feet. Her form is on point, pivoting at the hips for maximum impact. Her right arm curves in a hook straight for my face.

Her fist connects with my jaw with the force of some kind of supernatural beast. My head is thrown to the side and my body follows, slumping to the ground. Pain explodes in my jaw and I instantly taste blood.

"Holy fuck," I mumble while holding my now broken jaw.

Stars dance in my vision, but I hear Ellis gasp. She kneels in front of me with her hands pressed to her mouth.

"Oh my gods, Kai. I am so sorry." Her hands flutter over me, afraid to actually touch me.

I groan and close my eyes. Damn. That seriously hurts. My

heartbeat echoes in the side of my face where it's already swelling, the same rapid pace as Ellis's.

"Here," Cade says and pulls my hand away from my face. "Damn woman, you did a number on him."

Through my closed eyelids I see the violet glow of Cade's magic before his hand runs over the side of my face. The uncomfortable squeezing sensation of being healed replaces the throbbing from Ellis's punch.

When Cade steps away I open my eyes and see Ellis crouching across the room with her wide eyes trained on me and silent tears streaming down her cheeks.

"Shit," I mutter and walk over to her. "Hey, I'm sorry. I shouldn't have made you do that." I sit on the floor next to her and scoop her up in my arms. "I should have found another way to test you."

She looks at me through watery eyes before collapsing against my chest in great heaving sobs. I look at Cade as he sits on the floor beside us. His expression mirrors my own. Hopelessness. Desperation to make her pain go away. There isn't a lot we can do though. So we sit with her, we hold her, we rub her back. We let her know we're here, no matter what.

When her tears run their course, she sits up and rubs her face. "I'm sorry," she whispers. "This is just so much to take in. I feel like I don't even know who I am anymore."

My senses are shut down but the strength of her feelings seeps through anyway. She is so lost and confused. She's scared, and slipping back into the place she was in when we first met her. When she was stuck with an abusive fiancé and a father who didn't care.

"Ellis," Cade says gently as he brushes curls away from her face. "You are not alone in this. Please don't forget that. We are here for you, and we will be here for you until the end of time. Nothing will change that. Together we will figure out what's happening and we'll get through it. This won't last forever."

I hum agreement in the back of my throat. "A cabin in the

mountains with a crystal clear lake surrounded by pine trees. That's where I want to live when all of this is over."

"Just the four of us," Cade continues. "A whole cabin to ourselves, in the middle of nowhere. No one to bother us. Just snow, cozy fires, and hot chocolate."

"And lots of sex," I add.

Ellis huffs a small laugh, but I can feel her disbelief. I can only assume she's still wondering why we want to stay with her. Somehow we're going to have to find a way to prove to her the truth of our words.

"Come on, let's go to the kitchen," I suggest. "I've heard Cade makes an amazing chocolate cake."

3. Ellis

Baking a cake with a mage and a vampire is exactly what I needed to get out of my own head. These two are able to make me laugh even when I'm surrounded by the deepest shadows. They have a way of making me feel like I matter and that I'm cared for. Their words can only do so much to ease my fears, but their actions fill in the spaces where that fear festers.

"What the fuck is the difference between baking powder and baking soda?" Kai asks as he holds up the two containers side by side.

"Baking soda is sodium bicarbonate," Cade answers as he measures and pours ingredients. "It's an alkaline salt compound that creates carbon dioxide gas when mixed with an acid. Baking powder is a mixture of sodium bicarbonate and an acid, like cream of tartar, which requires moisture and heat to activate."

I can't help but giggle at the blank stare Kai gives him at the explanation. It doesn't help that he has a bit of flour on the tip of his nose.

Cade chuckles as well as he leans over and licks Kai's nose. "They help make the cake fluffy."

"Could have just said that," he mumbles and wipes his nose off with his sleeve.

Cade opens a container with a brown powdery substance inside. With the lid off, I catch a whiff of the most heavenly scent.

"Is that coffee?" I ask, leaning forward to get a better sniff.

"Espresso powder. The secret ingredient in my chocolate cake."

I'm pretty sure I'm drooling as he scoops out a large helping of espresso powder and adds it to the rest of the ingredients.

"Kai, can you crack the eggs?"

Cade tosses two eggs to Kai without a care of dropping them. Of course, Kai catches them with his supernatural reflexes. Reflexes I apparently have, too? I push the thought away and don't let it ruin the good mood the guys have brought out in me. Kai studies the eggs like he has never seen them before.

I watch with amusement as he holds one of the eggs above a separate bowl Cade provided. He struggles with cracking it. First, tapping the egg too lightly, then way too hard. The shell shatters and egg splatters everywhere.

"Son of a bitch," Kai curses. He looks down at himself, covered in flour and egg, and sighs.

"You're a regular Martha Stewart aren't you? Do you need help?" I ask, sliding off the stool to stand next to him.

He looks at me and relief flashes through his eyes. "Yes!"

He grabs my waist and slides me in front of him. Cade hands me another egg with a chuckle, and I crack both eggs without getting a single shell in the bowl. I look over my shoulder and grin.

"Easy peasy."

"Whatever." Kai pinches my ass and pushes me out of the way.

Cade mixes everything together and pours the batter in a cake pan. Once the cake is in the oven, he starts on the icing.

Kai, having had enough of honing his baking skills, sits with me at the island. We chat quietly about nothing in particular until Cade shoves a beater covered in chocolate icing under my nose.

"Well, sir, you certainly know the way to my heart." I snatch the beater out of his hand and take the first lick of chocolatey goodness. I moan as the flavor of chocolate and espresso explodes in my mouth.

When I look up, I see both guys staring at me with wicked grins and a sparkle in their eyes.

"No need to be so seductive doing that," Kai says as he adjusts himself in his pants.

I grin and scoop a dollop of icing from the beater with my finger and plop it on his nose. I watch as he goes cross-eyed to look at the blob of chocolate.

"Well, someone better lick that off of me."

Cade and I both go in for the icing at the same time and all three of our heads collide.

"Ouch," I laugh and rub my forehead, which I'm pretty sure ran into Cade's chin.

"Is it really that good that you guys would fight over it?" Kai asks. He scrapes the icing off and licks it off his finger.

Cade and I double over with laughter as his top lip pulls back from his teeth and he shakes his head.

"That is disgusting! How do you eat that shit? And to think, you almost knocked each other out to get to it."

"I think it was more the person it was on than the icing," Cade says in a dangerously low voice. "Although, the icing is pretty damn good. I'd lick that off you all day, every day."

I moan and nod my head. "Chocolate covered Kai dick. Where can I get me some of that?"

Kai chokes on a laugh and shakes his head at me.

"Come on you two," Cade says. He shoos us out of the kitchen and into the hallway. "The cake needs to cool before I ice it, but I'll be sure to save some for you, Ellis. I wouldn't want to deprive you of your chocolate covered dick."

All three of us are laughing as we round a corner and run into another vampire. Kai sobers immediately and pushes me behind him, but not before I've peaked the interest of the older vampire.

"Dad," Kai says cooly.

"I haven't seen you around much, son." His cold, dark gaze travels to me. "I think I can see why."

I shiver at the predatory look shining in those dark depths. He reaches a hand out and pushes Kai aside, and before I know it, I'm standing before Salvatore Thorne. King of the vampires.

Kai got his classically handsome facial features from his mother, but his height and build, and the dangerous glint in his eyes, he gets from his dad. Salvatore Thorne has dark brown eyes, so dark they're almost black. His brown hair falls to his waist in a smooth, silken sheet. If it weren't for the terrifying vibes he puts off, I would say he was attractive.

His dark gaze travels over my body and I see Kai stiffen out of my peripheral vision. Cade, standing behind me, steps closer and places his hand on my shoulder.

"We were just heading out, sir," Cade says respectfully.

"Were you now? Well, I'm glad I caught you. I have business to discuss with you." His lips curl in a cruel smile and his fangs lengthen as he runs his tongue over them. He hasn't looked away from me. "That can wait though. There's something more interesting standing in front of me."

Salvatore takes a step closer and Kai's entire body goes rigid. My heart thunders in my chest and I'm not sure if it's my reaction or Kai's. Perhaps it's both. Cade's hand tightens on my shoulder, almost to the point of pain.

The king of the vampires reaches out a hand and wraps one of my escaped curls around his finger. "You are a true beauty, aren't you?"

His dark eyes flash red at the same time he grabs more of my hair and yanks my head to the side, exposing my neck. His free hand comes up and traces the column of my throat. With his thumb pressed on my pulse point, he leans his head forward. Cade squeezes my shoulder, like he's debating pulling me away but is afraid of how Salvatore will react. If he's currently in predator mode, it will incite violence for Cade to yank me out of the way.

I whimper and my heart stutters. The vampire king feels it under his thumb and he grins. A low chuckle rumbles up his throat. I'm sure my fear is only making this game more fun for him.

Before he can move another inch, Kai slams into his dad with an inhuman growl. Cade uses the distraction to shove me behind him, his magic springs up to surround us. My fingers tingle but I suppress it. If I show this man I can use magic, I'll become even more interesting to him.

Kai presses his father against the wall with a hand at his throat. "Don't ever touch her again. Don't even think about touching her. I will destroy you if you do." His words are guttural and hard to discern over the insane length of his fangs.

Salvatore Thorne doesn't look a bit phased. He laughs darkly and studies his son. "Interesting," he mutters. He shoves Kai off of him and straightens his suit jacket. "I want you two in my office in ten minutes. We have business to discuss." Before he walks away his gaze lands on me hiding behind Cade. "I'll be seeing you again, I'm sure."

With that parting remark, the king of the vampires turns and disappears down the hallway.

"Fuck!" Kai screams. "Gods damn, motherfucking, asshole!" He shoves his hands through his hair roughly and paces back and forth in front of Cade and me. "I swear, if he so much as looks at Ellis again, I'll rip his fucking heart out of his fucking chest and shove it down his fucking throat!"

I swallow at his outburst. I've never seen Kai so angry before. His whole body is tense, almost vibrating with aggression that is begging to be let loose. I can feel an energy surrounding him that raises the small hairs on my arms. His gray eyes are burning bright red, like the fires of hell itself. This is the predator I was afraid of when we first met.

Cade sighs and pulls his phone out of his pocket. He sends off a quick text before grabbing my hands and tugging me toward the library. "Come on, I need to make sure the wards are still good before we meet with him."

Kai follows us, a thundercloud of anger and rage threatening to sweep us away. Cade keeps one eye on our surroundings and the other on Kai. I keep silent, afraid I'll do or say something that will set Kai off even more. I'm not sure how to handle this situation.

In the library, I settle on the couch while Cade walks around doing his thing to make sure the wards are all still in place. I keep my gaze on Kai as he paces back and forth. His fists clench and unclench causing his muscles and veins to pop with each squeeze. A muscle ticks in his jaw and his eyes are almost glowing red. Pissed doesn't begin to describe the state he's in.

The door opens and Sterling walks in, shirtless as always. I let myself appreciate his sculpted torso and the wolf and moon tattoo there. His gaze lands on me as soon as the door closes behind him, and our eyes lock. There is no denying the connection between us. I feel the tug in my middle that tries to propel me toward him. I could get lost in his icy blue eyes and the emotions swirling through them.

But then I remember what he did. Both lying to me as well as almost dying to protect me. I'm not sure how to process either of those things, so I get up and walk through the shelves, looking for a book.

I let my fingers trail along the spines. Reading has always been one of my favorite things to do. After my mom and sister died, I didn't read as much. I lost some of the joy I found from it. After Sam changed and turned into a monster, I lost all of the joy I found in novels.

I meander along the shelves until I come across a section with romance books. I hesitate a second before pulling one down. Romance books were always my first choice. I loved the idea of being the center of someone's world. Of being cared for and loved. My past has taught me romance books are just that. Books.

A fantasy that will never come true. Reading them began to depress me as my relationship with Sam turned uglier and uglier.

I hold the book in my hand, running my fingers over the cover. I'm no longer in that relationship. I have two guys, maybe three, who put me at the center of their world. They claim to love me. Even with everything going on and everything we're learning. I wasn't lying when I said I don't know who I am anymore.

In ten years, I lost my mom and sister, two people who meant the world to me. I was beaten and raped for two years by someone who was supposed to love me. The man I thought was my dad let it all happen. Then one day, I find out that man is not my dad. My real dad killed my mom and sister, tried to have me killed. Now, I find out I'm fated to be with three guys, and I'm supposedly a mythical creature who is feared above all the others. How does a person process all of that?

I take the book back to the couch with determination. I guess the first step is reclaiming the things I enjoy and not letting my past steal them from me. Curled up against the arm rest, I crack open the book and begin to read. I'm distantly aware of Kai's continued pacing and Cade walking the perimeter of the room to check the wards. I know Sterling is sitting across from me on the chair, doing something on his phone.

I'm halfway through the first chapter when Cade approaches. He pulls the blanket off the back of the couch and settles it over me, and my heart squeezes at the gesture. Kneeling in front of me, he takes my face in his hands.

"You're still safe in here, I promise. I added a few more protection spells just in case, but as long as you stay in here, he can't hurt you."

"Is Kai going to be okay?" I gaze at my beloved. He's still pacing, still cursing under his breath. Still tense and looking at the room through glowing red eyes.

Cade looks at Kai for a second before turning back to me. "He ... he'll ..."

I bite my lower lip. Cade always seems so sure. To see him hesitate like this makes me uneasy.

"Depending on what his dad wants us to do, it might take him some time to calm down. He will probably need an outlet for his aggression when we get back."

My stomach flips over at his words. I know what kind of outlet that will be. He gives me a knowing smile and a wink, but his smile falls and he turns serious again.

"Just, understand that he might be a little more protective of you for a while. If he feels like there's a threat to you, he might not be able to control himself. Try to be patient with him."

"Always," I whisper.

"I love you, Ellis." He kisses me softly before standing.

"Be careful, please."

Cade motions for Kai, but before he leaves, Kai kneels in front of me. His eyes are sparkling like the darkest ruby. He grabs the back of my head and kisses me with a fierce kind of possession, like he wants to swallow my soul.

I kiss him back, just as fiercely. "I love you, Kai."

At my words, the red in his eyes fades a bit, a tiny rim of gray returning to his irises. He rests his forehead against mine and inhales.

"I love you, too. Don't leave this room. Stay with Sterling no matter what. Don't let my dad anywhere near you."

"I won't. I promise."

Satisfied, he stands and follows Cade out of the library.

4. Sterling

I can't help but look at her. My mate. I never thought I'd get the chance to get to know her, yet here we are. Sitting in the same room but not talking, all because my idiot self was too scared and too selfish to come clean with the truth. I'll never forgive myself for that.

She's fucking beautiful. I want to bury my hand in her hair again and feel her curls tickle my skin. I want her amber eyes to shine with happiness when she looks at me. I want her secret smiles and soft touches. I want to know her thoroughly and completely.

She's been reading that book since I walked in. It's like she'll do anything to avoid me. Fuck. Watching her with Cade and Kai is pure torture. Seeing her face light up in their presence, watching them touch her and kiss her, it stirs angry jealousy in my chest. I don't deserve those looks she gives them. I don't deserve to even sit here in her presence.

I turn my attention back to my phone and continue my search. I've been trying to find as much information on harpies as I can. It's hard to discern truth from fiction on the internet though. While our visit to Allie's aunts was informative, we still haven't figured out why or how Ellis is bonded to the three of us, or why she seems to be able to use Cade's magic.

Like she's a magnet though, my eyes don't stay on my phone screen long before straying back to my mate. My fucking mate. Being in her presence and not touching her, not claiming her, is almost impossible.There is a constant itch under my skin, an urge my wolf needs to act on.

I shake myself and return to my phone. A couple minutes later, Ellis exhales heavily and drops the book to her lap.

"I'm bored," she claims.

I set my phone down and look at her. When her gaze meets mine, that tug in my middle, the urge to claim her, intensifies. I don't say anything though. This conversation that needs to happen between us has to come from her first. I won't push it on her if she doesn't want to talk about it.

She sighs as if she is reading my thoughts, and sets the book on the coffee table. With her legs curled under her, she lifts the blanket higher, using it like a shield. "Guess this is the perfect time to talk, huh?" she asks.

"If you want to, yeah."

She studies me for a minute before asking, "Why didn't you tell me?"

I knew this question would arise, but it doesn't mean I'm prepared for it. I rub my face before answering. "I really don't have a good answer to that question. At least, not one that justifies what I did. I was scared, honestly. I was so scared I would tell you and you would never look at me again. The thought of losing you before I ever even had you was crippling." Just thinking about it now makes me nauseous. I lean forward and rest my elbows on my knees. "As soon as I found out I had a mate, I knew I had to hide it. I knew it would be too dangerous to ever make it known, especially since Noah wanted you dead. I had accepted the fact I would never know my mate, never get to hold her or be part of her life. I accepted the fact you would never even know I existed."

I swallow thickly. The emotions I'm feeling are too much for me. I have a hard time dealing with them, but for her, I'll face them all. All the fear and heartache. The desperation and overwhelming desire.

"When Kai suggested he compete in the contest, I knew it was a bad idea. I knew I'd never be able to stay away from you. But there was no good reason to talk him out of it. You waltzed into my life, Ellis, and everything I had accepted as being impossible was happening. You were talking to me. You were looking at me. You wanted me. It's why I was always gone. I couldn't stand being around you and not claiming you."

I look away from her piercing stare. Shame and regret, riding me hard.

"I almost told you so many times, but each time I decided I would come clean, you would smile at me or look at me with those beautiful eyes and I'd crumple. I couldn't bring myself to do it. I was selfish. I didn't want to lose those looks. I didn't know if I could go back to knowing I had a mate and not being able to be with her. Especially after getting to know you. I was selfish and afraid, so I kept it to myself."

"You know, while it hurts that you didn't tell me and I had to find out from someone else, the thing that hurts worse is knowing that I shared my body with you."

Tears shine in her eyes, and it's like a punch to the gut, physically making me double over.

"It wasn't easy for me to do that, you know. After Sa ... after Sam ... I didn't think I would ever want that again. You three took the fear away, but it was hard to get out of my head and remind myself that you guys aren't him. I had to convince myself you guys wouldn't hurt me. And I honestly thought you wouldn't."

Her last words are whispered, and as she says them, the tears spill over and track down her cheeks. I squeeze my eyes shut, the sight of her tears undoing me. It never even crossed my mind that what I did to her would remind her of her past.

"I didn't want to hurt you, Ellis. I didn't want to cross that line with you. I knew it was wrong but I couldn't fight it anymore. My wolf and the bond, all of it kept pushing me forward until I just snapped. I regret it, Ellis. I regret all of it."

She wipes her tears and sniffles, and I want so badly to go to her. To comfort her and take her pain away—pain that I caused her. Gods dammit. I'm such a fucking idiot. I get a chance to be with my mate and I throw it away. The question I'm dying to ask but too scared to hear the answer to, slips out before I can stop it.

"Is there any chance you'll be able to forgive me?"

She looks at her lap and twists her hands together nervously. "I don't know," she says quietly.

My heart stops at her words. It fucking hurts. Like, really hurts. I bend over again and clutch at my chest. I seriously think I might be having a heart attack.

"I want to forgive you. I want a relationship with you. The connection is there, and I feel it everytime we're near. But," she pauses and takes a deep breath, "when I look at you, I see my mom and sister's dead bodies. I feel the pain at learning you lied to me and betrayed me. I'm not sure how to get past that."

I close my eyes. That was exactly what I feared she would say. And I know she's right. I don't even know how I would go about earning her forgiveness. I'm not sure I deserve it. No, I know I don't deserve it.

I'm saved from any further heartbreaking discussion by the sound of a text message. Ellis grabs her phone off the coffee table and reads the text, a small smile pulling up the corners of her lips. Jealousy burns through me. I know it was either Cade or Kai. Most likely Cade with the state Kai was in when they left. What I wouldn't give to be the reason for one of those smiles.

"They're on their way back," she announces. "Cade says Kai is pretty much out of control."

I spot the faint blush that creeps into her cheeks, and I know exactly what thought crosses her mind. The best way to bring Kai back from the edge is sex.

Unable to take anymore, I stand from the chair and walk into the shelves. I can't leave the room until they get back, but I can at least take a moment to get myself under control. It's my fault I'm in this situation. I have no one to blame but myself, and I'm getting damn good at doing that.

5. Ellis

I collapse into the cushions and pull the blanket over my head when Sterling gets up and walks away. Why does it have to be so hard? I wish I could just shove it all to the back of my mind and move on. I want to forgive him. I really, really do. I know he didn't mean to hurt me. And I know he cares about me. But, when I think about letting him in again, I freeze. My heart panics and protection mode sets in—it's been through too much and it's always on edge now.

I'm not sure how long I hide under the covers trying to talk myself into going after him and saying to hell with it all. I'm still there when the library door crashes open, causing me to jump. I fling the blanket off, fully expecting to see Kai's dad hovering in the doorway. Instead, I see Kai. Shoulders rising and falling with each heavy breath he takes.

His red-eyed gaze zeroes in on me and he takes a slow step into the room. Bright red streaks coat his face and hair, and dried blood flakes from his leathers. Those pointed fangs are on full display as he gives me a slow, wicked smile.

My stomach tumbles at the sight of him. I'm not sure what makes me do it, but I scramble over the back of the couch and back away. I know backing away from a predator is the last thing I should do, but a thrill of anticipation spreads through my body as his eyes darken and he takes another slow step toward me.

We continue this way, me backing away and him stalking me, until my back hits the pool table. Each step he takes makes my heart pound harder in my chest. His red eyes haven't strayed from me, despite Cade walking into the room and monitoring us with an expression that's both weary and eager.

With my back pressed against the pool table, I take a moment to decide which direction to go. The hesitation costs me. Kai pounces. His inhuman reflexes stun me for a moment. One second he is in front of the couch, the next he is vaulting over it and landing in a crouch in front of me.

I turn to my left, thinking hiding in the shelves of books might work, but before I can take a step in that direction, Kai is at my back. His hand circles my throat and he pulls me against his chest. My pulse flutters wildly and he rubs his thumb over the vein, right over the bite mark that he left the last time we fucked.

"I caught you, little bird," he breathes in my ear.

His words, his voice, his breath, his thumb on that mark. They all make my legs shake and my breathing hitch.

The adrenaline pumping through my blood combined with the liquid heat pooling in my core, spurs me into action. I'm not ready to be caught so easily. I throw my elbow back, connecting with his ribs. A soft 'oomph' flutters my hair, and his hold on my throat loosens enough for me to twist out of his grasp.

I take off as fast as I can. This time, I make it three steps toward the bookshelves before Kai's arm wraps around my middle, halting my escape. He lifts me off my feet and I kick blindly, trying to connect with his shins, but he pulls me too close and I can't get the right angle.

"What the fuck do you think you're doing? You can't run from me, baby girl."

I shiver as his deep growl runs over my skin. A fire has been lit inside me and I can't help but try to get away. I catch Cade's gaze. He's standing by the couch with his arms crossed over his chest.

The outline of his cock strains against his leather pants. I plead with him silently, and his violet eyes sparkle as he gives me a slow smile and nod. This time, I manage to break away by slamming my head back into Kai's chin.

"Fuck!" His arms loosen, and I drop to the ground.

I'm running before he has a chance to recover. I head straight for the door, having every intent of running out of the library, knowing I won't make it that far. As I reach for the door handle, I look over my shoulder in time to see Kai take a few steps toward me. I give him a small smile I know will set his blood boiling. He runs his fangs over his lower lip and the bite mark on my neck tingles.

Cade steps in front of Kai, blocking his path, and I turn back to the door. I hear a tussle behind me but pay it no mind. Just as the door cracks open, a hand slams against the wood, pushing it shut again. I whip around to find Kai with both of his arms on either side of my head, blocking me in.

"You should never run from a predator, little bird. It only excites us more." He presses in closer to me and I can indeed feel his excitement through his leather pants. "Not only that, you just got Cade in trouble. Now, I'll have to punish you both."

My pussy clenches at his words and I feel myself growing wetter. Kai's nostrils flare as he inhales, and I know he can scent my arousal. He smiles wickedly and throws me over his shoulder.

"You're going to regret playing the brat, baby girl."

Fuck. This side of Kai is something I could definitely get used to. I lift my head and look at Cade as Kai carries me past him. He smirks at me and rubs himself through his pants, just as turned on by this show as I am. Kai sets me on the pool table and pushes me down on my back with a hand on my throat.

"I'm going to make you beg for my cock, and I'll only give it to you if you're a good girl. Think you can behave now?"

His grip tightens just a little on my neck and I gasp. The last person to have their hand around my throat almost killed me. Surprisingly, this doesn't scare me. I'm so turned on I can barely handle it. The trust I have in these guys makes all the difference. I know Kai would sooner shove a stake in his own heart than harm me.

He squeezes a little harder, and this time he pinches my nipple through my tank top at the same time. "I didn't hear you answer. Are you still misbehaving?"

"No," I whisper. "I'll behave, I'm sorry."

He smiles, fangs on full display. "Good girl. Now, you're going to let me undress you."

I nod because I'm not sure I can find my voice. In my head I'm screaming. Yes, please take my clothes off. Take yours off, too. Kai pulls a knife out of his pocket and I eye it with a racing heart. Oh, no he isn't. He's not going to cut my clothes off of me, is he?

Kai does just that. He slices up my shirt and lets it fall open. I'm not wearing a bra, and his eyes devour me. He runs the tip of the blade over one breast, flicking my nipple with the edge. I know he can hear my blood rushing through my veins, pumping through my body by my heart that has never beat so hard before.

He grins and moves the knife lower. The blade drags over the center of my leggings as he cuts the fabric carefully and exposes my already wet undies. Holy fuck. This is the hottest thing I've ever done. He rubs the flat side of the knife against my pussy and when he pulls it away, I can see the wetness of my arousal on the shining surface.

I hear the sound of rustling fabric and I turn my head to see Cade pulling his leathers off. His cock is standing proudly at attention and I can see the glimmering bead of precum on the tip. I lick my lips, wanting to taste it. Kai notices where my attention has traveled and he chuckles. He rips my undies in half and I jerk in surprise, my attention returning to him.

Kai shakes his head and grins. "Cade, tie her up."

A sliver of fear worms through my desire. No. Not that. Anything but that. I squeeze my eyes shut and brace myself for burning fire to wrap around my wrists and ankles. It doesn't come. Instead, a finger under my chin turns my head to the side. I open my eyes and see Cade staring at me with his violet eyes full of emotion.

"Ellis," he breathes. "You don't have to."

That's all it takes. Those four words from my sweet and caring mage. They remind me this is different. This is Cade and Kai. My fated mates. My beloved and soul-bonded. If I'm going to erase those awful memories, this is the way to do it.

I relax and let my arms fall above my head with my wrists crossed. "Do it," I say.

"Are you sure?" he asks.

I nod. "I'm positive. Do it, Cade."

Cade leans over and presses the softest kiss to my lips. "Say the word, and they disappear."

He kisses me again and I feel the warmth of his magic slither over my skin. It's sensual and arousing, and I arch my back off the pool table. The warmth settles around my wrists, binding them together. It travels down my abdomen and over my hips. Kai's cool fingers grip my thighs and spread them wider as Cade's magic wraps around them, binding them to the pool table.

I tug against the bindings, finding them secure. My heart stutters in my chest for a moment, but then Kai steps back and runs his eyes over my naked body, spread and tied to the table for his pleasure. His throat works on a swallow, and the red in his eyes almost disappears as he looks at me. Knowing I have that kind of power over him even when I'm completely powerless is a heady feeling. It calms some of the fear I can't help but experience at being tied up.

"Cade," he says gruffly, not taking his gaze from me. "Help me undress."

"Yes, sir," Cade says quietly and places his hands on Kai's chest.

Kai's head snaps to Cade and a slow smile spreads over his lips. "Sir. I think I like that."

Cade chuckles and moves his hands to the hem of Kai's shirt and slowly lifts it up, exposing his pale skin and muscled abdomen. I watch the muscles of Cade's back shift as he struggles with the tight leather. I'm not sure where to look. Both guys are devastatingly beautiful and mouthwateringly sexy. I want to devour them both.

Cade manages to get the shirt over Kai's head and he throws it over the back of the couch. Then he places his hands on Kai's chest, running his fingers down over the bumps and grooves of muscle. He wraps his hands around Kai's waist and tugs him closer.

I lay naked and sprawled on the pool table, my legs and arms immobile, as Cade and Kai kiss. It's a brutal kiss. Nothing like the way they kiss me. It's like watching a battle for dominance. I whimper as need burns through me. I want to touch myself so bad. I need something to ease the ache and watching them—their strong bodies moving together, their passion for each other—is only making it worse.

They break apart, chests heaving, and look at me. I guess my whimper was a little louder than I thought.

"Look at that dripping pussy," Kai growls. "You'll leave a puddle on the pool table if we don't take care of you soon."

"Please." My voice is husky and almost hoarse sounding.

"I told you I'd make you beg for my cock. I don't think you've earned it yet, though."

No. No, no, no. Please. I need to be filled. I need my guys with their hands and mouths on me. Their cocks in me.

Kai takes Cade's hands and places them on the front of his leathers, silently instructing him to unbutton them. Cade does just that, sliding them down over Kai's hips and freeing his dick from its leather confines. Kneeling on the ground, Cade removes Kai's pants and throws them with his shirt, before grabbing Kai's cock in his fist.

Kai's head falls back and he groans as Cade begins working his fist up and down Kai's length. Kai watches me and I squirm as much as I can in Cade's magic bindings. This is pure torture. I'm so empty it hurts and by the little smile on Kai's face, he knows it.

Kai's hands land on top of Cade's head and he fists the other man's hair roughly before thrusting forward and slamming his cock down Cade's throat. This is also a brutal display of dominance that only makes me more needy. Cade's hands grab the back of Kai's thighs and he takes it with his eyes open and looking at Kai like he is the most wonderful person in the world.

These two are going to destroy me.

Just when I think I might cry from the need to feel something, anything, Kai steps back. He pulls Cade to his feet by his hair and kisses him again.

"Please. I'm begging you. I ache. Please, make it go away." I'm breathless and desperate as I beg Kai to touch me.

He steps between my legs and places his hand around my neck again. "Are you going to run from me again? Or are you going to be a good girl from now on."

"I'll be your good girl, I promise. Just please, touch me."

He leaves his hand around my throat as he bends down and licks up my center. I almost scream at the sensation of finally being touched. But it's not enough. He keeps the pressure of his tongue light and he doesn't go anywhere near my clit. I can hear him, the sound of my juices as he laps them up, and it's only making me wetter.

"Kai," I beg again. I'm almost sobbing at this point.

He stands with his mouth and chin glistening and fists his cock, pumping up and down. "You want my cock, baby girl?"

"Yes, yes, please, yes."

Movement catches my eye. Sterling is standing next to a bookshelf, icy blue eyes locked on what's happening on the pool table. Even from this distance, I can see his blown pupils, dilated from desire, his cock tenting his sweatpants. I know I should feel ashamed that someone is watching this. I know I should feel bad, knowing how much Sterling wants me. But I can't bring myself to feel either of those things. Instead, a heady rush of desire washes through me. I feel dirty letting someone watch, and I think I like it.

Cade climbs on top of the pool table and kneels next to my head. He gathers my bun in his hand and tips my head to the side.

"Open up, baby girl. I'll give you this cock if you suck down Cade's like a good girl."

I obediently open my mouth and let Cade slide his dick in. I swirl my tongue around the crown, tasting his precum and moaning at the taste. I'm distracted from my own desperate need for release at the moment, watching Cade's face as I pleasure him.

I'm not expecting it when Kai thrusts his cock inside me. I'm so wet he slides right in, and my walls clench tightly around him. I scream around Cade's cock at the feeling of finally being filled.

Kai is like a feral animal as he begins to well and truly fuck me. It's hard and rough. So much so, if it weren't for the magic bindings holding me in place, I'd be sliding across the pool table. As it is, the thousand pound table screeches across the floor with each thrust of Kai's hips.

I can do nothing except lay here, taking both cocks willingly as my guys take their pleasure. It's almost too much for me to process. The rough handling, the sensations, the sounds. It all stokes the fire inside me, and it grows and grows until I feel like I'll combust.

Sweat drips off of Kai onto me. His fingers dig painfully into my hips, and I love knowing I'll have bruises in the shapes of his fingertips tomorrow morning. Cade holds my chin just as roughly as I suck and lick his dick like it's the sustenance I need to survive.

I feel my orgasm building, each hard thrust from Kai pushing me closer and closer to the edge. When Kai grabs the back of Cade's head and draws him in for a bruising kiss, I lose it. My orgasm barrels through me so hard I black out for a second. When I regain awareness of my surroundings, I feel Kai stiffening above me a second before he finds his orgasm, filling me with his release. Cade follows and I swallow him down greedily, lapping up every last drop.

I can't move, even if I didn't have the magic bindings holding me in place. Tremors work through my arms and legs as little aftershocks of pleasure roll through me. My chest is heaving and my heart is pounding so hard I'm surprised it doesn't burst out of my chest.

Cade and Kai are breathing just as heavily. All three of us take a moment to collect ourselves, to reel ourselves back in from what just happened. Once Cade has control of his breathing, he removes his bands of magic, kissing my wrists gently as he does so. Kai kisses my thighs and closes my legs. I wince at the ache in my muscles—a pleasant pain from being spread so wide and fucked so thoroughly.

Kai gathers me in his arms and carries me to the couch where he sits with me cuddled against his chest. Cade follows and covers me with the blanket before laying down with his head in my lap. Kai wraps one arm around my back and the other around Cade. A sleepy smile pulls up my lips and my heart flutters happily in my chest. These guys are so fucking amazing.

I could easily close my eyes and fall asleep, safe in the arms of my two loves. Instead, Sterling steps out from the shelves and clears his throat. He opens his mouth and brings the real world crashing down around me.

6. Malakai

My fingers trail lazily over Ellis's bare arm. Her head on my shoulder and her naked body pressed against mine is exactly what I need after that display of dominance I had to get out of my system. The threat my dad posed to her left me feral. The monster inside me had to make sure she knows who owns her, body and soul. What that monster doesn't realize is that she owns me just as much as I own her. I mean, fuck, my heart beats at the same rhythm as hers. If that doesn't scream ownership, I don't know what does.

Cade sighs contentedly with his head in her lap. His heart beats steadily under my palm, and his hand covers my own with his fingers gently tracing the top of my hand. How the fuck did I end up here? With a beloved and a best friend who is rapidly turning into more than just a friend.

I only get a few moments to enjoy it before Sterling steps out from the shelves and clears his throat. That one sound drawing me out of my blissful thoughts and shoving reality back in. Has he been there this whole time? Watching us fuck on the pool table? Ellis tenses in my arms, and she takes a breath like she's preparing for war.

"I hate to break up cuddle time," Sterling says, sounding

anything but apologetic, "but while you were fucking around I used my time for something useful. I have a possible lead on where to find the information we're supposed to be looking for."

"Careful, Sterling," Cade mutters drowsily. "Your jealousy is showing."

Sterling growls low in his chest and his eyes flash as his wolf tries to break free.

"No, he's right," Ellis says. She pushes out of my lap, dislodging Cade and causing him to grumble. "We can't stop looking. I need to know what I am." She picks up her cut up leggings and glares at me. "Next time, can we keep my clothing intact? I don't have enough as it is."

I grin at her. "I'll buy you more, don't worry."

She rolls her eyes and grabs a shirt from the back of the couch —Cade's by the smell—and pulls it over her head. "What did you find Sterling?" She sits back on the couch between Cade and me and pulls a blanket over her lap.

Sterling takes the chair across from us and leans his elbows on his knees. "I text an old friend of mine from the pack."

I straighten. "Is that safe? Can you trust them?"

"He was adopted, and he's not a wolf, so he feels no allegiance to the alpha. He's the one who sends me updates on my mom." Shadows flash in his eyes before he forces them back. "Anyway, there is an old wolf in the pack, she's been alive longer than anyone knows. She's kind of like a healer, I guess. A wisewoman of sorts. She always seems to have knowledge of things no one else does. I had my friend ask her if she knew anything of harpies."

"And?" Ellis breathes. She leans forward, eagerly waiting for his response.

"She said there's a book that contains information about every magical being of the world. It's probably our best bet to find the information we need. It's in the Altair Library, but it's protected. They keep it in the vault, and you have to have special permission to get access to it."

"What kind of permission?" Cade asks.

"A letter from the leader of one of the races."

"Like my dad?" I ask.

"Yeah, but I doubt he'll be willing to give it to you, all things considered."

"Who said I was going to ask him for it?" I grin. "I've perfected his signature over the years. All those report cards from school I didn't want him to see."

Cade snorts and Ellis looks at me with raised brows.

"What?" I ask with mock innocence. "I hated school. I was lucky to graduate at all."

"Too busy getting high and fucking anything willing," Cade mutters under his breath.

I reach across Ellis and punch Cade in the arm. She rolls her eyes and shakes her head, but smiles at me with such adoration I actually find it hard to breathe. Fuuck, she's perfect.

"Okay, when can you get it?" Sterling asks, bringing us all back to the task at hand.

"Today, when he's sleeping. I'll sneak into his office. He'll never know."

"Then we should try to get some rest," Cade says. "None of us are used to being awake during the daylight hours anymore."

———

I DON'T THINK any of us actually slept, and as Ellis climbs out of the Land Rover covering a yawn with the back of her hand, I know she didn't. Her emotions have been assaulting my mental barrier ever since Sterling mentioned this book. Nerves. Excitement. Fear. Dread. They kept her awake, tossing and turning in my bed until she eventually gave up trying to sleep and perched in the window seat instead, peering out at the estate grounds. It was hard, but we left her with her thoughts. She needed to be alone for a bit, and we let her have that time.

I sigh and mentally prepare myself for the sun, sliding on a pair of gloves and my sunglasses. I hate the sun. As we approach the library, we keep Ellis in the middle of us while we scan our surroundings. The Altair Library is a three-story building of tan brick and soaring columns. There are only a few cars in the parking lot this early in the morning, which is lucky for us. We want to go as unnoticed as possible.

Cade pulls open the large wooden door and ushers us inside. The tension in my body immediately dissipates as I step into the darkened entrance out of the direct sunlight. I wait for my companions to sneak off into the stacks, before I pull the folded letter from my pocket and approach the main desk and lone librarian sitting behind it. I'd snagged a piece of official vampire court letterhead and scrawled some nonsense about needing the book for research purposes, and signed my dad's signature. I even added a wax seal of his signet ring. Something he rarely uses anymore. I wasn't about to risk being turned away or caught in the act of forging his signature.

"Can I help you?" the librarian asks in the quiet. Her eyes widen briefly when she realizes who she's talking to, but she recovers quickly.

"Yes, I need access to the vault. There is a book in there my dad needs some information from." I give her a small smile, making sure to keep my fangs hidden.

I slide the letter across the desk, and she quickly scans the contents before sliding it back. She produces a large ledger and places it in front of me.

"I just need you to fill this out, then I'll take you there."

I quickly write my name, date, and reason for needing the vault. I hate that I'm leaving a trail behind, but there is no way I can use a fake name. The librarian clearly knows who I am, and it would raise too many red flags. She signs next to my name and grabs a key from a drawer.

"Follow me."

I follow her through the library, and I sense the others following at a distance. The vault is in the very back of the building, behind a massive wooden door. The librarian waves her hand over the wood and pale blue light flares from her palm. A mage then. Once whatever ward has been dealt with, she slides the key inside and unlocks the door.

Turning to me, she gives me a stern look. "Nothing may leave this room. If you need copies made of something, let me know and I'll get them for you if I can. We have to keep a record of everything that leaves, and only certain things can be copied." She points to my bookbag. "I'll take that, and keep it at the front desk. I can't risk you copying anything without my knowledge. I'll also need your cellphone."

I knew this was the policy, but I still balk at giving this mage my cell phone. I roll my shoulders but hand both of them over. We don't have a choice.

"When you are ready to leave, stop by the desk to collect your things, and I'll make sure the door is locked again." She gives me a final nod, and turns back the way we'd come, taking my phone and bag with her.

When I'm sure she's out of sight, I open the door and the others quickly file through the doorway. Once inside, I close the door and pull a chair over to wedge under the handle. We can't risk her coming back and finding us in here with cell phones and notebooks.

"Okay, where is this book?" I ask.

Sterling pulls his phone from his pocket and scrolls through his texts. "*The Complete History of Magical Races in Lustros*." He strides to a computer and types the name into the search bar. "History section, shelf 42, row G."

With that information, it doesn't take us long to find the book. Sterling sets it on a table, and we all stand around it, staring at it with varying expressions. Sterling looks like he's going to battle, Cade looks nauseous, and Ellis looks like she's about to bolt.

"Okay," she says shakily. "This is it." She nervously twists a hair tie around her wrist.

"Here, sit down." I pull out a chair for her, and she falls into it, wiping her palms on her leggings.

I sit next to her and pull the book toward us. "Ready?" I ask, giving her an encouraging smile.

She bites her lip but nods. Cade sits on the other side of her and grabs her hands. "Remember, Ellis. Whatever we find in this book doesn't change anything. It's not going to make us love you any less. It's not going to chase us away. We'll be right here with you, no matter what."

She takes a deep breath, and I see something settle inside of her. She needed to hear those words again, the reassurance we weren't going to leave her.

"Here we go," I say and flip the cover open. I run my finger down the table of contents, scanning the names of various magicals. "Elves, fae, gargoyles, gremlins, goblins ... harpies. Page 376."

Ellis's fingers dig into my thigh as I turn to the page indicated in the table of contents. None of us have any idea what we're about to read. All we know of harpies is what Aunt Madge told us, and the stories we heard that apparently aren't real. How much will everything change with this new information we find?

I smooth the pages down with slightly shaking fingers. It's not just Ellis's fear I'm sensing, causing the tremors. It's my own fear. I'm scared of what this will do to Ellis. Whatever we learn will either have a positive or negative impact on my girl's life, and I'm praying to every god out there it's a positive impact.

The first thing I see is a drawn image of a harpy. A beautiful woman, naked and glowing, with long hair blowing around her body. In one hand, she holds a massive sword with flames licking up the blade. In the other hand, she holds an ancient tome, open with glowing light emitting from the pages. But it's the wings that catch my eye. Spread across the pages, the enormous, feathered wings sprout from her back and arch high over her head.

Ellis trails a finger over the image. "She doesn't look evil," she whispers.

Indeed, she doesn't. Her face is expressionless, but she gives off an air of peace I didn't expect to find.

"What's it say?" Sterling asks from the other side of the table.

I take a breath, and read the words on the page. "Harpies were created as a means to keep the balance between good and evil. They do this using the powers given to them by their Shields. Harpies are only brought into the world when there is a need for them. In times past, harpies have been heralded and praised at their birth, but as the views of harpies have shifted, their births have gone unnoticed to the public. Only when they start to develop their powers does a harpy learn what she is."

It went on to talk about the history of various harpies in the past, including the story of Maeryrea and Star Elves Aunt Madge had told us about. That was it.

Ellis slumps in her chair. "That didn't tell us anything new."

"Actually, it did mention powers. At least we know you being able to use mine isn't a random fluke," Cade says quietly.

"But, why? And, how? I have more questions now than I did before."

"Shields," Sterling mutters. "It said 'powers given to them by their Shields.' What are Shields?"

I turn back to the table of contents and suck in a breath when I see *Shields* on the list. Quickly, I flip to the page and find a short paragraph.

"Shields are a harpy's protectors. Given to her by the universe, they are destined to be her guardians and lend her their powers. A harpy may have anywhere from two to five Shields. It is up to fate to bring them together, and up to the harpy to secure the bonds. Oftentimes, her Shields will lay down their lives for her. Her life and her mission are their top priority."

I look up from the book, barely breathing, and catch Sterling's gaze. "Shields." I spin in my chair and grab Ellis's chin in my fingers, making sure she's looking at me. "We're your Shields. That's how you're bonded to all three of us. That's how you can use Cade's magic and my strength. We were meant to be with you from the very beginning."

Her shoulders relax, and a small smile pulls up the corners of her lips. I lean in and give her a quick kiss.

"See?" Cade says. "I told you we weren't going to leave you." He wraps his arms around her waist and drops a kiss to her shoulder.

"So, I'm a harpy and you're my Shields. I can use your powers, but what for? What's my purpose? What balance am I supposed to be restoring?"

"I think to find that out, we need to learn what this warehouse is that Sam kept mentioning," Sterling says. "Aunt Madge mentioned it, so it has to be important."

"I agree," I say as I stand from the chair. "Whatever Sam is doing is definitely the problem we have to solve."

"How do we find that out?" she asks.

"We keep looking for the warehouse." Cade pulls her to her feet and hands me his phone. "Take pictures of all of that so we have it for reference."

I snap the pictures and Sterling reshelves the book. I approach Ellis and pull her in for a hug.

"It feels good knowing I was meant to protect you. I love knowing you have three guardians, Shields, to keep you safe and happy. It's a job I'll never take lightly."

Cade comes up behind her and swipes her hair away from her neck, displaying the mark I left when I claimed her. He runs his finger over the two punctures before kissing the spot. She shivers in my arms.

"You are our world, Ellis," Cade says, his voice low and filled with sincerity. "From the first moment we met you, we knew you were special. You belonged with us from the very beginning."

She looks at me with amber eyes, wide and shining. My heart thumps in time with hers, and I close my eyes to revel in the sensation.

"We should get moving," Sterling says, once again breaking

into our little bubble of happiness. "The longer we stay here, the more likely we are to be noticed."

We sneak out of the vault and I make my way to the counter alone. After thanking the librarian she hands me my stuff, and I meet the others at the car.

"Well, that was productive," I say, climbing into the back seat with Ellis. "Now we just have to figure out Sam's game."

"I'll get working on that," Cade says. "After we all get some rest." He leans around the front seat and grins wryly at Ellis yawning next to me.

"Good deal." I look at Ellis. She's wiping her tears away from her yawn. "Come here. Why don't you close your eyes until we get home?" I stretch my arm out, inviting her in.

"Kai!"

Her scream and wide eyes are my only warning before the sounds of crunching metal and shattering glass fill the air and I'm hit with the force of a freight train.

7. Ellis

I'm thrown into the door as a truck crashes into Sterling's Land Rover. My head smashes against the window and stars burst to life in my vision. Glass from the driver side windows explodes inward, showering us with sharp, glittering pellets. The Land Rover careens to the side and slams into a telephone pole, whipping us back the other direction before it settles in the ditch on the side of the road.

My ears ring in the silence that follows the collision. All I can hear is my heart pounding in my ears and the breath rasping in and out of my lungs. The scent of burning rubber and gasoline meet my nose, and I know we have to get out of this car in case it catches fire.

I look around wildly, my vision blurred and the world tilting alarmingly as I turn my head. Kai is laying motionless, the door twisted and contorted around his body.

"Kai!" I shakily unbuckle myself and climb over the seat to him. He has to be alive, unless something pierced his heart or head, I rationally know he's alive. But he's so motionless, the panic wipes all reason from my brain. "Kai, please. Wake up!"

His chest rises with a breath and his heart pounds as fast as mine under my palm. I exhale on a sob and turn my attention to the front seats. Cade is stirring, blood trickling down the side of his head.

"Ellis?" he rasps.

"I'm okay." I lean around the seat, only to find Sterling pinned under the steering column, a shard of metal piercing his stomach. "No," I whisper. "Cade, you have to help him!"

"Fuck," he groans, holding his head as he sits on his knees in his seat. He spares a glance for me, ensuring I'm really okay. "Kai?" he asks.

"He'll be fine." My voice shakes, and I realize my entire body is trembling. "Sterling ..."

"I got him," Cade grunted.

Before he can reach for Sterling, voices penetrate the silence along with the sounds of car doors closing and gravel crunching. But it's one specific voice that freezes the blood in my veins.

"Make sure she's alive, and heal any of her injuries."

Cade's head whips in my direction. "Sam."

"No," I whisper.

"What about the others?" a second voice, one I don't recognize, asks.

"Kill them."

Those two words thaw the ice in my veins and set my blood on fire. Kai and Sterling are helpless, they can't protect themselves. Cade needs his magic to save Sterling. That leaves me, the only one left to keep them all safe. A hysterical laugh bubbles up my chest. How the hell can I protect them? Especially when I have to protect myself.

Cade reads all of this in my expression and he shakes his head. "No, Ellis. Do not do what you're thinking. Let me protect you."

"I need you to save Sterling."

"Ellis—"

I climb over the seat again, ignoring Cade's pleas. I doubt my car door will open, but I can climb through the broken window.

"Ellis!"

I look at him, his expression torn between saving my mate or protecting me. "Cade, there is no point if I lose one of you. You guys are everything to me. Not just my Shields, but my entire reason for breathing."

"Shields," he mutters. "That's it! Use my magic, Ellis!"

Violet light climbs up his arms and the tell-tale tingle in my palms responds. I don't wait a second longer. I slide out the window, wincing as the broken glass cuts into my skin. Climbing to my feet, I come face to face with my nightmare. I fight the instinct to cower. Instead, I draw on my years of training at the gym and the sessions I spent working with the guys.

Sam's lips spread into a grin that makes my stomach churn. I swallow down my fear, straighten my shoulders, and lift my chin. It's easy to slip into a fighting stance—legs spread, knees bent, fists guarding my face. I notice the purple light swirling around my hands and I wish I'd had time to practice using this magic with Cade.

Sam's smile falters and his eyes widen. "So it's true," he whispers to himself. He motions to the wrecked car with his hand, and says sharply, "Take care of them. Now."

My gaze is drawn to the three men behind Sam. Mages and shifters who step toward the wreckage and my mates. Without thinking of what I'm doing, I fling out my arm and a purple lightning bolt shoots from my palm and hits the ground in front of them.

Startled, I jump back. I honestly hadn't expected anything to happen. I don't even know how I managed it. Before Sam catches on to my shock, I straighten my shoulders.

"I can't let you do that," I say with a barely noticeable tremor in my voice.

Sam studies me with an intense gaze, his brown eyes swirling with his green magic. He tsks and shakes his head. "Doll, you don't want to go up against me. Just let them do what needs to be done. It's going to happen at some point anyway. Isn't it better if they're already unconscious when it happens?"

My body physically recoils at the thought of my mates dying.

"Not gonna happen," I growl. "I will fight tooth and nail to keep you from them."

Sam's hands curl into fists, his magic twining around his arms, and I can't stop myself from flinching. I remember the pain of his magic as it restrained me, and for a second, I falter. Sam notices the moment I lose my confidence. He takes one step toward me, and stops, his gaze moving over my shoulder.

"You're lucky there are people around, Sam, or you'd already be dead." Cade steps next to me, his magic swirling around him. Waves of angry energy flow from him as he stares down my ex-abuser.

With Cade at my side, my confidence returns. And I finally take in my surroundings. A crowd of onlookers have gathered, and sirens blare in the distance, steadily getting closer. Someone must have called for a medic.

Sam must realize the same thing, because he takes a step backward. A muscle ticks in his jaw and his magic disappears.

"This isn't over," he growls, before turning and heading back to his car with his cronies in tow.

Once I'm sure Sam is gone, I turn to the Land Rover. Seeing the damage from the outside causes me to miss a step. The right side dented in from the telephone pole, and the left side is completely destroyed from the car that hit us. Cade grabs my arm and keeps me upright.

"Sterling?" I ask, afraid to look inside.

"He's going to be fine," Cade reassures me.

With that knowledge, I approach the car and peer through the broken passenger window. Sterling is still trapped by the steering column, but the shard of metal has been removed. It's laying in the passenger seat, one end covered in his blood. The hole in his shirt is gaping and stained red, but his skin underneath is smooth and unblemished. I don't release my breath until I see his chest rise and fall.

My knees almost buckle and I grab onto the edge of the window to support myself, ignoring the jagged edge of broken glass that tears into my palms. I glance in the back at Kai, relieved to see him breathing as well.

"What do we do?" I ask Cade.

He gently removes my hands from the window and I wince as the pain registers through my receding panic.

"Come here," he says gently.

He tugs me away from the wrecked car and turns my bleeding palms up. Gentle warmth surrounds my hands and travels up my arms as he heals the cuts from the broken glass. He keeps his magic flowing, checking every inch of my body and healing any bruising from the impact.

"Thank you," I say and give him a once over. "Are you sure you're okay?" I lift my hand and brush a lock of hair from his forehead, exposing the cut that has already started healing.

"I'm fine." He glances behind us at the car. "We just have to wait for the medics. They'll be able to get Kai and Sterling out of the car. Once they do, Kai will need your blood. Sterling just needs to rest. He'll wake when his body is ready."

I exhale and lean my forehead against his chest. "That was so scary. Why won't he just stop?"

"It sounds like he knows what you are." He wraps his arms around me, tugging me close. "We'll have to be even more careful. And we need to start working on your training so you're more prepared next time"

"If ... " I can't continue and have to swallow. "If something happens to you guys, what happens to me? With the bonds and the Shield thing. If a harpy loses her Shields, what happens?"

He shrugs. "We'll have to do some more research. Maybe Sterling's connection will know. Or maybe Aunt Madge. But don't worry about that. Nothing is going to happen to us."

I look over his shoulder to the twisted mass of metal that used to be Sterling's car. Cade's words do nothing to ease my fears. This very easily could have gone horribly wrong. If Cade had been unconscious, would Sterling have died? What if a piece of metal had pierced Kai's heart? There were so many ways something could happen to one of them, and the thought is utterly paralyzing.

Cade leads me to the curb and helps me sit. I watch the medics and police pull up and examine the scene. The police interview me and Cade, but we leave out the part about Sam. The cops are probably in his pocket anyway.

It seems like it takes forever for them to extract my guys from the wreckage. They get Sterling out first and load him in the back of an ambulance. But it's not long after that, I hear a commotion from the vehicle.

"What's going on?" I ask and stand from my spot on the curb.

A medic pops his head out of the back of the ambulance and looks at me. "Are you Ellis?"

I nod and take a step forward, fear twisting in my gut. Did something happen?

"You better get in here."

I don't waste a second. I run to the vehicle and hop inside, gasping when my eyes land on Sterling. He is laying on the gurney, thrashing around, fighting against the bindings the medics placed on his wrists, ankles, and across his chest. Claws protrude from his fingers and his teeth have lengthened. His wolf wants free, but he's fighting it.

"Where is she?" he growls. "Where is my mate?"

The gurney rocks back and forth with the force of his thrashing, and the medic's assurances are doing nothing to calm him.

I rush forward and drop to my knees next to him. "Sterling, I'm right here."

His eyes snap to mine and his wolf looks out at me from the glowing, icy orbs. I brush his tangled hair from his face and rub my thumb along his cheek. He stills, the thrashing ceasing, but his chest heaves with gasping breaths.

"Ellis? Are you okay?"

"I'm fine," I assure him. "I had a few cuts, but Cade already healed me. I'm okay, Sterling."

His eyes close and his body shudders as he realizes I'm safe. "Can I ..." He swallows, and opens his eyes. Desperate yearning shines in the depths. "Can I hold you? I just ... I need to hold you."

I nod, needing to know he's okay as much as he needs to know I'm okay. He jerks on the gurney, still tied down.

"What the fuck," he growls. "Let me up."

I see panic flare in his eyes as he struggles against the bindings, and I quickly unhook the strap around his chest, while the medics release the ones around wrists and ankles. He sits up, gasping for breath and eyes wild.

"Sterling, it's okay. I'm right here."

His eyes snap to mine and he grabs me to him, holding me against his chest. As I let myself relax, I push away all the thoughts that try to intrude, all the feelings of hurt and betrayal, and just let him hold me. I hate how good it feels, how right. He buries his face in the top of my hair and inhales my scent. His racing heart calms under my cheek, and I know his wolf is finally relenting.

Cade is standing by the door with a smile and a raised brow. I glare at him, silently daring him to say something.

"They got Kai out," he says. "When you're ready, he'll need your blood. No rush though." He glances to the side where I assume Kai is loaded on a stretcher, and his whole body tenses. "Oh, fuck. Don't do that!" He yells and pushes away from the ambulance. "Ellis, come here!"

I push away from Sterling, fear once again bubbling inside of me. *What now?* I jump to the ground, and look around to find Kai on a stretcher with a bag of blood attached to an IV stuck in his arm. Cade reaches Kai and yanks out the IV, blood spraying as he tosses it away.

"What are you doing?" the medic yells. "He needs the blo ..."

He trails off as Kai's body starts to convulse on the stretcher. I rush forward, heart in my throat and eyes wide.

"What's happening? Cade, do something."

"They gave him blood. He can only have yours now." He

grabs my wrist and slices it open with a knife he pulls from his pocket.

I place my wrist to Kai's mouth, a difficult thing to do with his body convulsing, but as soon as my blood touches his tongue, his mouth seals around the cut and his shaking slows. I brush his hair back from his forehead as he drinks my blood, his body slowly relaxing. My heart pounds in my chest, and I'm not sure if it's mine or his that's racing, or a combination of both.

Kai groans, his grip on my wrist tightening. His face scrunches up and he rolls to his side, drawing his knees to his chest.

"Kai? Are you okay?" I ask, angling myself so he can keep drinking.

He groans again and pushes me away, leaning over the side of the stretcher and heaving. His body jerks violently as he vomits up blood. Cade and I jump back to avoid the splatter as it hits the pavement. Even knowing it's because he just drank a bunch of my blood, it's disconcerting to see.

He heaves again, vomiting more blood. After he coughs and splutters some more, he finally lays back on the stretcher, gasping for breath. "Fuuuck," he groans.

I rush forward, ignoring the blood on the ground. His forehead is clammy, and strands of his black hair are plastered to his skin. "Kai?"

"Son of a bitch, it hurts." He curls into a ball again, squeezing his eyes shut. "Why does it hurt?"

I look at Cade, unsure what to do. He steps around to the other side of the stretcher and rubs Kai's back.

"They gave you blood. I don't know how much they managed to give you, but I imagine you're going to feel like shit for a while."

He groans again and it breaks my heart. Seeing my strong, vicious vampire in pain is not okay, and I don't like it at all.

"Ellis?" he asks.

"I'm right here." I bend down and kiss his temple while running my fingers through his hair.

"Are you okay?" His words are slurred and pain laces each one.

"I'm fine. Do you need more of my blood?"

He shakes his head then grimaces. "Gods, that hurts. No, no more blood. I took too much already."

"You threw it back up, you need more, Kai."

"No more."

He sounds so pitiful I don't argue with him.

"When we get home you can give him more. Then everyone can pass out and let their bodies heal." Cade gives me a reassuring smile. "He'll be fine. Just miserable."

8. Ellis

I call Allie to drive us home since the Land Rover was totaled. As she pulls up to the scene, Cade and Sterling help Kai from the stretcher and get him situated in the back seat. I climb in with him, and Sterling follows. Wedged between the two of them in Allie's tiny vehicle isn't the most comfortable, but it's nice being so close to them. Kai curls into the smallest ball possible and lays his head on my lap, while Sterling's shoulder and thigh press against mine.

"Do you guys need anything before I take you home?" Allie asks. "Or I can drop you off first and then get anything you need. Either way, I'm happy to help."

"Thanks, Allie. But I think we're good," Cade says. He glances into the back seat and smirks. "Cozy back there?"

"I should have made you ride bitch, then you wouldn't be laughing." I glare at Cade, but keep running my hands through Kai's hair.

His occasional groans break my heart, and I just want to take his pain away. He tenses and quickly sits up.

"Oh fuck. Allie, pull over." His words are muffled by the hand he slaps over his mouth.

Allie complies, and the car has barely come to a stop when Kai throws the door open and heaves more of his stomach contents onto the pavement. I rub his back until his stomach settles and he collapses back into the seat, pulling the door closed. A sheen of sweat shines on his forehead and his hand is clammy when I grasp it in mine.

"Are you sure you're okay?" I scan his face, concerned by his grayish pallor and pain-filled expression.

"Yeah, just have to wait for this other blood to leave my system. It's just my body's way of rejecting it." His head lolls to the side, and gives me a pathetic grin. "Hey, at least now we know for certain you're my beloved, if there had been any doubts."

I'm too emotionally drained to react. This morning started with me learning the guys are my Shields, then the accident, Sterling freaking out, and now Kai doing ... this. And to top it all off, I got no sleep the night before. I'm exhausted.

When Allie pulls up the long driveway to Kai's place, I'm almost too tired to move. Cade and Sterling have to help Kai inside, he's too weak to make it on his own. The sight reminds me how close I was to losing them.

"I can still feel that, you know," Kai mumbles as the guys lead him to his room. "We're all fine, stop worrying."

"Stop reading me," I grumble. "It's rude."

"Hard not to when you practically shove your emotions down my throat."

I rush past them and open the bedroom door, closing and locking it behind us. Kai flops onto his bed and moans.

"Gods damn," he groans and bends forward, clutching his stomach.

I kick off my shoes and sit next to him on the bed. "Arms up," I say.

Cade has to help him lift his arms, and I pull his shirt over his head.

"Lay down. Both of you." Cade says, nudging both of our shoulders.

I collapse behind Kai, who curls up on his side again as soon as Cade gets his pants off. Reaching over him, I place my wrist by his mouth.

"Drink."

He shakes his head. "No. I don't want to take too much." He tries to push my arm away, but he's too weak to even manage it.

I press myself against his back. "Please, Kai. You need to feed."

He swallows and groans.

"She's right, Kai. I'll make sure you don't take too much."

Kai sighs heavily before turning to face me. His fangs have already elongated, and his eyes are red rimmed. He watches my pulse flutter in my neck with intense hunger, and my heart beats faster. I angle my head so he has better access, and the red in his eyes grows, swallowing more of the gray.

He presses a gentle kiss to my mark before sinking his fangs into my neck. There is no pain this time, no pleasure. Only a sense of calm as he pulls deep on my vein. There is something deeply sensual about this, even though there's no overwhelming sense of desire. The connection between us flares brightly, burning hotter than a flame. We are one and the same, in this moment, as Kai uses my life force to heal himself.

Cade settles behind me with an arm around my waist as he monitors us, and the sense of rightness settles within me. It's not complete, though, not yet. I have a feeling I won't feel complete until I accept the bond between me and Sterling. But this? This is everything I have ever dreamed of. All those nights spent crying in my bed, laying next to a monster I couldn't defeat, hoping and praying for someone to save me. And they did. They saved me in ways I will never understand, and I'll be forever thankful for them. My mates.

Dimly, I realize my vision is growing fuzzy. Blackness creeps in, swallowing the light. I hear Cade tell Kai he's had enough. A tongue laps at the puncture marks. A kiss on either cheek. And I contentedly fall asleep.

———

THE RED CARPET under my feet squishes with each step. Red carpet? I glance at the rug in confusion. It's supposed to be cream with flowers. Why is it red? I take another step and watch the crimson ooze between my toes. It's thick and sticky, and cool against my skin.

My gaze follows the rug, climbing the stairs. More red is puddled on the treads. I step in each one, fascinated by the contrast of the bright color against my tan skin. At the top of the stairs, two bodies lay sprawled on the wooden floor, a floor now soaked in the same red liquid.

I recognize the blond hair splayed out around the first body's head. The curls are the same as mine, only now, they are stained crimson.

"Mom?" It's so quiet in our house. My voice echoes, reverberating off of the wooden floors and walls. "What are you doing?"

I kneel next to her, the red soaking into my pants. It's so cold. I brush my mom's hair from her face. The sight is so unexpected and so gruesome. A scream tears from my throat.

"Ellis! Ellis, wake up!"

I scream and scream, but my mom doesn't open her eyes. I'm scared to look at the other body, but I force myself to take in the brown curly hair, the blood that's pooled around the body, and the unnatural angle of the limbs.

"Gracie?" I whisper.

Her head turns. Slowly and jerkily, like it's being pulled by a puppeteer. When she's facing me, her eyes open and there is nothing in her gaze but death. A grisly smile tugs at her lips, and I scream again.

"Ellis, baby girl, wake up!"

Kai's words and gentle shaking penetrate my dream and I sit up, gasping for breath. Tears stream down my cheeks and the sweat on my skin is already cooling, making me shiver.

Kai stares at me with wide gray eyes and he cups my cheek. "It was a dream, baby girl. You were just dreaming."

I collapse against him and sob into his chest. I haven't had that dream in years, and now I've suddenly had it twice since meeting the guys? The end though, that was new. I shudder as I remember the way Gracie's head turned and she smiled at me with dead, white eyes.

"Shh," Kai murmurs. "It's okay. It was just a dream. I'm here." He rubs circles on my back until the tears stop. "Do you want to talk about it?"

I shake my head. "I just want to forget it."

Wiping my eyes, I look around the room. It's just me and Kai in his bed. The moon shines through the window, providing a soft silver glow for me to see by. Kai looks better than he did when I fell asleep, but he's still more pale than usual.

"How are you feeling?" I ask.

"Better. My stomach still hurts like hell, but your blood helped to dilute what they gave me. I should be fine by tomorrow."

"Do you need more?" I asked, already raising my arm for him.

He smiles and brings my hand to his mouth, kissing the inside of my wrist. "No, I'm good. You need to replenish what I took yesterday."

"Are you su—"

He cuts me off with a kiss, but he quickly pulls away again, groaning and holding his stomach. "Fucking hell." He flops back onto the bed with a grimace.

"Can I get you anything? Pepto Bismol? Tums?"

He stares at me, bemused. "Pepto Bismol? Tums?"

I shrug and throw my hands up. "I don't know! How am I supposed to know what vampires need when they have an upset stomach? I just feel bad and I want to help."

He tugs me down to lay next to him. "Just lay here with me. That's more than enough."

My heart flutters and I cuddle closer, listening to his heart beat in time with mine. I'll never get sick of that feeling. I don't know how long we lay together before Cade joins us.

"Good, you're awake." He sits on the edge of the bed and looks down at both of us. "How are you feeling, Kai?"

"Like my insides want to become my outsides."

"So, not too bad, then." Cade grins at him, his violet eyes swirling with amusement.

Kai slaps his thigh and grunts. "Glad my misery is entertaining to you."

Cade chuckles before his smile slides from his face. "I think I may have found something on this warehouse. Get dressed and meet me in the library. I already sent a text to Sterling."

"Where is he?" I ask tentatively. I'm still not sure where we stand after everything, or how I feel.

"Out for a run," Cade replies.

"He does that a lot, doesn't he?"

Cade studies me for a second. "Do you want an honest answer?"

"Always."

"It's the easiest way for him to keep his wolf in check. Right now, I'm willing to bet his wolf is ten times harder to control. It's almost impossible for a wolf to not claim their mate, and it's been hard on him. On both of them."

"Well, doesn't that just make me feel like shit." I sit up and draw my knees to my chest. "I'm trying," I whisper.

Cade sighs. "That's why I didn't want to tell you. I'm not blaming you, Ellis. I get it, we all get it. But that's why he stays away so much. Sterling can only remain strong for so long." He leans forward to kiss my forehead, then pats Kai roughly on the cheek, earning himself a string of curse words, before heading to the door. "Hurry up. Library. Ten minutes."

"When did he become a drill sergeant?" Kai grumbles as he slowly climbs out of bed. "Shower together?"

I raise a questioning brow. "I thought you didn't feel good?"

He answers my question with a groan, clutching his stomach and hunching over. "I don't, but water conservation is very important to me," he says through gritted teeth.

I snort but follow him to the bathroom.

He eyes the sunken tub with longing. "Fucking Cade," he mutters. "Ten minutes my ass."

"Come on," I say, and lead him to the shower. "You're moving slower than a sloth, and we don't want to piss Cade off."

We shower together, and the only reason we are able to keep it PG is because Kai can barely stand up straight. It was a challenge of my self control that I managed to not jump him at the sight of him naked and wet, with water droplets sliding down his tattooed chest. By the time we stepped out of the shower and dried off, we were already late.

I shiver as I emerge from the steamy bathroom, a dull ache in my neck and shoulders making me wince. Before we leave the bedroom, I rifle through Kai's closet and pull out a black hoodie with the white Altair University logo across the front.

"Are you cold? It's the middle of summer." Kai says as I pull the hoodie over my head.

"A little. The wet hair doesn't help." I lift the hood and snuggle into the warm material.

He eyes me, but says nothing. We walk to the library hand in hand, and I have to take a moment to think about how far I've come. Never in a million years would have I thought I'd be walking through Thorne Estate holding the Prince of Nightmare's hand. I'm reminded of the conversation Allie and I had three weeks ago at the River's Edge, the little cafe in downtown Altair. We'd been looking at a sexy picture of Kai and I told her Kai would make some woman happy one day. She'd said something about him eating her first. I giggle. Who'd have thought I'd be that woman whom he makes happy, and yeah, maybe there is some eating thrown in there, too.

"What's so funny?" he asks as he squeezes my hand.

"Nothing. Just remembering a conversation Allie and I had a while ago."

He hums. "That conversation wouldn't happen to have involved me, would it?"

I slap a hand over my heart in mock outrage. "What? No! Never!"

"Mm-hm." He shakes his head, but pushes open the library door and ushers me inside.

"That took longer than ten minutes," Cade says from the couch. His face is lit up by the laptop screen, his violet eyes glowing.

Sterling snorts, but keeps scrolling on his phone. I have to force my gaze away from him and his naked chest. Always freaking naked.

"Sorry, mom. I'm moving at the pace of a sloth, according to Ellis."

"It's true, he is." I plop onto the couch next to Cade, and stifle a groan. Damn, my neck is really hurting.

Kai sits next to me and tucks me under his arm. "So, what did you find?"

"Well, Aunt Madge said to look for a building that caused a lot of controversy when it sold ten years ago. I dug through some old news reports, and there was one incident that created a stir eleven years ago."

I shiver, and I'm not sure if it's the fear of what Cade is going to say, or something else. I pull my arms inside the hoodie and wrap them around my middle.

"Do you remember when that elementary school on the outskirts of Altair sold without any warning?" Cade asks as he scrolls on his laptop.

"The one that closed and didn't tell any of the parents until the day of?" Kai looks down at me. "Are you hungry?"

"Starving, actually."

"I can get some food," Sterling says as he stands from his chair and exits the library.

Cade sighs. "Can you guys focus?"

"Sorry," Kai mumbles.

"Yes, that one," Cade says as he picks up his story again. "I was able to find the realtor who was in charge of the sale.

Hacking into his email was way too easy and the idiot kept all of the records and correspondence between the buyer and seller."

"And ..." Kai drawls.

"The seller was obviously the city of Altair. The buyer ... one Samuel Morris."

"How the hell did Sam buy a school when it wasn't even for sale?" I ask at the same time I grab the blanket from the back of the couch and bury myself under it. I can't seem to get warm. The pain in my neck and shoulders is spreading as well, and now my back and arms are achy, too.

"From the emails, it sounds like he blackmailed some city officials to make it happen and to keep it quiet." He glances at me shivering under the blanket. "Are you okay, Ellis?"

"Yep. Just cold for some reason." My stomach rumbles loudly, and I grimace. "And really hungry."

Cade watches me for a second longer, brow furrowed, before Sterling comes back carrying a tray laden with food. While Sterling hands me a plate with grilled chicken, mashed potatoes, and corn, Cade returns his attention to the laptop.

The aroma from the food makes my mouth water and my stomach rumble even louder. I dig in while the guys discuss this school building issue.

"So we know Sam owns this building, and we can pretty much assume it's the warehouse he mentioned. Now, we just need to figure out what he's doing with it." Kai says.

"Were you able to figure that out, Cade?" Sterling asks as he sits with his own plate of food.

"Not yet. And knowing Sam, it will be a lot harder than hacking into emails to figure it out. He's too smart. He'll have covered his tracks really well. I'm honestly surprised he let the realtor keep those emails. And his life."

I shudder. It would be so like Sam to kill the guy who sold the building to him. Less mouths to spread the tale.

"So how do we find out? He's been using that building for

ten years now for who knows what. We can assume it's nothing good." Sterling says between bites of chicken.

"Honestly, I think spying will be our best chance," Cade replies. "I can hack into the street cams around the building, but I'm guessing it won't give us any ideas. We'll need to get in close, possibly inside, to get the nitty gritty."

Sterling nods. "That's what I was thinking, too. My friend in the pack, the one who was adopted, is a crow shifter. He might be able to get in easier than us."

Cade purses his lips, and if I wasn't shivering from cold, I'd be tempted to lean forward and kiss him.

"Think we can hook a go-pro around his neck to get a look inside?" he asks.

Sterling snorts. "Yeah, I'm sure we can, it might make him more noticeable, though."

"Worth the risk," Cade mutters.

"Is anyone going to eat that last piece of chicken?" I ask and point to the plate on the coffee table.

Sterling shakes his head and Cade eyes me, but says, "You can have it."

I unbundle myself from the blankets and reach out to take it, grimacing as pain flares in my shoulder and arm.

"You sure you're okay?" Cade asks.

"Yeah, I'm fine." I take a bite of chicken and chew quickly. I'm still so hungry, even after eating my piece and all the sides.

Kai groans next to me and clutches his stomach. "I'm not okay. Why aren't you asking me?"

"Because, you're being dramatic, and you'll be fine in a few hours." Cade turns back his laptop. "When do you think your friend will be able to do this?" he asks Sterling.

"Give him a few days to scope the place and see if there are any guards or security he'll have to deal with. I'll talk to him later today about it."

"Perfect. Next, we nee—"

Kai groans, louder and longer, cutting Cade off.

"Really, Kai?" Cade asks, exasperated.

"Yes, really. My dad just texted me."

This time, it's Cade who groans. "Damnit. What does he want?"

"Fucking hell," Kai mutters. "There's a party tonight. He wants the three of us there."

9. Ellis

"A party?" Sterling asks. "One of us needs to stay with Ellis. This is too good of an opportunity for him to grab her."

"Agreed," Kai says. "And my guess is he is going to announce my engagement to Guilia."

I stiffen, all the food I just ate threatening to come back up. How did I forget about the engagement? We never really talked about what was going to happen with that. Is he still going to marry her?

"Relax, baby girl. I'm not going to marry her. But I'll have to play by his rules for a little longer. I don't want to mention anything about you until I know for sure you're safe and all of this shit with Sam has been settled."

I turn to look at him, but grunt as the muscles in my neck protest the movement.

"Okay, Ellis," Cade says, setting his laptop on the coffee table, and kneeling on the floor in front of me. "What's going on? You're shivering and wincing everytime you move. And don't tell me you're fine."

"I think I'm just sore from the accident. Really, I'm fi—"

He cuts me off with a look. "Can I make sure there is nothing going on?" he asks as he lifts his hand, purple light sparking to life on his fingertips.

I nod and hand Kai the plate in my lap. Cade gently grabs my face in both of his hands and his eyes widen.

"Ellis! You're burning up. What the hell? Why didn't you say anything?"

I notice Kai and Sterling sitting forward, all their focus on me, and I try to shrink back into the cushions, but Cade's grasp on my face stops me.

"I don't know. It didn't seem like a big deal," I say, looking down at my lap.

Cade scoffs, but the gentle warmth of his magic seeps under my skin and I moan. I don't realize just how cold I was until that warmth surrounds me. Suddenly, I need more of it. I crave it, the way I crave these guys. Before I can wrap my arms around Cade's neck to pull him closer, he frowns and worry lights his violet eyes. Just like that, I'm freezing again.

"There's nothing wrong," he mutters. "No injuries, no illness, nothing. Everything is exactly how it should be."

"So why the fever?" Kai asks.

Cade shakes his head. "I have no idea."

"It's probably nothing, you guys," I say. "Stop fussing over me."

Kai barks out a harsh laugh, and Cade and Sterling both shake their heads.

"You might as well get used to it, baby girl. We will never not fuss over you."

He runs his fingers through my curls, and even the movement of my hair on my scalp hurts. I groan and sink back into the cushions, cuddling under the blanket. "Don't you guys have a party to get ready for?"

"I really don't feel comfortable leaving you when you're like this. Especially since I can't find any reason for it." Cade scans my face as if he could see inside me to find the cause.

Kai sighs heavily. "I'll tell my dad you can't make it. Prior plans and all that. Sterling?"

"Yeah, I'll come to the party," he says, resigned. "Someone needs to make sure you stay out of trouble."

"Like I need a babysitter to look after me," Kai mutters as he pushes up from the couch. "Fucking hell, tonight is going to suck." He heads for the door, clutching his stomach and moaning.

Sterling follows, leaving me and Cade alone in the library. If only I was feeling better, this would be the perfect opportunity for some one on one time with my mage. Unfortunately, I shiver violently and Cade clenches his jaw.

"Lay down, Ellis."

I do as he says, and he drapes two blankets over me, tucking me in snugly. He places his hand on my forehead and his magic warms me as he sweeps my body again. Frowning, he shakes his head before grabbing me a bottle of water from the minifridge and a couple of aspirins.

"Take these," he says, and sits on the floor next to me with his laptop.

Again, I do as he says, before I close my eyes and doze off. I'm awakened when the library door opens. I open my eyes and gasp.

"Holy shit, you guys clean up good." I grin at Kai and Sterling.

Both are wearing tuxes, tailored and cut to fit them perfectly. Kai's is black with a black button-up underneath. It sets off his pale skin and gray eyes perfectly. Sterling's is charcoal gray with barely noticeable white pinstripes, and a navy blue button-up underneath. His silver hair is down and brushed, and I've never seen it gleam so brightly in the light before. I desperately want to run my fingers through the strands.

Kai grins at me, fangs on full display. I shiver, and not from the fever. He chuckles as he walks to the couch and fists Cade's hair in his grasp, tugging his head back roughly. Kai gives Cade a chaste kiss, for all his actions are possessive and incredibly sexy.

"Take care of our girl," he mumbles against Cade's lips.

"Always." Cade grins.

I huff and cross my arms over my chest under the blankets. Kai smirks at me before bending forward and kissing my forehead.

"Be good for Cade. If you are, you can have a reward when you're feeling better."

Even feeling like crap, his promise makes my toes curl. I can't wait for that reward.

"Yes, daddy," I joke, but as soon as the words are out of my mouth, I realize how much I like calling him that.

Kai's eyes darken, and I know he likes it, too. "Save that for later, baby girl," he says, his voice deep as it brushes over my skin.

Before they leave, I catch Sterling's gaze and we stare at each other. There is so much I want to say to him, but I just can't bring myself to do it. I'm not ready yet, and I won't force it just because we're mates. He hurt me, and I need to heal from that first or our relationship will start on the wrong foot.

He breaks eye contact first, turning to the library door and following Kai out. I sigh and let my head flop onto the pillow.

"Why does it have to be so hard?" I whisper.

Cade brushes a finger down my cheek. "You'll figure it out. Maybe you two should spend some time together again and just talk. No expectations besides that."

"Couldn't hurt," I reply.

I doze off again, and when I wake next, I'm drenched in sweat. I kick the covers off and sigh as the cool air hits my heated skin. Cade glances at me from his position on the floor.

"Have you been sitting there this whole time? And speaking of, how long was I asleep?"

"About two hours. And I've just been digging into this school and trying to get as much information as I can." He places his hand on my forehead. "Your fever broke. How are you feeling?"

"I feel fine," I say. I sit up and stretch, no achiness in my neck or shoulders. "Nothing hurts, either."

"That's good. Weird, but good."

"Must have been a little bug." I look around the library. "I'm hungry though, is there anything to eat here?"

Cade's eyes widen. "Hungry? You just ate two huge pieces of chicken not that long ago. How are you hungry again?"

I shrug. "I don't know, but I am."

"I can text Kai and have him bring some food from the party when it's over."

"When will that be?"

He checks the time. "I'm guessing another two hours or so."

"Two hours? I don't know if I can wait that long."

"Seriously?"

I nod, and my stomach rumbles, emphasizing my point. "See? Starving."

He sighs and shakes his head. "We really shouldn't leave the library with everybody in the estate, but I can't let you starve."

He stands and sets his laptop on the coffee table before helping me to my feet. Peering into my eyes, he says, "You sure you're okay?"

I stand on my tiptoes and kiss him. "I really do feel fine now. I promise."

He wraps his arms around my waist, and I try to deepen the kiss, but my stomach has other plans. Cade chuckles and pulls away.

"I think I better feed you before your stomach tries to eat me."

"After I eat, then," I promise him.

"Deal."

He leads me through the estate, keeping to the hallways far from the ballroom where the party is taking place. I try to keep track of my surroundings, just in case, but I'm too hungry to focus on anything other than getting food in my mouth.

Cade slows as we come to an intersection. "We have to be careful here," he whispers over his shoulder. "It's the only way to the kitchens, and the closest bathrooms to the ballroom are down this hallway." He points to the hall to the right.

He peers around the corner, and waits for a few seconds before motioning to me. "Come on. Hurry."

Cade grabs my hand and tugs me through the intersection. The rest of the way is clear, and soon we push through the kitchen doors, and into chaos.

Servers run every which way, picking up full silver trays and depositing empty ones. Food, so much food, waits to be plated and taken to the ballroom. Cook storms around, brandishing a wooden spoon like a scepter, bellowing orders and fully expecting to be obeyed. I inhale the heavenly aroma of meats, vegetables, and sweets, and my mouth waters.

Cade snags a plate off the counter and holds it out to me. "This good?"

I glance at the roast beef swimming in sauce and the mashed potatoes with gravy. My stomach rumbles again. "Yes, please." I snatch a baby carrot off the plate and pop it into my mouth. Honey bursts to life on my tongue and I groan.

Before we leave, I spot a chocolate cake on the island and grin. "Is that your cake?"

Cade smiles. "It sure is. Grab it, and let's head back before Cook yells at us."

With the chocolate cake in my grasp, I follow Cade back the way we came. When we reach the intersection, he stops and leans around the corner. He stiffens a moment before he looks back at me with wide eyes. I hear a woman's voice, just a soft murmur, and without thinking, I push around Cade. He tries to stop me, but with the plate in his hand, I'm able to slip through his fingers. What I see makes my stomach drop to my feet.

Down the hallway, Kai is leaning against the wall, his head thrown back while a woman presses herself against him. Her blond hair falls down her back in loose ringlets, and her dark red dress clings to every inch of her body, leaving nothing to the imagination.

The world seems to wobble around me as I watch her hands rove over his chest and inside his jacket. I quickly realize, though, he isn't returning her touch. His jaw is clenched tight, and his hands are balled into fists at his side. It's not pleasure on his face, but irritation. I narrow my eyes as her hands slide lower to his belt and she grabs the leather, sliding it through the buckle.

"Guilia, stop." Kai says through gritted teeth.

She doesn't, and I snap.

Anger floods my system, a rushing inferno that takes over all rational thought. All I can think of is the threat posed to my Shield, and I need to protect him. The chocolate cake falls to the ground, the plate shattering on the marble floor. Guilia and Kai whip their heads in my direction, and Kai's eyes widen.

"Fuck," he says. "Ellis, it's not ..."

He trails off as I march forward. I can't see my face, but I can guess my expression is pure thunderclouds. Cade grabs my arm, and I whirl around and shove him with my free hand. I'm so angry, I don't even realize he flies across the hall and slams into the opposite wall with a grunt.

I turn to face the reason for my anger. Her blue eyes are wide as she watches me stalk forward. She swallows and takes a step closer to Kai.

I grin. "Wrong choice." My fingers tingle, then burn. I raise one arm, a finger pointed directly at Guilia's chest. Violet light, Cade's magic, dances over my skin.

Kai steps in front of me, hands raised. "Ellis, baby girl, calm down. Don't do anything you'll regret later."

I meet his eyes. They shine so brightly as he looks at me. When he places his hand over his chest, a subtle reminder of our connection, my anger slips away.

"She's not worth it, baby girl. Let it go."

Cade's magic disappears, leaving me feeling cold. The inferno in my veins evaporates, and I shudder. Kai steps forward to wrap me in his arms, but before he touches me, the ground shakes under our feet. An explosion pierces my eardrums, and bits of dust and rock fall from the ceiling.

Kai knocks me to the ground, covering me with his body

while also keeping my head from smacking against the floor. My ears ring and I blink the dust from my vision.

"Are you okay?" he breathes.

I nod my head, unable to find my voice.

He hops up and pulls me to my feet.

"That came from the ballroom," Cade says as he slides to a stop next to us.

Down the hall, smoke curls from around a corner, and debris from the ceiling and walls is scattered in the hallway.

Guilia is staring wide eyed from her knees on the floor. "What was that?" she asks in a voice that sounds like ringing bells.

Before anyone can answer her, another explosion rocks the estate. I cover my ears as Kai grabs my waist to keep me balanced on the shaking ground.

"What the fuck?" Kai growls.

"Sterling!" I grab Kai's arm and look at him. My heart races in my chest. "Was he in the ballroom?"

"Shit," he mutters. "Cade, get her back to the library, I'll go find Sterling."

Before any of us can move, Sterling tears around the corner in his wolf form. He doesn't appear to be injured and I relax knowing all my guys are safe and with me. When he reaches us, he shifts in the blink of an eye, silver wolf turning into a giant naked man. I notice Guilia behind him staring wide eyed at my mate, and I glare at her.

"It's Sam," Sterling says, drawing my attention back to him. "He's taken down the wards around the estate and blew holes into the ballroom. His men are infiltrating as we speak."

"Son of a bitch!" Kai yells. He grabs my arm and yanks me in the direction of the library. "Sterling, scout outside. Make sure it's safe for us to leave and bring my Charger around. Cade, grab everything you think we'll need technology wise. I'll grab the weapons."

Behind us, Guilia shouts for us to stop, but no one spares her any mind. When we get to the library, Kai tosses Sterling his keys, and he dashes outside and shifts back into his wolf. Cade and Kai grab bags and shove weapons and tech into them, while I stand in the middle of the library and shake.

Sam blew up the estate. He probably killed a bunch of people, just to get to me. We thought I was safe here, but I'm not. Where can we go that he won't find us? Will I ever be safe again?

Kai's eyes pop into my vision. Red encroaches on the gray and his fangs have descended, his body's reaction to the threat against his beloved. "Hey, it's okay. Your heart is racing, Ellis. You need to calm down. We're going to get you out of here. You know we'll never let him get his hands on you again."

I try to calm my heart, but I can't. The fear is too real. Sam is here, right now. He can walk through that library door any moment and my entire world would come crashing to the ground. How do I just *calm down*?

"Shit, Cade she's starting to panic, and it's making me panic. I can sense her emotions, and my heart is racing in time with hers."

"We don't have time for you both to panic. Get it under control, Kai." Cade slaps the back of Kai's head. "Did you get the weapons? Sterling has the Charger ready."

Kai swallows. "Yeah," he says. His chest is rising and falling as rapidly as mine.

"Then come on," Cade urges. He pushes both of us to the door and out into the night.

The warm summer air barely registers in my mind, as Cade opens the back door of the car and shoves first me, then Kai inside. He runs around the front and hops into the passenger seat. Sterling takes off before Cade's door is fully shut.

My panic recedes the closer to the gate we get, and as my panic recedes, so does Kai's. He's able to get himself under control and he peers out the windshield at the approaching gate.

"They blew the gate up, too," Kai says. "How the hell did they get so far without any warning?"

"Someone on the inside?" Sterling asks as he maneuvers the car around chunks of stone and twisted metal.

We're almost out of the driveway when something hits the back window. Kai immediately shoves my head down and covers me with his body.

"Go, Sterling!" he yells. "They're fucking shooting at us!"

Sterling floors it, the car bouncing over debris from the blown-up gate and Kai curses.

"You better not have just fucked up my car," he mutters.

"What the hell do you want me to do?" Sterling shouts. "You tell me to go, then get pissy when I go. Make up your mind."

"Is anyone following us?" Cade asks from the front seat. Always the voice of reason, he reels the other two guys back.

Kai lifts off of me, but he doesn't remove his hand from my neck to keep me down. "I think we're good," he says after a while.

He lifts his hand and I slowly sit up, glancing at the back window. "How did that not break?" I ask.

"Bullet proof glass."

"You have bullet proof glass in your car? Do you get shot at that often?"

He chuckles. "No. But you never know when you'll need it. Case and point."

"Fair enough," I say.

Cade turns around to look at me. "Are you okay?"

The concern shining in his eyes does something to me. I know these guys all care for me. I know they will do anything to protect me. I know their purpose in my life. But experiencing their love for me first hand is something else entirely. I swallow the lump in my throat and nod.

"I'm fine. Just trying to process everything."

"Do you need anything?" he asks.

"I never got to eat that food. I'm still hungry."

He smiles. "We'll stop and get you something once we know we're for sure not being followed."

He turns back around and Kai tugs on my arm.

"Come here." His eyes are still red-rimmed, and the way they shine in the street lights as we pass them makes me shiver. He looks every inch the predator he is.

I scoot across the seat and rest my head on his shoulder. He wraps an arm around me, holding me tightly.

"Ellis, about what happened back there."

I look up at him, worried he's mad about my reaction.

"Nothing happened between me and Guilia. She was trying, but I never would have let her take it any further."

"I know that," I whisper.

His brow furrows. "You were so mad, though. The expression on your face was nothing I'd ever seen before."

"I wasn't mad at you. I trust you, Kai. Completely. It was her I was pissed at."

"You were going to use Cade's magic on her. Which, by the way, you used without him using it first. In the past, he's always had to already have gathered his magic to him in order for you to use it. That wasn't the case this time."

"Really?" I hadn't noticed where Cade was during that confrontation. My focus was solely on Guilia touching my man.

"I think your abilities are growing. We really should start training you in all of this."

I nod. "That would probably be a good idea." I raise my arm and touch his cheek, just under his eye. "Do you need to feed? Your eyes are red."

He tucks my head against his shoulder again. "I'm fine. It's the adrenaline. But, I wouldn't say no once we get to where we're going."

I huff a laugh. "Where are we going anyway?"

"Pack lands," Sterling says from the driver's seat.

"Is that safe?" Kai asks.

"Noah will never know she's there. My dad had a secret cabin in the mountains. He would take my mom there on the weekends to get away from everything. Only my family knows about it."

"I'll throw some wards up, too. It's the last place Sam will think of looking. He'll assume we're too smart to take her into the crosshairs of the guy who wants her dead."

Nervous butterflies flit through my stomach, but I trust these guys to keep me safe. If they think this is the best option, then we'll do it. I just hope I don't run into my real dad while we're there.

10. Malakai

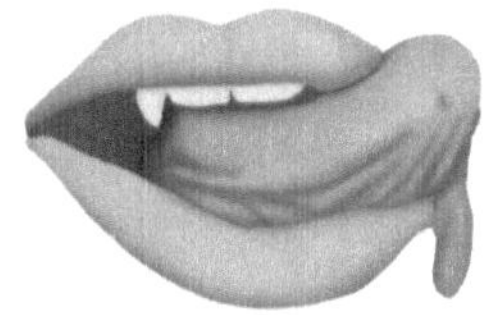

Ellis is asleep with her head in my lap. It's the only thing that's making this drive to the mountains bearable. I hate riding in the backseat. I'll never say so out loud, but it makes me carsick. I can't let people know the big, bad vampire gets sick when he rides in the backseat. It would ruin my street cred.

I focus on Ellis, instead. I trace her curls with my gaze and the line of jaw. Her lips are slightly parted, and they are too tempting not to touch. I rub my thumb along her lower lip, gently so I don't wake her. My palm and fingers graze her cheek, and I frown. She's warm. Warmer than she usually is to my slightly cooler skin. Placing my hand on her forehead, I curse.

"Cade, she's feverish again," I say to the mage in the front seat.

Cade turns around and frowns. He reaches back with a hand, purple light flowing over his skin as he places it on her arm. "Nothing. She's completely healthy. Just like last time."

"Think it's some kind of bug?" Sterling asks as he glances in the rearview mirror.

"If it were a bug, I think I'd pick up on that," Cade answers.

He looks about ready to climb into the back seat with us, although, I'm not sure what good that will do.

"Well, let's think about it," I say. "The first time it happened was after the accident. You said you checked her over at the scene, and besides some cuts and bruises, she was fine. Correct?"

"Yeah."

"Did anything else happen? I know Sam confronted you guys. Did he manage to do something? Something maybe you didn't notice or wouldn't be able to pick up on with your magic?"

"No," he says slowly, "but she used my magic to defend you and Sterling." His brow furrows. "She used it tonight, too. And not just my magic, but your strength. She pushed me halfway down the hall."

"You think that's it? Whenever she uses our abilities she gets a fever? Why would that happen?"

He shakes his head. "I have no idea, but it's the only thing I can think of. Maybe it's her body's way of adjusting to the sudden change?"

"What can we do about it?" Sterling asks.

Cade bites his lower lip. "I think we have to let it ride its course. We need to keep an eye on her, but I don't think there's much we can do."

I don't like the thought of not being able to help her when she needs it, but I think Cade is right. If he can't heal her, there isn't anything we can do except keep her comfortable when it happens.

"This might make training more difficult," I say. "If she gets a fever every time she uses our abilities, we'll have to limit the amount of time she uses them."

"Yeah, not ideal, but we'll figure it out."

We fall silent again. Cade doesn't turn back around. He continues watching Ellis, like he's prepared to jump in if needed. I smooth her hair back from her face and she whimpers in her sleep. The sound breaks my heart. I'm about to ask Cade or Sterling if they have any aspirin, when my phone rings.

Fishing it out of my pocket, I groan when I see who's calling. I swipe to answer, fangs extending and lips curled in a silent growl. "Kennedy. What do you want?"

Cade and Sterling both stiffen in the front of the car. Cade whips around to mouth something to me, but I'm too focused on my phone to make out what it is.

"Thorne, always a pleasure talking with you." Kennedy's smooth voice reeks of sarcasm.

"What do you want, Kennedy?" I ground out.

"I have the details for the second challenge. I figured you'd want to know what they were."

Disbelief stuns me to silence. We were just attacked at the estate, and this man, who isn't even Ellis's dad, wants to continue with the challenge? Not a fucking chance.

Cade finally gets my attention. "Go along with it," he mouths.

I glance back to my phone, making sure to keep Ellis out of the screen. "What's the challenge?"

"Have you ever heard the tale of the mountain troll who stole the gem of Lustros?"

I blink. Then blink again. He can't be going where I think he's going.

Kennedy smiles. "The second challenge is to get the gem."

Yep. He went there. "You're fucking crazy," I breathe. "First, that's a legend. There is no proof that gem exists. Second, if it does, it's suicide going into a mountain troll's lair."

"If you want to keep my daughter, you'll have to risk it."

It's on the tip of my tongue to say she's not his daughter, but I bite it back. Cade says to play along, so I will.

"When does this challenge go down?" I ask through gritted teeth.

"It starts now. The other contestants are being informed of the details as we speak."

"Perfect," I growl. "We'll talk later." I hang up and look at Cade. "Well? We're obviously not doing this. So what's the plan?"

"We need to get that proof Sam mentioned about Kennedy

not being her dad. If we can prove she isn't his daughter, this contest is over."

"And if we can't get the proof?" Sterling asks quietly.

After a beat of silence, Cade says, "It doesn't matter. This contest is over no matter what."

"What about your mom and sister?" I ask.

Cade doesn't reply, and I know the answer to that question tears him up inside. When it comes to Ellis, nothing is too great a sacrifice for her safety.

―――

THE DRIVE to the cabin is torture. With the winding roads and being stuck in the back seat, my car sickness has reared its ugly head. Nausea churns in my gut, and there's a steady throbbing behind my eyes. I just want to get out of this godsforsaken car. When Sterling pulls off the road and starts driving up the rocky slope, I cringe.

"What the hell, man? This car is not built for off-roading."

The undercarriage scraping against the ground emphasizes my statement. We hit a rut and the car jerks violently, causing Ellis to moan.

"Sorry. It's the only way to the cabin. My dad didn't want any roads leading to it. Less chance of discovery."

More scraping and bouncing, and I feel each one deep in my soul. "You're paying for any damage, asshole."

Sterling's only reply is a grunt.

It's almost daylight by the time we reach the cabin. My poor car is thoroughly battered, and the sound of scraping is forever etched into my brain. I swear I hear it sigh in relief when Sterling cuts the engine.

My eyes are burning and I have to ask Cade to give me the sunglasses out of the glovebox—they're always more sensitive to light when the red is showing. And for some reason, I haven't been able to calm down enough since the attack. I'm guessing it has to do with Ellis shivering in my lap, and there being nothing I can do to help her.

"Wake up, baby girl" I say as I rub her shoulder. "We're here. We'll get you inside and comfortable."

She groans and shudders, curling into a tighter ball. I check her forehead and she's still burning up. We'll have to run to a store to get medicine for her. And food. We never stopped to get food.

I run my hand down her back to try and wake her up. She gasps and flinches, her moan of discomfort turning into one of pain. I jerk my hand away, alarmed at her reaction.

"What's wrong?" Cade asks, turning around his seat.

"My back," she mumbles. "It hurts."

"Okay," I say quietly. "Let's get you inside and we'll check it out."

Sterling hops out of the car and opens the back door for me. Even lifting her as gently as possible she still whimpers. Tears form on her lashes through her closed eyelids, and each one is like a stake to my heart.

"I'm so sorry, baby girl. I'm trying to be gentle," I whisper.

I hurry up the wooden steps and through the front door Sterling holds open. Cade grabs a plaid blanket from the back of the couch and I lay her down on her side. Carefully, Cade lifts her shirt to look at her back. There is nothing but smooth, creamy skin. Not a single blemish or mark.

"Where does it hurt, love?" Cade asks.

"Upper back," she gasps.

He brushes two fingers down her spine from her nape to her mid back and she flinches again. She curls herself into a ball, trying to escape his touch.

"It burns when you touch me," she whimpers.

He pulls his hand away and a crease forms between his eyebrows. "I have no idea."

Anger and fear flash in his violet eyes. Having a puzzle before him he can't solve will drive him mad. I know him well enough to see the frustration. And with it involving his soul-bonded, it's bound to be a hundred times worse.

I tug her shirt down, careful to not touch her back, and cover her with the blanket. "Just rest, Ellis. We'll be here." I sit on the floor next to her and tuck a curl behind her ear.

"We need supplies," Sterling says. "Medicine, food, clothes. I'm going to call my friend and see if he can pick up some stuff for us. None of us should be seen in town if at all possible."

He heads for the porch to make his call, and I glance at Cade. He's watching Ellis sleep, shoulders tense and eyes creased with concern. Reaching out with my senses, I'm bombarded by his emotions. Fear, anger, helplessness, anxiety, love. It all swirls around so thickly it almost chokes me.

This is possibly the first time I wished my ability was more than just sensing emotions. Right now, I wish I could take what he is feeling away from him. I'd take it all for myself if I could. Instead, I grab his hand and tug him down to sit between my legs with his back against my chest.

"I know you're beating yourself up right now, and I get it. But there's nothing we can do." I massage his neck and shoulders, the muscles so tight under my hands. "You haven't done anything wrong, Cade."

"I feel like I'm failing her," he whispers. "What good is my magic if I can't heal her when she needs it? What good am I as a Shield if I can't keep her safe? I have one purpose in life, one job I was destined to do, and I'm failing."

"You are keeping her safe. You got us out of the estate when we needed it. I froze, Cade. I fucking froze. I let her emotions take over me, and if it hadn't been for you, we wouldn't have made it out. You are not failing her. This is something out of our control, and there is nothing we can do about that. You are not failing her," I repeat, punctuated by increased pressure on his muscles.

He moans and the sound shoots straight to my cock. When he tilts his head to the side and stretches out his neck, my gums tingle as my fangs descend. I swallow thickly and close my eyes, but the urge doesn't go away. Inhaling through my nose also makes it worse as his scent invades me.

Cade moves slightly. Just enough for his ass to brush against my erection. He stiffens and sucks in a breath. "Kai," he says in a low, raspy voice.

The control I had been fighting, snaps. I lean forward and lick up the side of his throat, tasting him, wanting so badly to bury my fangs in his neck. He grabs my thighs and squeezes tightly as I drag my fangs across his skin.

"Fuck, Kai." Reaching one hand back, he palms the back of my head and presses my mouth against his throat.

Needing no more encouragement, I bite down, sinking my fangs into his vein. The taste of his blood, like rich spiced wine, explodes on my tongue. He tastes so fucking good. We both moan at the same time, and his hips jerk, seeking friction. I slide a hand down his abs and into the waistband of his pants. I palm his cock and stroke it from base to tip, squeezing the head how I know he likes it. Cade's chest is heaving as if he's just run a marathon.

THE STRENGTH of his desire hits me like a ton of bricks when I open myself to his emotions again. It punches straight through my chest, and it amps me up even more. I retract my fangs, licking the puncture marks to seal them, and slide out from behind him. I push him to the ground and straddle him so I can kiss him. I have every intent to ravish his mouth, but for some reason, that's not what happens.

Cade frames my face in both of his hands, and it's such a gentle touch it calms my urgency. The kiss is soft, but deep. There is a thrumming in my chest, something intense that gives me pause. Each interaction between us has made this connection grow. I've loved Cade for a while now, as a friend, as someone who has such an important role in my life. But I think it's shifting. And that scares me and excites me at the same time.

I break the kiss to yank his pants down his hips and his

erection springs free. Cade kicks them off the rest of the way and I trail kisses down his chest and abs, giving him little nips here and there that leave him writhing under me. His hands on my shoulders try to push me lower but I resist, giving him a wicked, fang-filled grin. I can hear his blood rushing through his veins, pumped by his heart that's beating a mile a minute.

When I finally lick up the length of his cock, Cade is barely restraining his trembling. I love to think I have so much sway over this man. That I can turn this magnificent, powerful mage into a trembling mess with just my fangs. My tongue traces the slit at the head of his cock, lapping at the precum, and his hips jerk, desperate for more. I wrap my lips around his length and slowly tease him, keeping it just shy of what he needs.

"Fuck, Kai," he moans.

His throaty moan makes my dick twitch in my pants. It's straining and aching for pleasure of its own. I rub my hips against his leg as I continue to suck him, the pressure only a tease to me, drawing me higher but no closer to what I want.

I place my hands on the floor on either side of Cade's hips and set a punishing rhythm. His hips thrust up, matching my pace, and his fingers dig into my scalp, pulling my hair hard. I meet his gaze at the same time I graze my fangs along the top of his cock and he curses as he explodes in my mouth.

I've never thought about other men in the same way I think about Cade. I've never thought another man was attractive or beautiful, but Cade is. And when he's chasing his pleasure, he is infinitely more attractive with his cut muscles tensing and relaxing, a sheen of sweat glistening on his skin, and pure bliss lighting up his violet eyes. This man is absolutely beautiful.

I release him, wiping my mouth on my sleeve, and barely have time to take a breath before he flips us. His mouth crashes into mine and he kisses me with a passion we've never had before. It's like he's trying to devour my soul through my mouth, like he can't get enough oxygen so he has to steal mine.

That piece in my chest, the one I've felt slowly shifting, clicks into place. Right next to the piece that belongs to Ellis.

Cade pulls my pants down and wraps his hand around my cock, finally giving me what I've been desperate for. My head thumps on the floor, and I close my eyes, taking in each sensation. I do something I've never done before. I open myself up to his emotions while he sucks my cock into his mouth.

The combination of his mouth and the intensity of his affection almost makes me come. The thought that he might feel the same way about me as I do about him is overwhelming. Fuck. I close my eyes and thread my fingers through his hair. He's driving me closer and closer to that edge, and he knows exactly what to do to get me there. I groan as he squeezes my balls and lightning shoots through my veins. I come so hard, stars dance behind my closed eyelids.

Cade crawls up my body and places his hand on my cheek. He kisses me deeply, and my heart flutters. Is this really what I think it is? Is it possible I love him like I love Ellis?

He settles next to me, head on my chest, and palm over my heart. "Hey," he says after a while. "How come you can drink from me and not get sick now that you have your beloved?"

"That's a great question." I prod one of my fangs with the tip of my tongue. "I hadn't even thought about that. Maybe our connection as Ellis's Shields makes it possible? Whatever the reason, I'm not going to complain."

He huffs a laugh. "Oh, I'm not either. Not. At. All.".

11. Cade

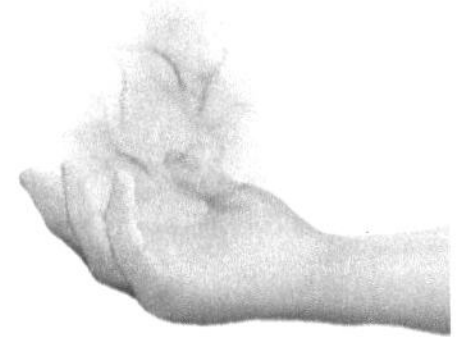

Ellis is screaming. Her voice breaks as her screams are torn from her throat. I drop the mug in my hand, ceramic shattering and sending tea splattering in all directions. Kai and I run into each other in our rush to get to her. He has a dagger in his hand, fangs elongated—fangs that were just buried in my neck minutes ago. My magic rears to the surface on its own, like it can tell my soul-bonded is in trouble and needs help.

She's on the couch, blanket tossed to the floor amid her thrashing. Kai reaches her first and grabs her shoulders, shaking her awake.

"Ellis! Wake up!" he yells. His eyes are wild, and red encroaches on the gray yet again.

I fall to my knees on the floor by her head just as her eyes pop open. She gasps, hand flying to her throat as she tries to suck in enough oxygen. Sweat plasters her curls to her forehead, and even I can see her vein pulsing in her neck as her heart hammers in her chest. Her amber eyes fill with tears, and she throws herself off the couch and into my arms.

I'm hesitant to touch her, afraid I'll hurt her if I do, but she buries her face in my chest and sobs. It's instinct to wrap my arms around her and pull her close. I say nothing, just rock her back and forth, and rub circles on her back, which doesn't seem to hurt anymore. Once she stops crying, I pull back so I can see her face.

"Are you okay?" I ask.

She nods and wipes her cheeks. "Just a bad dream." Little hiccups interrupt her answer and she continues to shudder.

"Do you want to talk about it?" Kai asks.

She shakes her head violently. "No. I want to forget it."

Kai purses his lips and hesitates. He looks unsure, like he wants to say something, but he's scared. He takes a breath and says, "Can I ask you something?"

She nods and rests her cheek on my chest.

"You seem to be having a lot of nightmares lately. Is that normal for you?"

She bites her lip and tries to bury closer to my body. "No," she whispers so quietly I barely hear her. "I used to have this dream after my mom and sister died. I haven't had one like it in years. Until recently."

"Can you do something to help her?" I ask Kai. With his abilities, he's able to walk in people's dreams. He'd be the one who could help her with this.

He shakes his head. "It doesn't work like that. The most I could do is pull her out if she gets stuck. I'm not able to manipulate a dream she is already experiencing."

"Any idea why you might be having it again so often?" I ask Ellis.

She snorts but there is no humor behind it. "Trauma?"

Fair enough. I kiss her forehead and notice she's no longer feverish. "I just hate there's nothing we can do to help you. With the dream or these fevers."

She shrugs. Her eyes are red and puffy from her crying, with dried tear tracks down her cheeks. "It's just a dream. I'll be fine. And these fevers are annoying, but don't seem to last long."

Kai leans in to kiss her cheek. "Can we get you anything?"

"Food? I don't think I've ever been this hungry."

"Food is on its way," Sterling says from the door to the porch.

I hadn't even heard him come in. Which reminds me I need to lay down some wards.

"Why don't you go take a shower and try to relax," he says, nodding to the wooden staircase by the kitchen. "The shower is upstairs in the bedroom. When you're done, I'm sure the food will be here."

"Thank you, Sterling." She stands and hesitates, staring at the wolf shifter with indecision on her face. Biting her lip, she turns away and heads for the stairs.

The three of us watch her until she disappears at the top.

"I hate this," Kai murmurs. "I hate seeing her hurting."

I don't reply, because I've already stated my feelings on the matter. Nothing has changed. Kai's words were nice, but they were just words. I get up and head for the front door. At least I can try to keep her safe while we're here.

"I'm going to lay down some wards. I'll be back."

I walk the perimeter of the house, my magic flaring as I set protective wards. It's a classic two-story wooden cabin you'd find in the mountains. Small but quaint. Perfect for a romantic weekend getaway. If only our purpose was for fun and relaxation.

I make it back around the front at the same time a small SUV pulls up the rocky slope. I vaguely recognize the man who steps out as Sterling's friend. We've met once or twice, but it's been years since I saw him last.

"Cade, right?" he asks as he shuts the car door.

I nod and hold my hand out. He grabs it in a tight grip.

"Drew Harper. I'm Sterling's friend."

"Yeah, we met a few years ago. Thanks for getting us supplies," I motion to the bags he's currently pulling from the back of the car.

"No problem. I don't know everything that's going on, but I know a bit, and I'm happy to help."

I jump in and grab the last few bags. Sterling opens the front door as we climb the wooden steps, and Drew and I walk in as

Ellis is descending the stairs. I set my bags on the kitchen table and smile at her.

"Food," I say.

She peers into a bag and her lips quirk. "Um, that doesn't look like food," she says with a raised brow.

I glance inside and chuckle. "Well, I guess that depends on what you consider food?"

Kai looks over Ellis's shoulder and laughs. Reaching into the bag he pulls out the bottle lube and turns to Sterling. "Really?"

Sterling shrugs. "Thought you'd appreciate it."

Kai tosses the bottle in the air and catches it. "Thanks man. Much appreciated."

He winks at me and I shake my head, but really, I'm glad Sterling thought of that. If we're stuck in this cabin for the time being, the tight quarters are bound to lead to some sexy time.

"Okay, but is there real food?" Ellis asks, rubbing her stomach.

"Of course there is." Sterling grabs the bags from Drew and places them on the table with mine. He digs around and pulls out some bread and lunch meat. "Sandwich?"

"Yes, please. A big one!"

He grins at her and I don't fail to notice her cheeks turning a faint pink. Those two need to work out their differences. Just imagine the fun we could get into with all four of us.

Drew steps forward and holds out a hand to Ellis. "Hey, I'm Drew."

Kai stiffens as Ellis places her hand in Drew's. His gaze never leaves the crow shifter and his stance is poised, ready to strike.

"Ellis. It's nice to meet you. And thanks for the supplies."

"Not a problem." Drew turns to Kai and appears to notice the predatory intent in Kai's posture. He pales and raises his hands, taking a few steps back.

"Kai," Ellis whispers, placing her hand on his chest. "Calm down."

This is really the first time we've seen Ellis interact with someone other than one of us—or an enemy. While I'm protective of Ellis, as a mage, I don't have the possessive instincts Kai and Sterling do. This will be a good experience for them.

He rolls his shoulder and gives her a sheepish look. She stands on her toes to place a soft kiss to his lips, and just like that, I see the tension leave his body.

"Here," Sterling says to Ellis, holding out a plate with a massive turkey sandwich.

Her eyes light up and she goes straight for the sandwich, grabbing it off the plate and taking a huge bite. "Mmm, fank yoo," she says around the food in her mouth.

I snort. "Such a lady."

She gives me the middle finger and takes another bite at the same time.

"Thanks, Drew," Sterling says. "Let me know how much I owe you."

"Don't worry about it. Hey, I saw your mom and brother the other day."

Sterling's head whips up from the second sandwich he is making. He looks like he's barely breathing as he slowly sets the bread on the table. "And?"

"I told her you would be close by with your mate. And dammit, the hope in her eyes almost broke me. I told her I'd sneak you in to see her."

Now he really wasn't breathing. Fine tremors work through his hands as he grabs the edge of the table, closing his eyes tightly.

"Is that safe?" he rasps.

"Probably not, but Noah is gone for the week. He's dealing with some shifter bullshit on the other side of Lustros. We could do it, but it's up to you if you want to risk them."

The wooden table groans under Sterling's grasp and his muscles flex in his arms. "Fuck!" He releases the table and runs his hands through his hair. His chest rises and falls with rapid breaths. "I should say no. It's not worth it to risk them. But ..."

He closes his eyes again, and his shoulders slump in defeat. "I haven't seen them in so long."

Ellis takes a step toward him, sandwich forgotten in her hands, but she stops herself from going to him.

"Say the word, Sterling, and I'll make it happen."

"Do it," he says, looking at the ceiling with his hands fisted at his sides. "Fuck me. I'm going to end up regretting this."

12. Sterling

I couldn't say no. How could I, when I haven't seen my family in almost 150 years? Drew has helped me stay in contact with my mom. Mostly letters that could be burned after reading to reduce risk of being caught. But there had also been occasional phone calls that were the most precious things to me. Being able to hear my mother's voice had been a balm to my aching soul.

Now, sitting on the steps outside the cabin, all I can think of is all the horrible ways this could go wrong. I already regret my decision to meet with them, but I can't make myself call Drew to cancel the plans. Another opportunity may never arise, and despite the risk, I really want to see my mom. I need to make sure she's okay. I need to see how big my little brother has grown.

The front door opens, and I know it's Ellis from the lavender and vanilla that surrounds me, and the way my wolf perks up. She hesitates before sitting next to me, leaving space between us that I absolutely loathe. But it's my fault that distance is there.

"You okay?" she asks.

My wolf practically melts at her concern. "Not really," I answer honestly.

"How long has it been since you've seen them?"

"150 years."

She exhales heavily. "Wow. I can't even comprehend that amount of time. I'm sorry. That has to be really hard." When I don't answer she scoots a tiny bit closer to me. "Tell me about them."

I turn to her, surprised she wants to know anything about me and my family.

She gives me a sad smile. "We *are* mates, Sterling. We have a lot we need to work through, and getting to know you is a step in the right direction."

She's right, so I sigh and nod my head. "Cole was young when I left. Barely five-years-old. He'll be grown now. He probably doesn't even remember me." I swallow back the emotion that threatens to pull me under. "Drew has helped me and mom pass letters back and forth, and the occasional phone call, but we always kept Cole out of it because he was so young. We didn't want to risk him telling someone and Noah finding out. I'm not sure if my mom ever talked to him about me or what he remembers, if anything.

"My mom, gods she has been through so much. But she never let anything get her down. When my dad was sick, and after he died, she remained so strong." I turn to Ellis again and smile. "You remind me of her. Despite everything you've been through, you've come out stronger for it. But my mom, her last few letters have seemed more ... depressing. It's a long time to live under someone's thumb, with the constant threat to your life and your children's lives. I think she's finally starting to break."

Ellis scoots closer again. There is only an inch between us and I desperately want to close that distance, but then she rests her head on my shoulder. I know it's supposed to be a comforting gesture, but all I can think of is how my mate is willingly touching me. It's not much, but at the same time, it's tremendous. I thought she'd never want anything to do with me after I fucked up so badly. But here she is, my mate, this amazing woman, comforting me when she could have just ignored the entire thing.

I close my eyes and soak in the feel of her. It's not the same as the one time I got to hold her in my arms, skin to skin. But it's almost more powerful because of the bad history between us.

"Why does he keep them captive like that?" she asks, bringing me back to the present.

"Initially it was to keep me in line. To make sure I did his dirty work. But when he eventually kicked me out of the pack, it became a way to make sure I never came back to try and take my place as alpha. If I tried, he'd kill them."

"Why did he kick you out of the pack? It seems like he had the perfect weapon. Someone who would do whatever he asked as long as he had something to hang over your head."

"As I got older, it became more apparent my role was to be alpha. My wolf was not easy to control back then, and Noah started to feel threatened. At some point my wolf would have challenged his, despite the threat to my family, and I would have won. In a way, I'm grateful he kicked me out. I would have beaten him and become alpha, but I would have lost my family in the process."

"I'm so sorry, Sterling," she whispers.

"Would you ..." I shake my head. I'm not going to ask her that. I can't do that to her.

She lifts her head from my shoulder and looks at me. "Would I what?"

I sigh and rub my hand down my face. "Drew told my mom I found my mate. Would you come with me to see her? It would give her so much joy to meet you." And I could really use the support of my mate, even if we don't have the best of relationships.

She studies me. Her amber eyes drill into mine and I hold my breath. If she says no, I don't think I could walk away from that. It would shred me to pieces. In a way, it would be like her rejecting me and the bond. The final nail in the coffin. I'm not prepared to walk away from her, but if that's what she wants, I'll do it. Even if it destroys me in the process.

She nods. "Yeah. I'll come with you."

I exhale, relief rushes through me so powerful it could knock me over.

"When do we leave?" she asks.

"Tonight. You should get some rest before we go. It's been an eventful couple of days."

She stands and turns to go back into the cabin, but I grab her hand and stop her.

"Thank you, Ellis."

She gives me a small smile and runs her fingers through my hair blowing in the summer wind. I lean into her touch and close my eyes, desperate for more. But it only lasts a second, and then she's gone.

———

I PUSH my wolf back and shift into my human form. After Ellis went inside, I couldn't keep my wolf contained. We shifted and spent the rest of the evening running laps around the mountain, trying to clear our head and mentally prepare for tonight. I snag my sweats from the porch and quickly pull them on, followed by my shoes before entering the cabin.

I pause at the threshold. Ellis is sleeping on the couch, her head in Kai's lap. Cade is sitting on the floor in front of them and Ellis's arm is draped over his shoulder. Cade and Kai are talking quietly, exchanging smiles and soft laughter. Fuck. I'm not expecting the jealousy that burns through me. What I wouldn't do to be part of that. To be in that pile of tangled limbs with my mate, satisfied in every way, looking at me the way she looks at them. I'm happy for her—for all of them—but gods damn, it hurts.

I clear my throat and close the door behind me. Violet and gray eyes zero in on me.

"Are you okay, Sterling?" Cade asks.

"Yeah, I'll be fine," I reply.

Cade's eyes narrow. "I feel like everything has gotten all messed up lately. I don't like it."

His fingers trail over Ellis's forearm absentmindedly, like he doesn't even realize he's doing it. That casual, habitual gesture sends a pang of sadness through me. Will I ever have that with her?

"Yeah, well." I shrug, unsure what to say. How do I tell them what they probably already know? I'm jealous, angry, and incredibly sad. I don't want to risk further damaging our friendship, especially because all of this is my fault.

"Everything is going to work out," Cade says quietly, seeing right through me.

Kai may be the empath, but Cade can read people better than anyone I've met. His caring and understanding nature are usually things I like about him. Right now, though, it just pisses me off even more.

I grab a shirt hanging on the back of a kitchen chair and tug it on. "It's almost time to leave. Wake Ellis up." I don't mean my words to sound as harsh as they do, but I'm teetering on the edge, and I need to keep myself from falling over. Too much is at stake to let myself fall apart.

Kai gently shakes her shoulder and whispers something in her ear, while Cade stands and stretches.

"We're coming with you. At least to the house. We'll remain hidden while you go inside, but we figure it's safer if you have someone keeping watch."

I jerk my head once in agreement and walk out the front door. I don't think I can handle watching them get ready together, making eyes at each other, smirking and laughing. I'd probably crack.

I hop in Kai's Charger and wait, forcing the negative thoughts from my mind. No one likes self-deprecation, and it won't do anything to help me get back in Ellis's good graces. I watch as the three of them descend the front steps. Ellis walks around the front of the car and opens the passenger door. She slides into the front seat and gives me a small smile, and I hate the flutter of hope that builds in my chest.

"Alright," Kai says as he shuts the door behind him. "Let's do this. Carefully! Don't hurt my car, please."

I ease the car down the rocky terrain with Kai groaning dramatically everytime I hit a particularly big bump. He heaves a sigh of relief as I pull onto the road and head toward town.

"I've never been on pack land before," Ellis says.

"It's nice," I reply. "We have everything we'd need in town so we don't have to go to the city. It's easy to keep a low profile, if that's what you want. Although, lately it's been going downhill. A lot of buildings are run down now, and everything could use a good sprucing."

"Noah has really made a mess of the lands and the pack," Cade says from the backseat. "It's a shame. The wolves used to be a powerhouse, but now they're more like corrupt criminals."

"Would you become alpha if you could?" Ellis's question is quiet and tentative, as if she's scared to ask.

"I don't know," I answer honestly. "I've thought a lot about it, but it would depend on a lot of things." I glance at her, my meaning clear. It would depend on her accepting our mating bond. There is no way I could challenge Noah and keep my family safe without the extra strength our bond would give me.

She looks down at her hands in her lap, her curls falling forward to hide her expression from me. I wish I had Kai's abilities, to know what she was feeling right now. I tighten my grip on the steering wheel and pull the car off the road and behind an ivy covered wall that used to be part of a mechanics shop on the outskirts of town. It has long since crumbled to the ground under Noah's rule.

"We go on foot from here," I say as I cut the engine.

A crow caws from the top of the wall as we climb out of the car, and I give Drew a wave. He flies off over the sparse forest the wolves frequently run in. We're lucky it's a new moon tonight. The phases of the moon don't have any impact on shifters like it does in the stories. But we do have a special relationship with it, and many of the shifters worship Luna, the goddess of the moon. As such, wolves mostly run during a full moon.

We follow Drew through the forest as he keeps an eye on the surrounding area for any wolves. The darkness is complete in the woods. There are no city lights to cast a harsh glow over the trees, and no moon to provide overhead light. Ellis stumbles, and I reach out to steady her. I forget she doesn't have any supernatural abilities, at least not like Kai and I do. Cade will be using his magic to enhance his eyesight, but Ellis is essentially human right now.

Without thinking, I grasp her hand in mine and help lead her over the fallen branches and protruding rocks. She doesn't pull away, and again that flutter of hope grows in my chest.

When we come to the edge of the forest, we stop. This will be the riskiest part of this entire plan. Noah's house is situated next to the forest, but a wide expanse of flat grass lies between them. There is no cover for us to hide behind as we cross it. I wait for Drew to signal that everything is clear, and Ellis and I sprint across the clearing, leaving Kai and Cade to keep watch from the woods.

I pause briefly at the top of the back steps, my hand hovering over the doorknob. My heart is pounding in my chest, and not from the run. This is it. This is the moment I have been waiting for for almost 150 years.

Ellis squeezes my hand. "You can do this. You're not alone."

I glance down into my mate's amber eyes and take a deep breath. Her presence here makes all the difference. Even with our history, I can feel her support and encouragement, and it gives me the strength I need to turn the knob. I step through the door, and almost fall to my knees.

She's there, standing in the kitchen, shaking hands covering her mouth, and tears gleaming in her bright blue eyes. She's aged since I saw her last. Fine lines crease around her eyes, and streaks of gray adorn her raven black hair. But she is still as beautiful as ever.

"Sterling," she whispers.

I take three steps toward her and wrap my arms around her trembling body. She clutches the back of my shirt and sobs into my chest. She's as tiny as Ellis is, barely reaching my shoulder. And for some reason, she seems smaller, more fragile than she was before. My wolf howls inside me, his anger and grief washing through me and combining with my own.

"Mom." My voice is a hoarse croak, and I breathe in her scent. Flour and vanilla. She was always baking, the aromas clinging to her like a cloak. I found them comforting when I was child, and now as an adult, I find it just as comforting. I pull back to look at her, and I realize I'm crying when she reaches up to wipe my cheeks.

"My baby. I miss you so much, Sterling." Her voice wobbles as she fights more tears.

I can't speak. The lump in my throat is preventing me from doing so. Gods, I miss my family. I hadn't realized how much until I'm standing with my mom knowing I'll have to say goodbye again.

A gentle touch on my back draws my attention behind me. Ellis stands there, her eyes gleaming with unshed tears. I swallow the lump and clear my throat.

"Ellis, this is my mom, Shari. Mom, this is Ellis. My mate." If my voice cracks on the word *mate* I can't help it. I haven't introduced her to anyone as my mate yet. Saying it aloud feels so right.

My mom smiles a blindingly bright smile and pulls Ellis in for a hug.

"Oh, dear. I am so happy to meet you."

Ellis is stiff at first, but then she relaxes into the hug. It makes me wonder if she's been hugged by a parent since her mother's death. Of course, on the heels of that thought, comes the reminder I'm part of the cause of her mother's death.

There are so many emotions whirling through me right now, I'm not sure what to do. I want to fall to the ground and cry. I want to beg Ellis for forgiveness I don't deserve. I want to grab my mom and take her away from here. Instead, I stand stupidly in Noah Martin's kitchen and watch my mate and my mom hug. I take a deep breath and force all the emotions down. I'll deal with them later. Or never.

"Come, sit down," my mom says as she pulls away from Ellis. "We don't have a lot of time. I want to learn as much as I can."

She leads us to the living room, and I sit next to her on a pale green sofa while Ellis sits in a matching chair.

"Where's Cole?" I ask, finally realizing he isn't here.

"Right here."

I spin at the sound of the deep baritone voice and gape. My baby brother isn't a baby anymore. I knew he wouldn't be, but I wasn't fully prepared to see a man leaning against the wall with his arms crossed. His black hair, like our moms, is long and tied back. A full beard covers the lower half of his face, and his bright blue eyes shine with anger.

"Cole," I breathe.

He snorts and shakes his head. "Unbelievable. You come back here and act like we should fall over ourselves to welcome you home. Like you haven't abandoned us to go live your life of fame and luxury."

Shocked, I jerk back. My mouth opens but nothing comes out. I don't even know what to think, let alone say. The last time I saw Cole he was a five year old pup filled with joy and life who laughed at everything and hung onto every word I said. Now he looks at me like I'm the enemy.

"Cole, stop," mom says quietly. "I haven't seen my son in years. Don't ruin it for me."

He says nothing else, but his eyes seethe with anger. Satisfied, my mom turns back to Ellis.

"Ellis, tell me about yourself. I feel like I have so much to learn."

Ellis shifts in her chair, shoulders turning inward as everyone's focus lands on her. Her uncertainty is endearing and it makes me smile.

"Ellis likes to box," I say, stepping in to save her. "Actually, the first time we met she broke my nose."

My mom gasps, but her eyes shine with mirth. "And how did you meet?"

I look at Ellis, letting her answer this question. It's up to her how much she wants to share.

"Well, I'm sure you've heard about the contest my ... my dad created. Sterling joined Malakai and unofficially participated in it." Her brows furrow and a slight frown pulls her lips down. "If it hadn't been for that, I never would have met him," she says quietly, almost to herself.

I wish I could know what's going on in her head. Why does she look so contemplative?

"Fate," my mom says, smiling brightly. "Fate will always find a way."

Ellis looks at me, and it's as if a weight has been lifted from her shoulders as she exhales. The contemplation leaves her eyes, and it's replaced by something I've never seen when she looks at me. Not love, but something similar. Affection, perhaps. I suck in a breath as I stare at her, wanting her to see everything I feel for her. Love, respect, regret, need. All of it. Her eyes gleam as tears build on her lashes and she looks back down to her lap.

"You've got to be fucking kidding me," Cole mutters.

"Cole!" mom admonishes.

"No, I won't be quiet. This is bullshit. The golden child returns, after having done absolutely nothing for 150 years, despite that fact he has a mate who could help him take his spot as alpha, and everyone overlooks that! What a fucking joke. Some alpha you'd be. We're probably better off with Noah."

Ellis and I both jerk as if we'd been slapped. Shame burns through me, because a lot of what he said is absolutely true. I say nothing in response, I'm too stunned to even formulate a coherent thought.

"Cole, please," my mom begs. "Don't ruin this moment."

"We should probably be going, anyway," I say woodenly.

I stand and Ellis follows. She walks over to me and places her hand on my arm, concern shining in her eyes.

"Wait," my mom says.

She pulls a necklace out of the collar of her shirt. I recognize it immediately. I've never seen her not wear it. The delicate silver links shine in the light, and the opal dangling from the chain sparkles. She unclasps it, and hands it to me.

"I want you to have this. For Ellis." She gives us both a sad smile.

"But, dad—"

"Your father gave it to me when we first mated. I want you to have it." Her eyes fill with tears as she looks at Ellis. "I only wish I could get to know you better. But you'll never know how happy I am to know he's found his mate."

I see the devastation on Ellis's face. The guilt and uncertainty causing her cheeks to flush. I tuck the necklace into my pocket and grab Ellis's hand, leading her through the kitchen to the back door.

"Don't come back," Cole says from the living room. "You're not needed or wanted here."

My steps falter and Ellis's hand tightens around mine.

"Sterling," my mom whispers.

I turn around, tears blurring my vision of the woman who raised me.

She wraps me in a hug. "I love you, Sterling. Please be careful."

"I love you, too, mom."

I kiss the top of her head before pushing through the back door and out into the warm night.

13. Ellis

I MAKE TO FOLLOW STERLING OUT THE DOOR, BUT pause. Turning back to his mom, I give her a small smile. "It was nice meeting you."

Her smile is sad as she looks at me. "Please, take care of him for me."

I swallow thickly. "Always," I force the words from my throat. I turn to the door, but stop again. I'm not sure what possesses me, but I turn back around to level a look at Cole. "One day, you might regret this. One day, you might wake up and realize you lost your only sibling. I know how that feels, and I don't wish that on anyone. Put yourself in his shoes next time you feel the need to attack him. You don't know the whole story, and you sure as hell don't know how much this tears him apart."

I don't give him a chance to respond. Pushing through the door, I hurry after Sterling, who is already across the clearing and entering the tree line. I have to run to catch up with his long, angry strides. Cade and Kai open their mouths to speak, but I shake my head and continue into the forest, following Sterling's silver hair, the only beacon in the darkened woods.

He stops and presses his hands to the trunk of a tree, his head hanging down in defeat. Without thinking, I wrap my arms around him and rest my head on his broad back. He turns around and pulls me to him, sinking to the ground and dragging me with him. I realize he's crying. His shoulders shake with silent sobs, and my heart breaks.

"I am so sorry, Sterling," I whisper. Guilt spears through me. All of this time, I could have accepted the bond and we could have saved his family. Instead, I've been selfish. I've pushed him away for something that wasn't his fault.

"He's right." His voice is rough and filled with pain. "Everything he said is true. They've been living in captivity, basically, while I've been off riding the fame and fortune being Kai's friend gives me."

"That's not true, Sterling." I shift so I'm more comfortable in his lap. My hand moves on its own, and before I know it, I'm cupping his cheek, forcing him to look at me. "You can't blame him for being mad. He's bound to be hurt, especially since he was so young when you left. He wouldn't have understood, and he probably thought you had abandoned them." I brush a tear away with my thumb. "He will never fully understand what you did for him. Your hands were tied, and the choices you made were the best ones at the time."

As I talk, I realize I'm not just speaking of Cole. Our situation, mine and Sterling's, isn't so different. That night my mom and sister were murdered, he was doing what he had to in order to keep his family safe. I can't blame him for that. I can't blame him for not grabbing me that night and taking me away. I wouldn't have gone willingly, and I probably would have hated him for it. Him not telling me he was there that night, that was a mistake. He made a choice, and it turned out to be a bad one. I can't blame him for being scared of losing me again. We all make mistakes. Don't we all deserve forgiveness, too?

And, yeah. He shouldn't have slept with me. But I kind of forced it. I didn't let him say no, and he fought it as hard as he could. In the end, the bond and his wolf won. Again, I can't blame him for that.

Something his mom said tonight hit me. It forced me to think of things in a different light. *Fate will always find a way.* Fate put him in that situation ten years ago. Fate put him back in my life with this contest. Fate is not giving up. We are supposed to be together, and even my heart knows that. I can *feel* it. And I'm so tired of being mad at him. I want to let it go. I want to know him better, as my mate, my shield. I want … him.

His icy blue eyes are so sad. He's carrying so much weight on his shoulders, and I want to take that away. And I can. I can take all that despair away. I just have to accept the bond.

"Sterling, if I—"

He cuts me off. "No. I know what you're going to say, and I don't want you to accept the bond because you know it will help me get my family back. That's not what I want. My intention in bringing you tonight was not to make you feel that way. I wanted to give my mom something to hold onto when things get dark. If you accept the bond, I want it to be because you want to. That's it."

His eyes shutter, and my heart drops to my stomach.

"That's not what I meant," I say.

"We should go." He stands abruptly, and sets me on my feet.

I stand frozen in place as he walks away. My chest is hollow and cold. Kai brushes my arm as he walks past to join Sterling, and Cade stops in front of me, lifting my chin with a finger.

"Give it time, love."

I blink back my tears. "I don't know what to do," I whisper.

Now he'll never believe me when I say I want the bond. He'll always question my motives. Suddenly angry at everything, I brush my tears away and stomp past Cade. How the fuck is any of this fair? Why has fate made it so difficult? If we're meant to be together, why make it such a fight?

We reach the car hidden behind the ivy covered wall, and I climb into the backseat, slamming the door shut behind me. Kai cringes and opens his mouth to say something, but one scathing look from me, and he quickly changes his mind.

The ride back to the cabin is filled with tense silence, and Kai's curses as the car bumps over the uneven terrain. I ignore all of it and seethe in quiet anger until we reach the cabin.

———

"Ellis?" Cade pops his head into the bedroom. His expression is weary, as if he's afraid to say the wrong thing.

I guess I've been a little pissy since meeting Sterling's mom.

"We're gathering in the living room. We have some things we need to talk about."

I set down the book I was pretending to read. In reality, I've been skulking around the cabin for the past day, content to ride my anger. "Meeting about what?" I ask. I don't fail to notice the bleakness in my voice. When was the last time I sounded like that? Back when I was with Sam, no doubt.

Cade's jaw tenses, but he says, "We need to work on getting the proof that Kennedy isn't your dad."

I sigh, standing from the bed and brushing past him. Before I can descend the stairs, he grabs my hand and turns me to face him. His violet eyes scan my face, and based on his expression, he doesn't like what he sees. I want to pull away, but something stops me. Underneath the concern in his eyes, something else shines brightly. Something I desperately need to see.

He leans forward and gives me a gentle kiss. "I love you, Ellis." He fans his hands on either side of my face, tilting my head up to make me look at him. "Don't forget I'm here for you. Kai and I both are here for you. Don't shut us out. We will do anything you need us to. All you have to do is ask."

I sigh and let myself collapse against his chest. His arms immediately surround me and the fight drains away. "I just don't know what to do," I say for the hundredth time. "I've done so much thinking on this thing between me and Sterling, and I know things aren't perfect between us, but I'm ready to accept the bond." Rubbing my chest, I look up at Cade. "I don't want you and Kai to think you're not enough for me. Because you are. But, I just don't feel complete inside without him."

Cade takes my hand and pulls me back into the bedroom, sitting on the edge of the bed. I sit next to him and stare at my hands in my lap.

"Now that I know what you guys are, what I am, I've been able to really think about things," I say quietly. "I've never really been afraid of you, which is huge for me. There was always some part of me that knew I could trust you. And while my brain tried to fight that, my soul recognized you for what you were, even if I didn't realize it at the time." I glance into his eyes, and tears blur my vision when I see the adoration in his gaze. "As soon as I learned what you guys are to me, it's like a piece of the puzzle fit into place. I felt whole for the first time. But without Sterling, it's like part of me is still missing. And I don't know how to make him understand that."

Cade wipes away the tears that track down my cheeks. "Have you really tried to talk to him?"

I shake my head. "I just came to terms with everything the other day. When I tried to talk to him, he stopped me and he wouldn't hear me out."

"Give him some time to work through everything. It's the first time he's seen his family in decades. Let him process what happened, then try again. He wants to be your mate, Ellis. Don't think otherwise."

"I want to help him process everything. I want to be there for him, but he won't let me."

"Sterling has always handled situations like this without help from anyone. He's always held personal things close to the chest. Don't take it personally. It's just who he is. But, tell him you're here for him. Make sure he knows you really mean it. Then, if he wants to, he can come to you."

I wipe my cheeks and sniff. "Okay. Thank you, Cade."

He smiles and leans in to kiss me. "Anytime, love," he mumbles against my lips.

When he tries to pull away, I stop him. I wrap my arms around his neck and bury my fingers in his hair, deepening the kiss. When I finally let him pull away, I stare into his eyes.

"I love you, Cade." It's the first time I've said it out loud. I've said it with my emotions, so Kai can pick up on it. I've said it to myself. But I've never voiced it aloud before.

His eyes shine and he shudders. Pushing me down to the mattress, he leans over me, brushing hair away from my face.

"Fuck, Ellis. I could listen to you say that for the rest of my life."

He lowers his mouth to mine and kisses me. It's deep but sweet. The tenderness steals my breath and leaves my head spinning. I slide my hands under his shirt and run my fingers up his back. From the first moment I met him, Cade has been able to calm the rising tides in me. It's like he just gets me. He knows when I need someone to be gentle, or when I need an encouraging word.

"Fuuck," Cade groans, breaking this kiss. His chest rises and falls rapidly, matching my own. "We have to stop." Even as he says this, he kisses me more.

"Says who?" I'm breathless, but craving more. It's never enough.

He leans up on his elbow, trailing his fingers over my cheek. "There really are important things we need to talk about." His breath fans over my neck as he leans down.

I tilt my head to the side and let out a breathy sigh. "Can't it wait?" This is so much more fun, and whatever we have to discuss will still be there when we're done.

Cade groans again and runs his nose up my throat to my ear. "It really can't." He tugs my earlobe between his teeth and gently pulls. "One of us has to be responsible here."

"It sure as hell won't be me." I emphasize my point by sliding my hand down his side and around to the front of his hips. Palming his hardness, I bite my lower lip and moan, knowing it will drive him wild.

"Dammit, Ellis." With quick, jerky movements, he shoves off of me and takes a few steps away from the bed.

Sticking out my lower lip and widening my eyes, I pout, hoping it's enough to change his mind. His erection pushes against his sweatpants, and I want to get my hands on him. He stays strong though.

Pointing a finger at me, he shakes his head. "Don't look at me like that. It won't work." He runs his hands through his hair, mussing up the brown strands. "Go downstairs. Now. I'll be down in a few."

I sigh as he walks to the bathroom and closes the door, locking it behind him. Damn. I thought for sure that would work. The sound of the shower turning on followed by a not so manly yelp kind of makes it all worth it though. Serves him right. He started it anyway.

When I enter the living room, Kai looks up from his phone, wariness evident in every line of his body. He watches me closely as I walk toward him, muscles tense and gaze searching, like he's preparing himself for battle. My shoulders slump as guilt weighs me down like a heavy blanket.

"I'm sorry," I say quietly, situating myself on the couch so I'm facing him. "I haven't been the nicest person to be around. Sometimes everything just kind of ... gets to me. I shouldn't have taken it out on you guys."

"I knew I should have sent Cade up sooner," Kai mumbles under his breath. He quickly continues when I narrow my gaze on him. "You know you can talk to us about anything. We're here for you, baby girl. Always." He tucks a curl behind my ear and kisses my forehead, making my stomach flutter at his gentleness.

I curl up next to him and rest my head on his shoulder. "Thank you, and I know. I'm just used to dealing with everything on my own." A sense of peace settles over me as his arm circles my waist and tugs me closer.

It doesn't last long. Frustration smothers the peace as Sterling walks through the front door. His steps falter when his gaze lands on me, but he quickly averts his eyes and steps to the side so Drew can enter. I can't pull my attention from my mate, though. The connection between us grows taut, and I don't know how he ignores it. The tugging in my stomach makes me want to throw myself at him. I clench my hands into fists and shove them against my belly, attempting to curb the desire. It doesn't work. And through it all, Sterling looks as unphased and uncaring as ever.

Tension grows in my shoulders and a fire ignites in my veins, slowly burning away the frustration and turning it into anger. Why won't he just listen to me? It's not fair he gets to judge the reasons behind me wanting to accept the bond. He doesn't get to make my decisions for me.

I'm opening my mouth to say something I'll probably regret, when Cade walks down the stairs, distracting me. With his wet hair and the small shivers of his body, I can't help but grin.

"You look a little cold there buddy," Kai says, cracking a smile.

"Yeah, well," Cade tosses a look in my direction, and growls, "She's a fucking temptress."

I give him my best sultry look, which to be honest, isn't very sultry. With lowered lids and pouty lips, I wink. Apparently he agrees, because he busts out in laughter.

"Well, that certainly takes care of any lingering desire," he says through his chortling. As he sits next to me on the couch, he ruffles my hair with his hand.

I flop back on the couch with my arms crossed over my chest. Jerk. Kai chuckles and elbows me playfully in the side. I give him some side-eye. Also a jerk.

Sterling clears his throat. "I asked Drew to come because I think he can help us get into Noah's office." With those words, reality crashes back around me. "We don't have a lot of time. Noah is supposed to return in a few days. So we have to move quickly."

"I've been hanging out by his office to monitor things, and I think I have it figured out." He crosses his ankle over his knee, and settles into his chair. "His secretary leaves every day at 11:30 for lunch. She returns at 12:15. So that gives us a 45-minute window, which should be plenty of time to find the document.”

“What about other security?” Kai asks. “Alarms, cameras, locks. There is no way he has nothing to protect his office.”

“That’s where Cade comes in.” Sterling sits forward, leaning his elbows on his knees and looks to Cade. “You do your techy stuff to figure out his security camera and alarm system set-up. We’ll also rely on you to make sure there are no magical wards in place, which I doubt there are. Noah doesn’t play well with other races.”

“Has anyone heard from Thomas?” I ask tentatively. It seems strange he’s been so quiet.

“Yeah,” Kai says, rubbing his hand down my arm. “He called while we were on our way to the cabin. You were asleep.”

I swallow, nerves flaring to life in my belly. “What did he say?”

“He gave me the details for the next challenge. I played along, because we don’t have the proof yet we need to make this all stop.”

I whip my head in his direction, shock coursing through my veins. “He called to talk about the next challenge when we had just been attacked?”

“I’ve been thinking about that,” Cade chimes in. “I’m not sure how much Kennedy is aware of what Sam is doing. I mean, he might be. But I get the feeling, Sam is working behind Kennedy’s back for some other purpose.”

“What purpose do you think that is?” Kai threads his fingers through mine, giving a little squeeze. “You think all Kennedy was working toward was getting Ellis married to Sam because he’s a prominent mage?”

Cade nods his head side to side, pursing his lips. “I think Sam has played him. Everything I saw while working for Kennedy made me believe Sam was just sucking up to Kennedy, trying to get in his good graces. He played a part that Kennedy wanted to see. Someone who was desperately trying to weasel his way into the Kennedy family for the fortune. And Kennedy allowed it because he was desperate to marry Ellis off and find a powerful mage to carry on his legacy."

"But you don't think that's really the case?" I ask, shifting so I can look at him better.

"Not at all. Nothing I saw from Sam while working would account for his attempts to get his hands on Ellis. If it were really a case of him trying to marry her for the fortune, I can't imagine he wouldn't just give up after she proved so difficult to get a hold of." Cade pauses and rubs his chin, thinking through what he wants to say next. "After the accident, while I was healing Sterling, I kept my attention on Ellis. Sam's reaction to her using my magic surprised him but not in the way it should have had he not known what she is."

"You think Sam knows Ellis is a harpy?" Sterling growls, his knuckles as white as the arm rests of his chair.

"I think he had to have some suspicion there was something special about her. Maybe not necessarily a harpy, but definitely something powerful that he wanted to get his hands on." Cade shrugs his shoulders and grimaces. "It's almost like he was treating her the way he was to get some kind of reaction out of her. Like if he pushed her far enough, her powers would manifest. The day of the accident, she proved his theories right when she used my magic. Whether that means he knows she's a harpy remains to be seen."

"If he knows anything about harpies, he would have to know what he was doing to her wouldn't make her powers manifest," Kai muses. "My guess is he doesn't know what she is. Just that he wants her. For what reason, I don't ever want to find out."

All this talk about Sam and what he's done to me, has me withdrawing into myself. It's been easy to forget about him, to sweep my memories under the rug when I have three men who are the exact opposite of him. The reminders tear off the scabs and reopen the wounds. What would have happened had I not found my guys? If my dad never created that stupid contest, I'd still be living in that hell with Sam. He'd still be trying to beat and rape my powers out of me.

What will he do now to get his hands on me? He knows I have powers now. He'll stop at nothing to get me in his possession. My throat closes up as fear grips my spine. And then what? What does he want with my powers? How will he use and abuse me then? My heart beats rapidly in my chest, the rush of blood making my head spin. As the room tilts precariously, callused fingers grip my chin firmly, and the next thing I see is Kai's gray eyes. They're an anchor I grasp onto, holding myself afloat from spiraling further into my panic.

"Breathe, Ellis." His fingers contract on my chin, digging in just short of pain.

I try. I really do. But I can't get my lungs to expand. It's like they're frozen in my chest. As darkness creeps into the edges of my vision, I know I'm going to pass out.

Swirling luminescence gathers in Kai's eyes and they take on an eerie glow. "Breathe, Ellis." His words, softly spoken but with command, resonate inside my head. Echoing through my mind and into my bones.

The hold my panic had on my lungs releases, and I'm able to suck in a breath of air. I collapse against Kai's chest, hearing his heart beat at the same quick pace as mine. Tears burn my eyes, and I squeeze them shut.

"It's okay, baby girl," he says soothingly to the top of my head. His arms come around me and hold me tightly, giving me the peace I desperately need. "We're not going to let him touch you again. You have three Shields that won't allow any harm to come to you. Trust us in that."

I do trust that. I know they will keep me safe, but at what cost? Everyone of them would sacrifice their own life for mine, and that thought almost sends me into another spiral. But now is not the time to think about that. I can't let my fear of them getting hurt rule my life. Instead, I nod against Kai's chest, and his arms loosen enough for me to sit up.

Taking a deep breath, I focus on the task at hand. "So, we need to prove Thomas isn't my dad so we can stop this ridiculous contest and take one thing off our plate."

Sterling nods, eyes somber. "We do. And Drew and I have a plan. Tomorrow night, we'll get the proof we need."

We all fall silent for a moment, until Cade looks at Kai. "Have you talked to your dad? I've been wondering if he's been able to link Sam to the attack on the estate. If he has, I would assume he would take this to the court. And if Sam is found guilty, it might solve some of our problems."

Kai nods. "I called him earlier. While we all know it was Sam, there is no concrete proof. That bastard is too good at covering his tracks. My dad is currently questioning all of the staff, because the only way Sam could have gotten so far was with help from the inside."

"Was anyone hurt?" I ask quietly.

"No. Luckily, the guests were all vampires, so no serious injuries. Although, I wouldn't mind if Guilia had been hurt."

I snort, because I agree. That bitch deserves something bad to happen to her.

"I also told my dad we were taking a vacation, so he won't bother us about new missions," Kai adds. "He wasn't too thrilled with it, but he's so focused on finding the proof he needs to blame Sam, he didn't put up much of a fight. The fucker did mention making sure I brought Ellis back when I come home. Not likely, asshole."

"Good deal," Sterling says, standing from his chair. "Everyone get some rest. Tomorrow we'll get that proof we need."

14. Sterling

Ellis is pissed. She won't look at me for longer than a few seconds, and the not so subtle glares out of the corner of her eyes speak volumes. Not to mention the acid dripping from her voice every time she has to speak to me. I regret taking her to my moms. I regret the entire visit. Cole's words have sunken deep, pierced flesh and bone, and left gaping open wounds that won't stop bleeding. I understand his anger. Perhaps that's why it hurts so much. Because I know it's deserved. Every word he spoke was true, and if our roles were reversed, I'd react the same way, I'm sure.

But Ellis suddenly changing her mind about the bond after hearing his words, and meeting my mom? I know she doesn't really mean it. How can she after what I did to her? And Ellis being who she is, caring and supportive, would tie herself to me just to ensure my family is safe. I appreciate the gesture, more than she'll ever know. But I can't let her accept the bond for that reason alone. If she is going to tie herself to me, she's going to do it for the right reason. Because she wants me.

The front door to the cabin opens, and the scent of cedar and lilac hits me where I'm sitting on the steps. I groan inwardly, really not wanting to have this conversation. Cade lowers himself next to me on the steps, and for a few minutes, we sit in silence, enjoying the mountain view and the sounds of birds chirping in the pines.

Eventually, Cade sighs heavily and turns to face me. "Do you think this plan will work?"

I keep my gaze focused on the lake in the distance with the setting sun glinting off the surface. "Yeah. Drew is thorough when he does his research. And with you gaining access to Noah's security cams and alarm system, I have no doubt we'll get what we need and be out in minutes."

Cade snorts. "Noah's security was a good challenge. It's been awhile since I had to work so hard to hack into something."

"I figured it would be. That's why I gave us a day to figure everything out. He's not an idiot."

We lapse into silence once again. In just a few minutes we'll be heading out to find the proof we need to end this bullshit challenge. Then all we have to worry about is Sam and what his plans are.

"You know, it's crazy to think about where we were just a few weeks ago," Cade muses, violet eyes growing distant. "How different life was for us. It makes me realize this whole time I was just skating through life. Not really working toward any one goal. Looking back, it seems like such a sad existence."

I swallow thickly. He's not wrong. But at the same time, it hasn't changed much for me. I always knew Ellis was my mate. The misery of knowing she's out there, of watching her from afar, has not been easy on me. This time I've spent with her, the one time I slept with her, it's all only made it harder. While Cade and Kai have found the other half of themselves, I'm still floating in limbo. Self-inflicted limbo, that I just can't seem to climb out of.

"You need to talk to her," Cade says quietly. It's like he can read my mind. "Sit down with her and talk about everything. Listen to what she has to say."

I shake my head. "I don't know what good that will do. I'm scared it's too late. There is no way she can honestly accept the bond for the reasons I want." The ache in my chest grows at the thought and I rub the spot, hoping to ease the pain. It doesn't work. "I won't let her accept it just to help me keep my family safe. She'll regret it later, and I don't want that. I don't want her to hate me more than she already does."

Cade snorts. "You're both too stubborn for your own good. Give her a chance, Sterling. Don't make a decision without at least talking to her first." He stands and slides his hands in the pockets of his black cargo pants. His violet eyes pin me to the spot, weighing and judging. "Don't hurt her more than you already have."

Fuck, his words sting. Like pouring salt into my already gaping wounds. Why the fuck would fate give Ellis a mate like me? She deserves so much better.

My muscles burn with the need to move. My wolf paces back and forth inside me, desperate to run, to escape this pain that constantly weighs us down. As fur ripples under my skin, I know I won't be able to focus tonight until I get this energy out.

I send a quick text to the group chat telling them I'll meet them at Noah's office and strip out of my clothes, leaving them on the porch for the others to bring. The change overcomes me, lengthening and shifting my bones until I'm standing on all fours. It doesn't make the ache disappear. If anything, being in wolf form makes it worse. Like the connection to Ellis is stronger in this form, and the pain is more fierce, more constant than in my human form.

Tipping our head back, we lift our muzzle to the sky and let out all of the pain and heartache in a soul-wrenching howl before tearing off into the night. The wind in our fur, the scent of pine and mountain air in our lungs, our muscles burning as we run faster than we ever have, it focuses us like nothing else can. We lose ourselves to the motions and the scenery blurring by as we race down the mountain and through the woods. Cool water splashes between our paws as we dash through streams. Our ears and nose twitch as the scent and sound of running prey reaches us, but we ignore it. Tonight is not for hunting.

As we dash around trees and over fallen logs, the moon provides a path for us to follow. The silver light reflects off the ground, leading us through the darkness. I wish it could lead me through my own darkness. We take the long way to Noah's office, needing to burn off the energy and distract ourselves from the negative thoughts threatening to drown us. We can't let our emotions get in the way of being able to think rationally.

When Noah's office comes into view, we slow to a steady lope. We can hear the Charger down the street, and we wait to approach the building until we know Cade has disabled the cameras. A crow caws as it lands on the roof of Noah's office, and we give Drew a nod of our head in acknowledgement. As the car pulls up, our gaze is immediately drawn to Ellis sitting in the front seat. She's a magnet that draws us in no matter where we are.

Cade pops out of the car with his iPad in hand and nods toward the office. "We're good. I have the cameras feeding back a loop and the security system has been disarmed."

I shift back into my human form as Ellis climbs out of the car and walks around the hood. Her gaze is like a brand on my skin, and just knowing she's looking makes my dick harden. She stumbles, catching herself on the hood with a curse that would make Kai proud. Hurrying to the car, I grab my clothes from the backseat and throw them on in record time. Normally, I would have no problem teasing her. It just doesn't seem right to do so with whatever is happening between us.

I glance at everyone, my gaze snagging on Ellis as she sidles closer to Kai. "Are we ready?"

"Let's do this," Kai says, wrapping his arm around Ellis's shoulders.

Cade climbs the steps first and violet light flares around his hand as his magic slides inside the keyhole and flips the lock. He slowly turns the knob and lets the door swing inward. While we wait for Cade to scope the place with his abilities, my gaze travels to Ellis again. She's looking at Kai like he hung the fucking moon as he tucks a stray curl behind her ear and says something that makes her smile.

My wolf growls low in my chest. It fucking hurts. Like a hot knife slicing through my heart. What have I done in my life to deserve this fate that has befallen me? Why can't it all be easier than it is? Rubbing my chest, I force my gaze to the front door.

"We're clear," Cade says, popping his head out then disappearing inside again.

I nod one last time to Drew, who will remain on the roof keeping watch, and follow Ellis and Kai through the doorway.

The main entryway of Noah's office is surprisingly nice. A pair of leather chairs sit in front of a gas fireplace with a low side table between them. The secretary's desk sits along the far wall with a vase of fresh flowers that scent the air with their floral aroma. Cade motions us to a door to the left of the desk, and we file in. Noah's desk takes up the majority of the room, with a couple of book shelves and a filing cabinet along the wall behind it.

"I'll make sure everything is unlocked," Cade says, heading to the desk. "Ellis and Kai, take the desk. Sterling, you can help me with the filing cabinet."

With Cade's magic unlocking everything, we get to work searching for what we came for. The first drawer is useless. We leaf through property titles and deeds for the pack lands, census paperwork, and criminal records. None of it is what we're looking for. Cade closes the drawer and opens the second one. As if something possesses me, my fingers move on their own accord, rifling through files to stop on one particular folder. I pull it out and flip it open, eyes scanning the first page. The world blurs around me as the words register in my mind.

"Cade, can you unlock this lockbox?" Ellis's question is a distant echo in my head.

My finger shakes as I drag it down the page, certain words jumping out at me and making my heart stop in my chest.

Project Bellona.
Experiments.
Powers.
Weapon.
And hidden in the midst of a list of names:
Ellis Kennedy.
Grace Kennedy.
"Cade," I breathe, my voice trembling as much as the folder in my hand.

I sense him next to me, looking at the file. His breath leaves him in a harsh exhale. "What. The. Fuck."

Kai's stunned voice whispers against my mind as he says, "That's it. Ellis, we found it."

"Wait," she says shakily. "What's that?" Papers rustle, then she says, "There's one for Gracie, too."

"Okay," Kai says. "We have what we need, let's get out of here."

I ignore them and keep flipping through the file in my hands. At this point, I'm not really seeing anything except Ellis's name on the first page. It's like it's imprinted in my memory, a fear I never knew I had coming to fruition.

"Sterling, take as many pictures of those documents as you can. Quickly." Cade keeps shuffling through the files in the cabinet, just in case there is anything else we need to find.

"What did you find?" Kai asks, coming to stand behind me.

I block Ellis as much as I can from what I'm doing, however I get the impression from her silence she's either reading what she found or she's in shock over what she found. "I'm not sure yet. We'll have to go over it together." My voice shakes a little, despite how I try to make it strong. The moment my fingers closed on that file, dread sluiced through me like a bucket of ice water had been pumped inside my veins. Nothing good will come of these documents.

The door to the office crashes open. I drop the file and jump up, heart pounding. Claws are already forming on my fingertips, and my teeth have sliced my tongue where they elongated so fast I didn't have time to open my mouth. Kai and Cade have Ellis shoved behind them, and I grab her hand, ready to run or fight or something. But instead of a bunch of wolves I expected to find in the doorway, it's just Drew, panting and wild eyed.

"They're coming." He hasn't fully shifted. His feet end in talons and his arms still sport shiny black feathers. "About fifteen wolves, all headed in this direction. They'll be here in minutes."

"Fuck." Kai grabs the papers from Ellis's hands. He shoves them in his jacket pocket and grabs her hand, tugging her away from me and toward the office door.

I grab the file I dropped and quickly place it back in the cabinet and close the drawer before following Kai and Ellis. Cade stays behind, locking everything again and sweeping his magic through the room to wipe away our scents. I push past Ellis and Kai, and run through the front door as Drew points to the south. Letting my ears shift so I can hear better, I try to tune out the frantic rhythm of my heart pounding against my ribcage. When I gaze through the trees, I realize I didn't even need to shift my ears. I can see them clearly, just fifty feet away, and I recognize the wolf leading the charge.

Alex, Noah's nephew, is a massive gray wolf, and one whom I have a bad history with. Without thinking, my wolf surges to the surface, ready to fight. My scar tingles, and I itch to rub it. As the change starts taking over, I'm jerked backward by someone grabbing the scruff of my neck, halting the shift.

"Don't even think about shifting," Cade growls, pulling me away from the oncoming wolves. "Get in the fucking car."

My wolf doesn't want to listen. Instinct rides him, the need for revenge is greater than anything. Almost anything. A gust of wind blows Ellis's scent my way, lavender and vanilla, and I'm able to push my wolf back enough to turn toward the car, and my mate. Her eyes meet mine over the hood before she climbs into the passenger seat. Worry and fear shine brightly, and she swallows, shoulders slumping as I make my way to the car.

I hop into the backseat, Cade following after another blast of his magic sweeps the area and erases our scent. It doesn't matter though. Alex saw me. There's no way he wouldn't recognize me.

"Go, go, go!" Cade yells at the same time Kai steps on the gas.

The tires squeal and spin before they gain purchase on the asphalt, and then we're launched forward. I can hear the growls and yips of the wolves behind us. We just need to make it to a straightaway where Kai can really let loose, and we'll leave the wolves behind. In the rearview mirror, Kai's eyes are alight with excitement as he tears down the streets, flying around curves and pushing his car to the limits. His fangs glint in the moonlight, on display from the grin that splits his face in boyish enthusiasm.

Ellis, on the other hand, is clinging to the grab handle with both hands, knuckles white and arms trembling. The squeaking sounds coming from her whenever Kai throttles around a corner is fucking adorable, and I find myself smiling despite the situation.

"Just a bit further, Kai, and you can probably slow down," Cade says, turning around in his seat to peer out the back window.

"Psh, fuck that," Kai mumbles. "I don't get to do this very often. I'm taking full advantage of it."

Ellis whimpers. "Please don't kill us," her words almost drowned out by the screeching of tires as we fly around a corner.

"Relax, baby girl," Kai chuckles. "I'm a pro." He reaches across the space and pats Ellis's knee, which causes her eyes to about pop out of their sockets. She grabs his hand and pushes it back to the steering wheel.

Cade snorts. "I don't know if I'd go so far as to say you're a pro, but you're the only one I'd trust to drive this crazy and not crash."

"Well, thank you. I think." Kai's eyes flash to the rearview mirror and a look passes between them that makes my heart squeeze.

I just want to be a part of their little ... thing. Not necessarily the sharing of the dicks, but I want to be in it deeper. I want the connection. The closeness. The ... family. Kai, Cade, and I have that. Or, we did. As things developed between Cade and Kai, and when Ellis joined us, I removed myself. I didn't want to watch as their relationships grew, while mine suffered. I also didn't want to make them feel awkward that I was around, when I wasn't really part of what was happening.

Kai finally slows when we approach the mountain where he'll have to drive his precious baby up the rocky slope. Indeed, as the underbelly of the car scrapes along the ground, his smile drops, replaced by a scowl.

"Son of a bitch," he growls. "I swear, any work I have to get done when this is over, you're paying for Sterling."

"Yeah, yeah. I hear ya," I placate.

When we reach the cabin, Ellis jumps out and sinks to the ground, mumbling her thanks for making it back alive under her breath. A chuckle slips past my lips as I climb out of the car, and she glances at me, her amber eyes searing straight to my soul. I look away before she can say anything, and her sigh reaches my ears, making my shoulders curve inward in defeat.

"I'm going to double check my wards, and lay down a few more," Cade says, closing the car door. "When I'm done, we have a lot to talk about." He glances at me, his intent clear.

What I found needs to be discussed. We need to know what's happening. Shoulders rising on an inhale, I head for the cabin, preparing myself for something horrible.

15. ELLIS

THUNDER RUMBLES IN THE DISTANCE AS I SIT ON THE couch. My stomach twists uncomfortably as I wait for Cade to return. I'm positive he and Sterling found something while they were looking through the filing cabinet. While my attention was pretty focused on what I was doing, I heard enough of what they said to raise my suspicions. Knowing it could be absolutely anything—most likely nothing positive—has my insides tangled and writhing in nervousness.

Kai hands me a bottle of water from the kitchen and sits next to me. His weight on the cushions displaces me, and I tumble into his side. Rather than try to sit back up, I curl in closer, reveling in the weight of his arm as it settles around my middle. I watch Sterling as he sits in the chair across from us, texting someone on his phone. Silently, I beg him to look at me. And like I somehow managed to push that thought into the ether, his icy blue eyes raise from his phone and meet mine.

Just like that time at River's Edge with Allie, I'm sucked into his presence. Everything around me disappears until it's just me and him. All I know is his piercing blue stare, the weight of his gaze on me, the all-encompassing realization that I am the center of his attention. My heart kicks up, hammering in my chest. It's hard to draw a breath, because he has stolen all the air from my lungs. I try my hardest to make him see how much I want him. I hope it's reflected in my eyes as I trace his features. My lips part, I don't know if it's to try to breathe or to say something, but it doesn't matter, because he blinks and looks away.

Just like that I'm released from the spell. Dropped back into reality like being thrown into an ice cold pond. Every muscle in my body sags and my heart falls into my already roiling stomach. I just don't understand why he keeps fighting it. Sensing my emotions, Kai squeezes me tighter and kisses the top of my head.

The front door opens and Cade enters, just as the first drops of rain fall from the sky. More thunder rumbles, closer this time, and through the windows I see the pine trees blowing in the wind.

"We're good," he says, kicking off his shoes by the door. "If any wolves come within five miles we'll know." He plops onto the couch on the other side of me with a sigh. Violet eyes meet mine, and he says, "You got what you need?"

Kai reaches into his jacket pocket, jostling me in the process so I shift to lean against Cade. He pulls out two folded pieces of paper and hands them to me. My fingers tremble as I grasp them, even though I already know what they say. Spreading the papers open on my lap, Cade ducks his head to look at them and Sterling sets his phone down.

"DNA test results," Cade breathes.

"Yep." I pop the 'p', trying to affect nonchalance. None of them fall for it though. "For both me and my sister. Noah Martin is our father."

Silence settles in the room like a heavy cloak, broken by the claps of thunder that have steadily grown louder. It doesn't come as a surprise for anyone, but it's still a lot to process. Especially for me.

Kai's hand rubs up and down my back. "Are you okay?" His eyes are narrowed like he's trying to understand the emotions I'm putting off.

Taking a deep breath, I give myself a second to think about

my answer. "Yeah, I'm okay," I say slowly. "In a way, it's a relief. To know it wasn't my real dad who let me suffer through all that abuse under his roof. Although, I don't know if it's much better that he raised me as his own and still treated me the way he did. I mean, before my mom died, he was never very affectionate toward me and Gracie, but he was never coldhearted." I shrug, trying to play off the confusing mix of emotions. "I guess it was easy to not care since I wasn't flesh and blood."

Of course, this brings out even more confusing emotions knowing my real dad murdered my mom and sister, and wanted me dead as well. What did my mom see in him? Why have an affair, not once, but twice? At least that we're aware of.

Cade clears his throat. "So we have the proof we need. How do we go about letting Kennedy know this contest is over?"

"I think the best option is to meet him somewhere neutral," Sterling says, running a hand through his hair. He winces as his fingers tangle in some knots, and my own fingers itch to brush through them. "We tell him when and where, and that he is to meet us alone. No Sam. We also need to make copies of the results so we at least have something in case he decides to ruin the originals."

Kai nods and folds the papers, setting them on the end table. "I'll call him tomorrow. We'll meet somewhere public, too. Less chance of him going crazy on us."

"What about you, Cade?" Sterling asks quietly. "Have you heard anything lately? Will this impact your situation?"

I glance at Cade, brows furrowed. "Heard about what? And what situation?"

He sighs heavily, rubbing a hand down his face. "It's a long story. One I probably should have told you already, but," he pauses to swallow. "It's not easy to talk about." He turns to me, eyes wide and pleading. "I promise, I'll tell you sometime. It doesn't affect you, so don't worry about that. I just ... I need to prepare myself for it."

I nod and take his hand, threading our fingers together. "I get it. Take whatever time you need."

He leans over and gives me a soft kiss. "Thank you," he says against my lips, before pulling away. "I haven't heard anything. But I'll deal with whatever fallout this brings."

"You sure?" Kai asks worriedly. His quiet words almost drowned out by the boom of thunder outside the windows.

"Yeah. This needs to happen. I won't let Ellis stay under Kennedy's thumb any longer."

"Okay, then I think we need to discuss what I found in Noah's office." Sterling glances at me, eyes creased with concern, before he looks down at his phone. "I'm going to send you guys these pictures I took. I snapped as many as I could before we had to run, so I'm sure there is more in that file. Possibly more in the cabinet."

Bile climbs up my throat as dread sinks in. I wait impatiently for the pictures to send, and when lightning flashes through the window and thunder booms on its heels, I jump. Kai's phone lights up first, so I lean over to him and hold my breath as he clicks the first picture. A printed copy of an email, sent to Noah Martin from Sam Morris.

My eyes scan it at the same time Cade reads, "Top Secret: Project Bellona. Noah. The building has been secured. Equipment has been ordered for the experiments we discussed. We'll need to reinforce the basement walls to protect against any rogue powers we may pull out of the subjects on accident. I have a contractor working to get a plan together to create a room where we can test the weapons as well. Below is a list of names I think may be worth looking into for possible subjects."

As my gaze travels down the list of names, I already know what I'll find. Still, ice floods my veins when I read mine and my sister's names. The room is silent save for the rain pounding the roof and the almost constant rumble of thunder. Kai's muscles are hard as a rock under me, vibrating with the strain to keep himself in control. I latch onto that sensation or else I'll probably end up shutting down again.

"What's next," I ask hoarsely.

Kai slides his thumb across the screen. The next picture is a copy of the deed to the elementary school Sam bought. The warehouse, as he calls it. Kai slides his thumb across the screen again. This is a document detailing the progress made with Subject 1. I'm able to read that they didn't find what they were looking for, but Kai swipes again right as I got to the descriptions of Subject 1's treatment. It's probably for the best I didn't see it.

We spend the next half hour looking at various documents that detail the progress made on various subjects, the reports from the builders on the renovations to the building, and random email threads between Sam and Noah. Through it all, the rain continues to pour down, thunder booms, lightning flares, and wind batters the cabin. The weather is appropriately fitting for the situation.

A soft rumbling growl from Sterling catches my attention. I peer over at him, but he's focused on his phone, his grip so tight I'm surprised the device doesn't crack in half. Kai stiffens under me, and I look down at his cell. Immediately, my name pops out at me. I quickly scan the document, realizing it's an email from Sam to Noah detailing his plan with me. And by detailing, I mean *detailing*.

"Don't let her read that!" Cade jumps up and grabs Kai's phone, but not before Kai exited out of the picture.

It doesn't matter though, I saw enough. Cold sweat breaks out over my skin at the same time heat courses through me, shame no doubt turning my tan complexion flush. *Oh, gods.* The guys have read what Sam did to me. In detail. My body trembles, and I want nothing more than to run upstairs and lock myself in the room. It's one thing for them to know what he did in my own words. It's another beast entirely to read it in detail from the monster himself.

Kai grabs my face in a not-so-gentle grip and forces me to look at him. I try to break free, too embarrassed to meet his gaze, but he's stronger than me. "Do *not* be ashamed, Ellis. It wasn't your fault, you were a victim. I *never* want to sense that shame and guilt from you again." His words are stern, but the undercurrent of love can't be ignored.

I swallow past the lump in my throat. Logically, I know his words are true. But getting my heart on the same page is a battle I'm not sure I'll ever win. "I don't want you guys to think differently of me. Or treat me differently." My whispered words are almost lost in the rain pelting the windows.

Kneeling on the floor next to me, Cade grabs my hand. "Love, nothing will ever make us think differently of you. You're our mate. Our soul-bonded. Our beloved. We will love you, cherish you, and protect you, *no matter what*. You never need to hide yourself from us."

My gaze wants to travel to Sterling, to see his reaction, to get his confirmation nothing will change. But I'm too scared. If I see his rejection of me right now, I'll crumble. So I stare into Cade's violet eyes, letting myself drown in the adoration I see shining in their depths.

"Tell me you understand," Cade whispers, his thumb rubbing soothingly across the back of my hand.

I nod my head, unable to voice the words for fear they will betray me. Cade narrows his eyes at me, like he knows exactly what I'm thinking. Knowing him, he probably does. Eventually, he sighs and returns to his spot on the couch, but his hand never leaves mine. Tucked tightly between two of my guys, their steady strength a pillar I can lean on, my anxiety slowly fades to a mere trickle rather than a raging torrent.

"Okay," Cade says, running his free hand down his face. "Now we know what Sam's plan is, and we know Noah is in on it. What do we do about it?"

"Drew said he needs at least another week of casing the outside of the warehouse," Sterling says, leaning back in his chair.

"After that, he'd need probably a couple more weeks to scout the inside before we'd even be able to develop a plan."

My stomach plummets again. "Three weeks? I just want all this to end." The despair in my voice is clear. "And what will we do once Drew finishes his scouting? Blow the place up? Tell the authorities?"

Sterling's eyes are understanding when he looks at me. "I think we would need to figure out if the authorities are in Sam or Noah's pockets. If they are, things will get a lot messier."

I slump against the back of the couch as exhaustion crawls through my limbs. Why can't anything be easy for me? Just once, I'd like something to go my way and not be dramatic. I'm so tired of always fighting, always being on guard. What would my life look like without a threat hanging over my head? Would Kai and Cade take me on dates like normal couples? Not that we're normal by any stretch.

Sterling continues to stare at me, but I'm too overwhelmed to even think about it. Those icy blue orbs travel over my face, taking in the exhaustion no doubt lining my features and the dejection in my eyes. The tendons in his neck stand out as he clenches his jaw.

"Don't le—" Cade doesn't get to finish his sentence as the power flickers, then goes out.

The room is plunged into darkness, the only light provided by the lightning that flashes through the windows. We wait in silence, listening to the storm rage outside, to see if the power comes back on. When it doesn't, Sterling pushes up from the chair and heads to the kitchen.

Kai leans over, running his nose along my neck. "Well, this is kind of romantic. Don't you think?" Shivers erupt over my skin as he inhales my scent and groans low in his throat.

Sterling returns with a flashlight, steps faltering as he reads the sexual tension that has suddenly grown in the room. Our eyes meet, and I silently plead with him to join us. His gazes shutters, and he sets the flashlights on the coffee table before stepping outside into the storm.

I sit up straighter, prepared to chase him outside and tell him not to leave, but Cade stops me with a hand on my cheek, turning my head toward him. "Leave him," he says, voice low and gravelly. "His wolf likes to run in storms."

I don't get a chance to respond. Cade's mouth captures mine and I'm lost.

16. Ellis

"Let us take your mind off things," Kai breathes against my neck, his fingers skating along the skin just above the waistband of my leggings.

I don't have the breath in my lungs to tell him they already managed that. Every touch drives my anxiety and fear a little further away. Every press of lips to my skin wipes away the exhaustion that has settled over my body. Each heated glance and whispered word makes me crave them in every way possible. They know how much I need them to show me nothing has changed because of what they read today.

"Upstairs?" Cade asks, pulling away to stand from the couch. He reaches out a hand and I let him tug me up and lead me to the steps.

It's dark, with the power out and the moon hidden behind the stormy clouds, it's difficult to make out the steps leading to the second floor. Before I can ask Kai to grab the flashlight, he scoops me up and throws me over his shoulder. I squeal as the world lurches. Kai's hand lands on my ass, a stinging slap that sends heat pooling in my core. I try to ease the growing ache between my legs by squeezing them together, and Kai chuckles darkly.

When we get to the bedroom, Kai drops me on the mattress and I gasp at the sudden sensation of falling. Bouncing a few times, I watch Cade approach with butterflies swirling madly in my stomach at his hooded look and obvious arousal tenting his pants. Both guys are still dressed in their cargo pants and henleys, and they look every inch the assassins the world thinks they are. Dark. Dangerous. Sexy. It's fucking hot as hell.

Cade slowly pulls my shirt over my head and tugs my leggings down my legs, careful not to touch an inch of my skin. He swallows hard as he unclasps my bra, his eyes dilating further. The lack of his fingers on my skin is driving me insane. I need his touch.

"Touch me, Cade," I breathe. "Please."

His only response is a wicked grin and he steps back from the bed, leaving me naked and alone.

Kai steps up to Cade's back. "Arms up," he says darkly in Cade's ear. When Cade does as he's asked, Kai slowly pulls the shirt over his head, fingers grazing the sides of Cade's torso. The shirt hits the floor, and Kai's fingers land on the button of Cade's pants, deftly undoing them. His pants and boxers quickly join the tee, and my mouth waters at the sight of Kai's hands trailing down Cade's chest and stomach.

A whimper climbs up my throat when Kai's hand wraps around Cade's dick and Cade's head falls back onto Kai's shoulder. Gray eyes seer into me, making me squirm. As my heart thumps in my chest, Kai works his hand up and down Cade's length. He gives me a crooked grin, one fang on display, before gently biting Cade's shoulder. Not hard enough to draw blood, but enough to make Cade moan.

I don't realize the position of my hand until Kai says, "Touch yourself, baby girl."

Cade's head pops up and his gaze latches on to my hand slowly moving down my stomach to the apex of my thighs. I hesitate, breath catching in my throat. I haven't done this in so long, and never when someone watched me. Uncertainty makes my skin prickle uncomfortably. Kai must sense my emotions, because he does the one thing that would make me forget my insecurity. He grabs Cade's chin and roughly tugs his head back for a dominating kiss.

My hand slides a little lower.

When Kai pulls away, he nips at Cade's lower lip with a fang, a drop of ruby blood beading before Kai licks it away with a low growl.

My hand slides even lower.

Breaking out of Kai's grip, Cade turns and pulls Kai toward him for a deeper kiss. His hands drop to the hem of Kai's shirt and drags it over his head. Cade falls to his knees and unbuttons Kai's pants, freeing his erection. Staring at Kai with desire and love, he sucks Kai's cock into his mouth.

That's all I needed. My fingers slide through my wetness and my legs fall open. Kai's gaze is lasered in on my hand as I slowly and gently touch myself. His chest heaves, and his hands tangle in Cade's hair. He watches my reaction when he roughly slams his hips forward, choking Cade on his cock.

"That's right, baby girl," he rasps. "Spread those legs wider, let me see how wet you are."

I barely hesitate as I do what he told me. Even sucking on Kai's dick, Cade manages to turn his head enough to watch me. Two sets of eyes, one gray and one violet, hone in on my movements. Watching both of them get distracted gives me enough courage to spread myself wider and increase the pressure as I slide two fingers through the growing wetness.

Kai growls, tightening his fingers in Cade's hair and reminding him to keep sucking. "Don't stop, Cade. That feels so fucking good." His head briefly falls back, tendons in his neck popping as he grits his teeth, fangs digging into his lower lip.

It's so erotic, watching them pleasure each other. Seeing how much they want each other's touch, and how much they love each other. That affection is almost more of a turn on than watching their beautiful bodies move against one another. Almost. My fingers slide lower, and I slip one finger inside. A soft moan escapes my mouth and Kai's head snaps up to watch.

"Fuuck," he groans, and pulls away from Cade. Tugging Cade up by his hair, he says breathlessly, "Your turn," and falls to his knees, swallowing Cade down in one motion.

Cade grunts, and threads his fingers through Kai's silky black strands. "That's right, Ellis. Watch what he does to me. Watch him make me come undone."

His violet eyes swirl seductively as I add another finger. The stretch pleasant, but not enough. Not compared to either one of them. I need more pressure, more friction. My hips lift as I try to get a different angle, something to ease the ache that only grows more each second. It doesn't work.

Cade's hips buck harder as I bring one hand to my breast and roll my nipple between my fingers, pinching the peak tightly. I gasp at the added sensation. The pleasure pain brings me closer to the release I'm dying for.

"We want to watch you come, Ellis." He tugs Kai off of him, but the vampire doesn't stand.

He kneels at the foot of the bed, watching with Cade's fingers still tangled in his hair. "Do it, baby girl. Make yourself come for us."

I whimper, the intensity of their heated gazes making a flush crawl over my skin. My fingers work faster, the heel of my palm rubbing the over-sensitive bundle of nerves while I tug harder on my nipple. Heat builds in my belly, spreading outward. I arch off the bed, pressing harder with my hand, and I cry out as my orgasm crashes through me in waves of pure electric pleasure.

As my body settles and the waves of my orgasm ebb away, my gaze lands on my two guys at the foot of the bed, their eyes glued to my body. Both of them are breathing heavily. Their cocks stand rigid from their bodies, beads of precum glistening in the flashes of lighting from the window.

A jolt of insecurity washes through me, tightening my muscles and making my stomach clench. But Kai quickly crawls onto the bed and grabs my hand, licking my juices off my skin. His slow smile eases the uncertainty, and he kisses me deeply.

Cade walks to the table by the bed and opens the drawer. I'm too lost in Kai's kiss to pay attention, until he says, "Roll over, Ellis. On your hands and knees."

Kai doesn't give me a chance to look at Cade or think about why he wants me to do this. His strong hands grab my hips and he flips me over. I gasp as the world turns, and my hands and knees sink into the mattress. With a dark chuckle, Kai grabs my thighs and spreads my legs wider. "Look at that dripping pussy. So fucking tempting."

Already, my arousal is building again. That orgasm was not enough to satisfy me when I have two men who do a much better job at it. The pop of a cap lets me know Cade has the lube, but I'm unprepared for the sudden cool wetness that slides over my backside. Instantly, I tense. My muscles contract and I try to sit up.

Kai prevents me with a strong grip on my hips. "Trust us, baby girl. We're only going to make this feel so much better." He doesn't give me a chance to respond before he slides under my body, and runs his tongue through my folds.

With my mind preoccupied with Kai's tongue working me higher and higher, Cade runs his palm down my spine and over my ass. "Relax, Ellis. Focus on Kai." His hands spread my cheeks apart, and something hard presses against my back hole.

I tense automatically, but Kai adds a finger with his tongue and my focus returns to what he's doing. A few seconds later, the pressure against my hole increases, and Cade mumbles nonsense words, and he slowly works something smooth into my ass.

The stretch is uncomfortable. It doesn't hurt, but the slight burn distracts me from what Kai is doing. It doesn't take long before the plug settles into place, the pain gone, leaving only a pleasant tightness.

Kai slides out from under me and runs his hand over my ass. "One day, you'll be able to take both of us at the same time."

His words make my breath catch and desire build. What would that be like? To welcome both of them into my body at the same time. I can almost imagine the closeness, the connection, that would create, and I want it.

Kai chuckles and leans up to whisper in my ear. "All in good time, baby girl. We have to work our way to that point."

Once again, he doesn't give me a chance to respond. He flips me back over and I land on the mattress with a soft thump. The plug in my ass getting pushed deeper makes me moan.

Cade's eyes are practically glowing as he climbs up my body and kisses me deeply. "You are perfect for us, love. Your body is a work of art that was made for us." His words make me flush again, this time with happiness. It's quickly replaced with raging desire, as Cade steps back. "What do you think of Kai and I switching places this time?"

My breath gets stuck in my chest, and my eyes widen. "You mean ..."

"Say it, baby girl. Or it won't happen." Kai's wicked grin grows, his fangs lengthening slightly.

Dirty talk has never been easy for me, but I know there is zero judgment with these guys. Whatever I say will turn them on, and they won't care how awkward I sound. I swallow, glancing at Cade. "You mean Kai takes your cock?" They've never done that. Cade has always been the bottom. Just the thought of Kai giving up that control makes me clench.

Cade runs a finger over my nipple and down my stomach until he reaches Kai's thigh. He trails his finger up Kai's thigh and runs it along the underside of Kai's cock, making it twitch. "These piercings will feel even more pronounced with that plug inside you."

My mouth pops open as I try to imagine that, but it's impossible. "Then what are we waiting for?" The breathy tones to my voice don't sound like me at all.

Kai chuckles and leans forward to kiss me. "So eager," he says against my mouth at the same time he settles in between my spread legs. My hips rise to meet his when he rubs his piercings through my folds, everything still so sensitive from my first orgasm. "You ready, baby girl?" His gray eyes pierce my own, and I don't fail to see the emotion in those dark depths.

I wrap my legs around his waist and nod. "Always ready for you," I whisper. He guides himself to my entrance and slowly slides inside. "Oh, gods," I moan as he fills me with small rolling thrusts of his hips. The added pressure from the plug makes everything more pronounced. His size, the piercings, each subtle shift of his hips. I can feel it all so much more. "Kai," I gasp.

He moves slowly, pulling out then pushing back in. "Oh, fuck," he grunts and stills. "I can feel it. Just imagine if that were Cade and not a plug." He rests his forehead against mine and breathes deeply.

At the mention of his name, Cade is shaken from his staring at Kai disappearing inside me. He hops onto the bed behind Kai and opens the lube again. "Ready, Kai?" The gravelly quality of his voice sends shivers over my spine, and Kai's too.

Kai shudders on top of me, nodding his head. "Yes. Hurry up."

We both still as Cade lubes up and presses his hips against Kai. He doesn't prepare him, just slowly pushes inside. Kai grits his teeth at the intrusion, but I can tell it's not painful. His eyes glaze over and he pants. With each inch Cade gains, Kai's cock twitches inside me. When Cade stills, fully seated in Kai's ass, the sound of our breathing fills the space. The waiting is too much. I need Kai to move. I need him to take care of the ache he created.

I whimper, and the sound sets Cade into motion. He pulls back and gives Kai enough room to move. Soon we're all lost to the sensations. The sounds of slickness and heavy breathing. The moans and skin slapping against skin. We're all covered in sweat as we chase our pleasure. Pressure builds behind my spine, a tingling warmth that grows with each thrust of Kai's hips.

Angling my head to the side, I meet Kai's lust glazed eyes. His fangs scrape his lower lip as he drops his head to my neck. The rough slide of his tongue up the column of my throat is my only warning before he plunges his fangs in deep.

I scream as my orgasm overtakes me like a freight train. With each pull of blood from my vein, my pussy clenches around Kai's cock. My toes curl and vision fractures, my breath stuttering out of my chest as my body shakes from pure ecstasy. The fluttering of my inner walls sets Kai off, and he stiffens above me, pulling his fangs from my neck as he comes. Cade follows with a grunt, his thrusts shoving Kai into me, drawing every last bit of pleasure from me.

Kai licks the puncture marks, and pulls back to look at me with blood dripping down his chin. My heart flutters at the sight. My sexy, tousled, bloodied vampire. Cade flops onto his back at the foot of the bed, his chest glistening with sweat and rapidly rising and falling as he catches his breath. He rolls his head to the side and catches my gaze. That sweet smile tugs at the corners of his lips.

"Wow," I breathe, brushing damp curls from my forehead with a shaky hand.

"Wow is an understatement." Kai grins.

I whimper when Kai gently pulls the plug from me. He walks to the bathroom, and my eyes fall shut. Slowly, my heart calms and my breathing returns to normal. Soft footsteps on the carpeted floor announce Kai's return, and he gently cleans me up before settling next to me. The bed dips as Cade crawls to lay on my other side. With their warm, comforting presence on either side of my body, my breathing slows even more as my mind slips closer to sleep. They successfully took my mind off of the worries that this recent mission created.

The last thing I notice before I fall asleep is the gentle kiss Cade places on my forehead, and Kai's fingers tucking my hair behind my ear.

———

I JOLT AWAKE, my limbs tangled with Cade and Kai's. Normally, waking up between them after mind-blowing sex is my definition of perfect. However, something isn't right. My stomach is uneasy, tumbling and rolling. An urgency I've never felt before settles over me, making my muscles twitch with the need to move.

Carefully, I disentangle myself and slide out of bed. I spare one glance for my sleeping boys, faces lax with sleep. The constant edge of danger that always surrounds Malakai is gone, replaced by an almost boyish appearance with his lips slightly parted and black hair falling across his forehead. Cade's sweet smile makes an appearance as he rolls over and tucks in close to Kai. My heart can't handle it. I love how much they love each other.

A sharp tug in my gut makes me stumble and drags me from the moment. Scooping Cade's shirt from the floor, I pull it on and let instinct draw me out of the room. The storm has stopped, but rain still falls gently, a soft pitter patter on the roof of the cabin. I pad silently down the steps to the front door. Without a second thought or care for what could be outside, I open it and step into the cool early morning air. The sky is still dark, but a lighter shade of black is just starting to transform the horizon.

I know what caused my body's reaction before I spot him. Sterling is halfway across the yard, back to me, as he heads for the edge of the pine tree forest surrounding the cabin. I know exactly what he plans on doing, whether that is instinct, the bond, or just knowing the wolf shifter. However I know, I know I can't let him do this.

"Sterling," I say quietly, taking a step to the edge of the porch.

He stops mid-stride, shoulders hitching up around his ears and back muscles tensing. With a huge exhale, his body seems to deflate, and he turns to face me. I'm moving before I realize what I'm doing. The grass is wet and cold under my feet, and rain quickly soaks through Cade's shirt, making it cling to my skin uncomfortably. I push wet curls from my eyes as I approach him, my heart thundering in my chest.

"Don't do this," I plead with him, blinking away the rain and searching his icy blue gaze for something that will give me hope about our future.

"I have to. You can't keep living like this." He shakes his head, a frown pulling his mouth down. "I need to make things right."

"Just wait. Wait until we have the information from Drew." I lift my hands and cup his cheeks. Even with the cold rain sliding down his face, his skin is warm. "This is too dangerous," I whisper. He doesn't answer, so I stand on my tiptoes. "Please."

His gaze searches mine and raindrops gather on his lashes. Then he lowers his head and kisses me. I'm swept away. He kisses me like he has all the time in the world. Deep and searching. Like he's trying to find my soul through my mouth to consume it. I'd let him have it. Happily. My heart flutters so fast in my chest I'm scared it will stop completely.

Warmth surrounds me as he wraps his arms around me and pulls me against him. My fingers tangle in his wet hair, grasping the strands like I can keep him here with me by that action alone. Of the three guys, I think Sterling's kisses are my favorite. Maybe it's because I've only kissed him a few times. Maybe it's because we both know it might never happen again. Whatever it is, it makes his kisses more meaningful. They hit me right in the chest and consume my very being.

His hands land on my bare thighs and slide up, lifting the shirt as they go. He grasps my ass and picks me up so I can wrap my legs around his waist. The kiss never falters. He keeps devouring me as one hand slides under the shirt and up my back. Fire trails in the wake of his fingers, making me shiver from the temperature difference between the rain and his skin.

Sterling finally pulls away, breathing deeply. "Kitten," he says softly against the skin of my throat.

I bury my face in his neck, and we both inhale each other's scents. Pine and winter air flood my lungs and I hold my breath, hoping to keep it there for as long as possible. My heart hurts—it's like a crack has formed and is slowly splitting wider and wider. Why does this feel like goodbye?

He tries to lower me to the ground but I cling to him tighter. Not ready to let go yet. Not ready to say goodbye. "Please come back to me," I whisper against his neck.

He shudders, but doesn't reply. When I finally let him lower me to the ground, his icy eyes appear duller than normal. He steps back, fingers grazing my hand, before he turns and heads toward the forest. His pants hit the ground, but I'm not drawn to marvel his ass like I usually would be. Each step he takes makes it harder to breathe, like he's taking all my oxygen with him as he leaves.

I blink. When I open my eyes, a silver wolf stands on the edge of the forest. It turns back to look at me, blue eyes shining in the rising sun. Lifting its muzzle to the sky, it releases a howl that pierces my heart, and I gasp, clutching at my chest to make the hurt go away. With the howl still echoing across the mountains, the wolf takes off into the trees, quickly disappearing in the darkness.

I stand rooted to the spot for who knows how long. The rain continues to fall, but I don't feel it, even as I shiver and wrap my arms around my middle. My gaze never strays from the forest. A desperate, foolish hope that Sterling will return keeping me there. The sky brightens, the black and deep blues turning to vibrant purples, pinks, and oranges. I don't notice them, though. I don't notice my teeth chattering or the chill that has settled into my bones until a warm hand lands on my low back.

"Ellis?" Cade comes to stand in front of me, his violet eyes creased with worry. "Are you okay?" The warmth from his palm on my cheek makes me shudder.

I watch a raindrop travel down his bare chest, and take a breath. "He .. he left." The words barely make it past the lump in my throat. "He's going to the warehouse."

Cade sighs. "Fuck." Brushing a wet clump of hair from my face, he turns me around. "Come on, love. You're freezing. Let's get you warmed up."

17. CADE

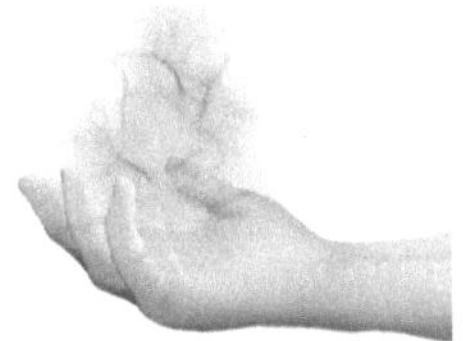

WAITING SUCKS. AND I KNOW IT'S EVEN HARDER ON Ellis not knowing what's going on with Sterling. I hate seeing her worry and not being able to help take that fear from her. We spent the day sleeping and cuddling—Kai and I doing our best to keep her mind off of the missing wolf. In the silences though, I see her eyes go distant and a frown replaces her beautiful smile.

Deciding now is probably the best time to talk about my story, I drag Ellis from the bed and down the stairs. Outside, the sun is just beginning to fall below the horizon, staining the sky orange and purple. The rain stopped sometime during the day, but the temperature remains chilly this high on the mountain. Ellis shivers and rubs her arms to ward off the chill as she sits on the swinging bench on the porch.

"Wait here," I instruct, and run inside to grab a couple of blankets. When I return, I drape one around her shoulders and the other over her lap.

"Thank you." She cuddles into the warmth and leans against me, stealing even more warmth from me.

With an arm around her, I hold her close and stare at the lake in the distance, reflecting the colors of the setting sun. "I guess now is as good a time as any to tell you my story." I can't help the slight tremor in my voice. Talking about this is never easy, and it's only gotten harder since Ellis came into my life. I don't want her to ever blame herself for what's happened, or what may happen.

She shifts against me, getting more comfortable. "You really don't have to tell me if you're not comfortable with it."

Her consideration for my feelings warms my heart, but this needs to happen. "Thank you. But, I want you to know. It's part of who I am, and I want you to have all of me." I'm quiet for a moment as I try to sort through what I want to say and how to say it. Releasing a breath, I start at the very beginning. "Do you know how Thomas Kennedy started his empire?"

"Um, no," she says, shifting against me. "I never really talked to him about it."

"Well, he found the most powerful mages he could, and asked them to work for him. The ones who refused, he either bribed or blackmailed. My dad was incredibly powerful. A violet mage, and at the time, the only one. He was a healer, and a damn good one. That's where my love of healing came from. He would take me with him to the clinic where he worked." I pause, remembering the times I spent with my dad at the clinic. "I learned so much from him. And not just about healing.

"Kennedy came to him, offering a job high up in the ranks of his new company. My dad refused. He was happy where he was, doing what he loved. Money and status never mattered to him. Kennedy didn't like that. And when my dad continued to refuse, declining massive amounts of money, Kennedy took the next route."

Ellis shifts against me again, like she can sense where this story is going and she knows she isn't going to like it. "What did he do?" she whispers.

I hate telling her, because she for sure isn't going to like it. And I know her. I know exactly what she is going to say when I reveal the whole story. This is the part that gets hard. Sighing, I continue. "Kennedy abducted my mom and older sister while my dad and I were at the clinic. He used them to make my dad work for him. And instead of releasing them after my dad agreed, he kept them locked away somewhere in the Kennedy building, probably with other family members he used to force more mages to work for him."

"Cade," she breathes, her hand gripping my thigh hard enough to leave bruises. "What happened?"

"It tore at my dad. For ten years he worked for Kennedy, while half of his family was held captive. We got periodic updates. A phone call once a year. But that's it. My dad's mental health started declining. He couldn't take it anymore, knowing he was the reason they were in that position in the first place. If he'd only accepted the offer the first time, none of it would have happened." My voice cracks as I continue, unable to keep the emotion contained. "He took his own life after ten years of working for Kennedy. I think he also partially hoped Kennedy would release my mom and sister if he was no longer alive."

Ellis sniffs and wipes at her cheeks. "He released them, didn't he? Tell me he let them go." Her words tremble slightly, like she's scared to know the answer because she really already knows it.

I shake my head. "He did not. He moved his attention to me. He didn't even give me a choice. I would have willingly worked for him if he released my family." The next sentence is so hard to say. My words sound forced, like the lump in my throat is trying to keep them contained. "They're still there. I have no clue how they're being treated. I still only get periodic updates and a phone call once a year."

Ellis sits up, eyes wide as she stares at me in disbelief. "How long? How long has he kept them hostage, Cade?"

"80 years. 83 to be exact." My voice sounds numb even to my own ears. Bleak and hopeless.

Her breath leaves her in a heavy exhale. "What happens if you quit? What will he do to them?"

I shake my head, unable to voice the words she already knows I'd say if I could. It wouldn't end well for them.

"Then what the hell are you doing here?" She pushes to her

feet, her voice raising an octave as she stares at me. Blankets forgotten, she runs her fingers through her curls with agitation. "You have to go back, Cade! Why are you helping me when helping me is basically defying the man who holds your family's fate in his hands?"

This is exactly why I didn't want to tell her. She'll never forgive herself if something happens to them. "Because, I don't have a choice, Ellis."

"What do you mean, you don't have a choice?" In the moonlight, I can see her cheeks turning rosy as anger and frustration build inside her. "You absolutely have a choice. Go back, Cade. Don't do something that will hurt your family."

"You're my family, Ellis." I stand from the bench and grab her shoulders. "I don't have a choice because as my soul-bonded, you are always going to be my first priority. I was made for you, Ellis. I will never, can never, walk away from you."

She stares into my eyes, I see the swirling of my magic reflected back at me in her amber gaze. "It's not walking away from me. It would be temporary until we can figure things out. But I can't be the reason you abandon your family. Don't put me in that position." Tears line her lower lashes, building until a tear escapes and falls down her cheek.

I wipe it away with my thumb. "Don't make yourself that person, Ellis. It's nothing you've done. I'm working on a plan, but for now, this is where I'm supposed to be. Where I *want* to be. With you. Always with you, Ellis. You need me as much as I need you."

Her eyelids flutter shut as more tears fall, and I hate myself for telling her the story. This will only cause unnecessary stress, and that is the last thing she needs. I tug her against me, trying to tell her through touch alone that I mean every word I just said. Yes, I worry about my family. Yes, I want to get them out of there. Yes, it would destroy me if something happened to them. But, I *need* Ellis. On a cellular level, my body, my magic, needs her. Nothing will ever change that.

"Why does this world suck so much?" she mumbles against my chest. "Both you and Sterling have similar, horrible stories. Why are the races like this?"

I don't have an answer for her. Power. Greed. Hatred. While all appropriate answers, they aren't what she's looking for. Maybe this is also part of her reason for existing. Maybe, as a harpy, she's supposed to change the way things are done in the magical world. I keep that thought to myself for now. She has enough to deal with already.

"Let's go inside. I'll make you some dinner." I pull away, dropping a quick kiss to the top of her head.

She grabs my forearm, halting me. "Just, keep an open mind," she pleads. "If you ever need to go back, I will completely understand. And I'll support you. Always."

This is why I love her. I give her a kiss, before tugging her back inside to the comfort of the cabin.

———

"It smells like a human bonfire in here." Kai steps behind me and shoves his head over my shoulder, sniffing. "Whatcha making?"

"A human bonfire?" I mutter, leaning back into his body. "You are so fucking weird. I'm making me and Ellis hamburgers. But, since there's no grill, I'm doing it on the stove."

"Oh, so a cow bonfire. I was close." His chest moves against my back as he shrugs.

"Still, so incredibly, fucking weird." I flip the burgers, and the sizzling renews with vigor as the juices seep from the other side of the patty.

Kai nuzzles my neck, his tongue teasing the bite mark he left not too long ago. "Yeah, but you love it," His voice has deepened, and it vibrates his chest against my back.

I shiver as heat spreads through my body. Damn, those bite marks are really fucking sensitive. "Mmm," is the only thing I can say to reply. My throat seems to have dried up, and my tongue is stuck to the roof of my mouth. I tilt my head to the side, exposing my neck even more, and Kai's hands travel over my abs and down lower, past the waistband of my pants.

"Stop distracting him, Malakai!" Ellis's voice calls from the living room. "I'm really hungry and burnt burgers do not sound appetizing."

Kai's hands freeze as if he's just been caught doing something he shouldn't. "Damn," he whispers. He kisses the mark and backs away. "Can't let her starve, now can we?"

I shake myself, trying to tamp down the desire Kai drug up in me. The burgers are pretty much done, so I reach for the plate with buns and drop a burger on each one. "Can you grab the ketchup and some waters?" I ask Kai, and pick up the plate of fixings I prepared earlier.

In the living room, I set the food on the coffee table and sit on the floor. Ellis slides down the front of the couch to join me. Making our burgers together is such a domestic activity, and my heart aches for the time when we'll be able to do this without threats hanging over our heads.

"We should probably take this time to figure out a plan for meeting Kennedy, Ellis." Kai sets the ketchup and waters on the table and sits across from us. "I want at least two backup plans in case things go to shit."

"Shouldn't we wait for Sterling?" Her voice is so quiet, the trembling of her words is barely noticeable. But it's there.

"I really want to get this settled. It's one less thing we would have to worry about." Kai leans back on his hands. "Besides, I don't think Kennedy is very fond of him. It's probably best if he isn't there."

"What about you?" She turns to look at me, burger forgotten in her hands.

"What about me?" I ask, although I already know what she's thinking.

"Is it a good idea to make him mad when he has your mom

and sister?" Worry pinches her brow, creating a crease between her eyes.

Rubbing the wrinkle away with my thumb, I give her a reassuring smile. "I won't be there." Her eyes flare with concern, so I quickly continue. "I mean, I'll be there, but I won't be with you. I plan on keeping my distance, but staying close enough in case of trouble."

She nods reluctantly, and sets her burger on the plate. "So, what's the plan then?"

Kai nods to her uneaten food. "Eat while I tell you."

She levels a flat stare at him, but grabs her burger and takes a bite. All without breaking eye contact with him. With one raised brow, she says, "Better?" the word distorted around her half chewed food.

He snorts, but draws one leg up to rest his forearm on. "We'll meet somewhere neutral and public. I want us to get there early, and scan the area for any threats and make sure he abides by our rules of bringing no one with him. While we meet with him, Cade will keep his distance but remain in our line of sight in case we need his help."

"It might be a good idea to have some sort of signal for us to look for," I chime in. "That way, if one of us spots something we can signal and get the hell out of there."

"Good idea," Kai nods.

"Where are we going to meet him?" Ellis asks around a bite of food. I'm happy to see her eating. Since we met her, she's already put on some weight, filling out where she was too skinny.

"What's a good public place?" I ask, taking a bite of my own burger.

"What about River's Edge?" Ellis offers. "It's right along the river, in the center of everything."

"I think that would work." Kai nods. "There's a good vantage point a couple of buildings up the street, too. Cade could hang there and keep an eye on us."

"Do we tell him I'm your beloved?" Her eyes burn with an

inner fire when she asks this. Like just the thought of being his beloved heats her from the inside.

"No. I still don't want anyone to know. Not until all of the threats have been dealt with, and I know you're safe."

I set my burger down. "We also need to keep the harpy thing on the down low. If there is any reason for him to be interested in you, we need to keep that under wraps, or he'll never let you go."

"Agreed." Kai pulls his phone from his pocket. "Should we call now? Get this over with?"

Ellis swallows, and her hands flutter in her lap. I grab one and give it a squeeze, trying to reassure her that everything will be okay. Nodding at Kai, I give him the go ahead to call Thomas Kennedy.

18. Sterling

There's a hot poker shoved inside my brain. It's the only thing that could cause this kind of pain. I groan and slowly crack one eye open. It's dark, thank the gods. I think even the slightest bit of light would cut through me in waves of agony. My other eye opens, and I stare up at the darkness.

I can't tell where the ceiling is. If there even is one. For all I know, I'm in some vast, empty void. Except under my hands is a smooth surface. It's unforgiving on my back, and my muscles are cramped and aching. I grit my teeth and roll onto my hands and knees, sweat breaking out over my skin at the effort it took for me to do that. My limbs are shaky, like noodles, and the longer I hold myself up, the harder it gets.

I collapse onto my side, gasping for breath, as my arms and legs twitch uncontrollably. *What the hell did they do to me?* I lift my head and look around, but I can't get any idea of where I am. It's all just dark. I know I have to be in that damn warehouse, because that's where I stupidly got captured, but that's all I got.

Reaching inside me, I call my wolf forward—he'll be able to see better in the dark. But nothing happens. It's like trying to hold smoke in my hands, but it leaks out between my fingers. There's nothing to grab on to. No link to my wolf. He's silent in my head and my chest is empty where he's usually felt.

The lack of my wolf's presence leaves me reeling. I gasp and clutch at my chest, digging my fingers into the skin like I can tear into my body and pull my wolf out. He's been with me my entire life. His absence is like losing a piece of myself, like losing a limb. *Where the fuck is he!*

A sound draws my attention. It's close but distant, like whatever it is is behind a door. I hear a key slide into a lock, and the lock clicks. Light creeps into the room as the door swings open, and I slam my eyes shut. When I peek through my closed lids, my heart drops to my stomach.

Sam Morris stands in the doorway. Green light twining around his arms.

"You're awake. Good." He grins, and it's a dark and twisted thing. "It's time to play."

19. Malakai

Ellis's emotions are battering against my shields. I've long since mastered blocking powerful emotions. But with her, even the smallest brush against my barriers gets sucked inside. And once inside, it's like it gets amplified. The only thing I can think of, is that her being my beloved is the cause of this. It's been distracting, because she feels everything so hard in the first place, and to top it off, her emotions are caused by extreme circumstances. I need to find a way to block them so it doesn't distract me during times I need to remain focused.

Right now, her anxiety shoves past my barrier, seeping into my blood and making my limbs itch with the need to move. Underneath that thick layer of nerves, hope flutters softly, like a butterfly tickling my skin. I want so bad for this to work. To get her out from under Kennedy's thumb will be one step toward securing our future together.

I take a deep breath to push her emotions down, and grab my phone. Switching it over to speaker, I meet Ellis's gaze, and give her an encouraging smile.

"Malakai Thorne," Kennedy's slimy voice projects from the speaker. "To what do I owe this pleasure?"

"There are some things I would like to discuss with you," I say, keeping my voice cool and uncaring.

"And what would that be? Shouldn't you be on your next mission? Or is this a conversation about you dropping out of the contest?" His glee over that prospect is not lost on me.

A slow grin pulls up the corners of my lips. It's not a pleasant grin, and my fangs descend slightly. "I won't discuss anything with you over the phone. Meet me tomorrow. River's Edge at noon. We can talk there."

"Will my lovely daughter be joining you?"

A growl rumbles low in my chest, and I swallow, giving myself time to get the monster under control. "She will. I can't let her out of my sight, after all. Wouldn't want her to fall into the wrong hands."

Kennedy chuckles drily. "Indeed. Tomorrow at noon, you say?"

"Alone. Do not bring any mages with you, no reinforcements. If I sense any other presence, we're done."

"That goes for you as well," he counters. "Just you and Ellis."

"Of course."

"Then I'll see you tomorrow. Tell Ellis I'm looking forward to seeing her."

He hangs up before I can growl a retort. It's probably for the best. I need to remember to keep myself in check tomorrow. I can't give him the idea that Ellis means anything to me. Ellis's amber eyes are wide in her pale face. Her knuckles are white from gripping Cade's hand so tightly. I wince. That has to hurt, especially if any of her supernatural strength is seeping through. Cade looks unfazed, though. His hope brushes against my barriers, and I let it in. It bolsters my own. Maybe this really will work.

Ellis exhales heavily and leans her head on Cade's shoulder. He kisses the top of her head, and my heart warms at the sight. Knowing my beloved has someone else to keep her safe, knowing she is getting even more love and affection, is a blessing I never thought I'd enjoy. If you were to ask me a year ago if I'd ever share my girl with someone, even Cade and Sterling, I'd have called you crazy. Now, I can't think of any better situation.

"I'm going to go crazy waiting," she mumbles. "So much waiting."

I slide my gaze to Cade, a wicked gleam shining in his violet eyes. "I'm sure we can keep you distracted."

———

"Have I mentioned how much I hate the fucking sun?" I pull the baseball cap lower and adjust the sunglasses when they get knocked astray from the movement. It's hotter than a demon's ballsack, and I'm sweating to death in pants and a hoodie. I can't wait for winter. Not only for the cooler weather, but the longer nights as well.

"Only a million times," Cade drawls as he parks the car in a public downtown lot. I briefly worry about someone—Sam— doing something to my car, but it's too late to worry about that now. We should have rented something they wouldn't recognize. Something I'll remember for later. Ellis's anxiety has been rolling against my barriers the entire drive here, and I haven't been able to keep my leg from bouncing as a result. Being an empath fucking sucks sometimes.

Ellis waits for me to get out before she climbs from the backseat. I immediately wrap my arm around her. There is no way someone is going to grab her from under my nose.

She looks sexy as hell today. It's the first time she's actually dressed in something other than leggings. I gave her my credit card and told her to shop to her heart's content when we first got to the cabin. The jean shorts and strappy white sandals were one of her purchases. So was the light pink shirt with fluttering sleeves that hang off her shoulders. The hem stops just above her belly button, teasing us with a sliver of tan skin..

I run my fingers along the exposed sliver of skin above her

shorts and lean down to her ear. "You look amazing today, by the way."

She smiles, the sight beautiful enough to make my heart thud heavily in my chest. "It's nice wearing actual clothes for once. I don't feel as frumpy."

"Frumpy?" Cade asks as he walks on her other side. "You never look frumpy, love. Those leggings make your ass look edible." His gaze travels the length of her body, and when he looks up, they're swirling with his magic. "But you do look amazing today."

A warm blush crawls up her chest and settles in her cheeks. Damn. I wish we had to time to find a shadowy spot behind a building for a quick fuck. It would probably help calm her nerves, too. But, we had to stop to make copies of the DNA results, so we're short on time.

We come to the building where Cade will hang out. It's a bookstore with two stories that has floor to ceiling windows on the second level. The view of the cafe is unimpeded, so he'll be able to keep watch.

Cade tugs Ellis from me, and wraps her in his arms. "We won't let anything happen to you, love." Her shoulders lose some of their tension, and he pulls away to frame her face in both of his hands. "Don't worry about anything. Leave it to Kai and me. We'll keep you safe."

"I know you will," she says quietly. Her faith in us is an unwavering force that briefly overpowers her anxiety. Standing on her toes, she kisses Cade before pulling away. "Let's get this over with."

Before we can walk away, Cade grabs the strings of my hoodie and tugs me close. I know what he's going to do before he does it, and I'm stunned into immobility for a second. His lips press into mine, and I smile against his mouth. While the crowd around us isn't huge, there is no doubt someone has noticed us and snapped a picture. I give it two minutes before this goes viral on social media. Two of Altair's most eligible bachelors, two of the triad, kissing in public. We've just started a new rumor for the gossip mill.

"Be careful," he whispers as he pulls away, making sure to keep his voice from traveling to Ellis.

I wink, and tuck Ellis under my arm again, and we watch Cade disappear inside the store. We wait for a text from him, letting us know he didn't pick up any magical traces that could be harmful to Ellis, then make our way to the cafe. The place is a popular spot for locals to grab a bite to eat and have a fruity cocktail with the river as a backdrop. There is usually a wait to get a table, however, as one of the Triad, we get seated right away.

"Breathe, Ellis," I murmur. Her heart rate has kicked up. Mine matches it, and I know if she doesn't calm down, we'll both end up spiraling. "We'll celebrate after this. How does that sound? We can make our own challenges. Starting with finding a shadowy nook somewhere. Cade and I will do our best to make you scream. If you don't, you'll get a prize."

Her heart races for a different reason now. Her anxiety faded to the background as her desire washes over me. That was exactly what I wanted to happen. "What kind of prize?" Her breathy question makes my cock harden in my pants and I shift to get more comfortable.

"Whatever you want it to be, baby girl."

Her eyes dilate and she parts her lips, but before she can respond, a shadow falls across our table. I whip my head around, cursing myself for getting distracted, and find Kennedy pulling out the chair across the table. Ellis's desire falls away, and her fear almost chokes me. The bite of pain from her fingers digging into my thigh through my jeans helps to center me, and I'm able to take a deep breath and focus on the man taking a seat across from us.

"Kennedy," I growl.

He sneers at us and leans back in the chair, crossing his arms over his chest. "Ellis, you look well." His brown eyes travel over Ellis's face, and her fingers tighten on my thigh.

I have to bite my tongue. *No shit she looks good, asshole. She's out from under your fucking roof and being taken care of the way she should have always been cared for.* "Let's skip the pleasantries, shall we? We all know they're fake." I flash a bit of fang, the intimidation tactic failing on the idiot. I could be across this table in .2 seconds to rip his fucking throat out. The temptation is real. I turn to Ellis and give her an encouraging smile.

We discussed in length who should be the one to bring up stopping the contest, and in the end we settled on Ellis. It seemed more appropriate she be the one to break the news to him, since we're trying to keep my involvement with her as secret as possible. Obviously, he will suspect there's more going on than we let him know, but it's better than confirmation.

Ellis swallows and squares her shoulders. "I want you to stop this ridiculous contest."

Before she can say more, Kennedy snorts and shakes his head. "Not going to happen, girl. You should have thought about the consequences before you almost killed your fiancé."

"Well, I'm so very sorry to inform you, you have no say over my life, *dad*."

His eyes widen, but he says nothing. A slight thread of anger pulses around him, mixed with curiosity and disgust.

"I know the truth," she continues. The more she talks, the less her anxiety controls her and the more her wrath grows. "You're not my father. You have no control over me."

A vein pulses in Kennedy's forehead, but he smirks smugly. "You have no proof, girl. Although, I'm interested to learn where you heard this from?"

Ellis smiles back. It's the first time I've seen her smile with that tint of darkness to the twist of her lips. It's fucking hot as hell. She holds out her hand, and I pull the paper from my back pocket, never breaking eye contact with the bastard across from me as I place it in her palm.

"Actually, I do have proof." She slides the DNA results across the table and sits back. Nerves once again flutter to life and pulse against my shield. This is the big moment.

Kennedy snags the paper and glances at it. As his eyes scan back and forth across the page, red infuses his face. The thread of anger quickly grows to a raging torrent. He says nothing, though, knowing he's been outmaneuvered.

"I think we're done here," I say cooly. "The contest is over. There will be no more contact between you and Ellis. She's free of you. Let me hear you say you understand."

Kennedy's jaw clenches, a muscle feathering under the surface. "I understand," he grounds out.

I smile, fangs on full display. "Excellent." I go to stand, but Ellis remains sitting, staring at Kennedy with a furrowed brow.

"I don't get it," she says. "You never wanted me, so why are you so angry that you don't have to deal with me anymore? Wasn't that always your end game?"

"My end game was to get Sam in the company," he sneers. "He only agreed if he could have you."

Ah, that was it. Kennedy didn't know about Sam's side hustle, and Sam only wanted to get close to Ellis to see what powers she was hiding. Ellis nods and stands, but there is something in the way she holds herself that tells me a weight has been lifted. I push her ahead of me, making sure to stay between her and Kennedy as we walk out of the restaurant. With my heightened vision, I can see Cade keeping watch from the bookstore, and we quickly make our way up the street.

He joins us as we pass the front door, a brown bag in his hand. "How'd it go?"

"It's over," I say. Ellis flexes her hand in mine, and I loosen my grasp, realizing I'm probably squeezing too hard. "Let's get back to the cabin. I won't feel safe until we're back in the safety of your wards."

20. Ellis

"Wʜᴀᴛ's ɪɴ ᴛʜᴇ ʙᴀɢ?" I ᴀsᴋ Cᴀᴅᴇ ᴀꜰᴛᴇʀ ᴡᴇ'ʀᴇ pulling out of the city.

He turns around to face me with his classic sweet smile. "Just a little something for you. For a celebration. We have one less thing to worry about."

I smile, but it feels forced. "Yeah. But in a way, it just gives us another problem. Kennedy isn't my dad, but Noah is. And he wants me dead."

"Eh," Cade shrugs. "I feel like he goes along with our bigger problem of this warehouse. I'm taking this one as a win." He hands the bag back to me, and I take it. My heart thumps happily as I pull the book from the bag. "It's not much, I didn't have a lot of time, but I think you'll enjoy it."

I run my fingers over the cover depicting a beautiful red-headed woman sitting in a forest. My eyebrows raise to my hairline as I read the blurb on the back of the book. "She's a witch, with an eccentric grandma, and ... four men?" Looking up, I catch Cade's grin.

"Seemed appropriate. Maybe you can pick up some pointers and we can act out some of the scenes?" He waggles his eyes, making me giggle.

"As long as you're not adding any more guys to the group," Kai chimes in. "Also, why the fuck am I driving?"

"It's your car, asshole." Cade turns back around, leaving me to flip through the pages.

"Yeah, but my eyes hurt." It's not quite a whine, but it's damn close. And if anyone ever tells Kai he's whining, they'd find themselves missing their throat.

Cade heaves a sigh, and slouches down in his seat. "Quit being a baby."

What is this? There is a lightness in my chest I haven't felt in years. It's like, my lungs have room to breathe and my heart can beat freely. I'm almost scared to let myself sink into it. I know this won't last. I know there's more coming. Sterling is still gone, Sam and Noah are still out there, I'm still a harpy. But Kai and Cade are with me. And that stupid contest is done. I never have to deal with Thomas Kennedy again.

Kai glances in the rearview mirror and he smiles. Whatever emotions I'm putting out there, he's obviously picking up on. "Enjoy it, baby girl. You're allowed to."

Fighting my own smile, I settle into my seat and open the book. I'm halfway through the third chapter when we pull up to the cabin. Looking out the window, I spot Drew on the front porch, naked, as if he flew here. All the light and fluffy feelings drop straight into my stomach.

"What's he doing here?" Cade mumbles as he opens his door.

I beat both Kai and Cade to the porch, heart pounding erratically in my chest, fear making my stomach roil to the point I think I'll be sick. "Where is he?" I gasp.

Drew swallows, his eyes not meeting mine and I'm already shaking my head. "He was captured."

Kai catches me around the waist as my legs give out. *Captured.* It echoes in my head, bouncing from one side to the other. Sterling. My mate. My Shield. He left for me. He went to the Warehouse to help me. And he got captured. The initial fear, the roiling of my stomach, slowly ebbs away as a spark fans to a flame in my chest. Each second I stand with Kai's arms around me, the hotter the flame becomes. It grows, burning like a wildfire through my veins, lighting me up and wiping away all coherent thought.

"Fuck!" Kai lets me go abruptly.

Drew backs away, eyes wide in a suddenly pale face.

Cade and Kai walk around me, coming to stand in front of me. Their expressions are the same. Eyes wide, but not with fear—it's awe shining in their gazes. Cade reaches his hand out, and hisses, pulling it back to his chest quickly. I see their mouths moving, but their words aren't getting through the ringing in my ears.

Sam has my mate.

"Ellis, baby girl, calm down," Kai says gently. I hear him, but I don't understand.

Calm down? How the fuck am I supposed to calm down. My mate has been captured.

The guys take another step back, Cade cursing. "Shit. You made it worse, Kai."

Kai looks at Cade from the corner of his eyes. "What the hell am I supposed to do? I'd like to see you do better."

Cade takes a step toward me, his violet eyes swirling and fracturing beautifully. Purple light envelopes his arms as his magic climbs to his shoulders. "Hey, love." He reaches out, slowly grabbing my hand. "I know you're upset, and that's okay. I'm upset, too. But, I need you to close your eyes and take a deep breath." His thumb rubs back and forth across the top of my hand.

I guess I can do that. For him, and his pretty eyes. My eyes fall closed, and I hear him murmur encouragingly. As I take a deep breath and my lungs inflate, it's like cool water rushes through my body. All the burning in my veins evaporates, leaving nothing by smoke and ash. Slowly, rational thought filters back in and my eyes snap open. They land on Cade, and the shaking starts again.

"What happened?" I whisper hoarsely.

"You were ... on fire." His gaze scans my body. "But, the flames were golden, and your eyes. They shimmered and swirled with golden light."

My legs tremble, and I'm second from falling to the ground when he wraps his arms around me, and pulls me close.

"You are so fucking amazing," he whispers in my ear as he leads me into the cabin.

I follow on numb legs and let him set me on the couch. "What ... what happened?" My voice is hoarse and everything seems as if it's underwater. Like I'm slowly resurfacing and coming back to reality. "Fire?"

"Golden fire," Kai says. He pulls his phone from his pocket and scrolls until he finds what he's looking for. He shows me the picture from the book about magical creatures we found in the library. The one that told me about my Shields. The picture of the harpy. It's black and white, so there are no colors, but she's surrounded by flames. "I think it's another of your powers manifesting."

"Fire?" I squeal, rearing until my back hits the cushions. *What the hell else can possibly happen?*

"Hey," Cade says quietly, sitting next to me and grabbing my hands. "It's a lot. I get it. You have more questions than answers at this point and it's overwhelming. But you're not alone. We're going to help you through this. I promise."

His words hit their intended mark. The rest of the uncertainty melts away, leaving nothing but disbelief standing in its wake. He's right. I know I'm not alone. It's still hard for me, but I need to lean on them. I need to let them help me shoulder this burden until we figure it all out. With this new—somewhat —calm mentality, I remember the reason for my magical outburst.

"Sterling!" I gasp, hand flying to my throat.

Drew takes a seat in the chair opposite the couch and sighs heavily. "It's not good." He runs a hand down his face and sits back.

Kai tosses him a blanket, muttering something about covering himself, and I sit on the edge of the couch. "What happened?" My voice is shaky, matching my hands clasped in Cade's.

"They had some sort of magical ward set up around the perimeter of the building. As soon as he crossed it, it immobilized him. It was … it was awful to watch." His eyes shutter and he shakes his head. "Two mages came and dragged him inside. That's all I know. I didn't try to fly past the barrier. I don't know if it just works crossing on the ground or if it protects against flying shifters as well."

Fear floods me, making my body prickle and sweat break out on my skin. I glance at Cade with pleading eyes. "We have to help him. Please. We can't leave him there."

"Of course we won't." He reassures me with a kiss to the top of my head before standing. Grabbing his iPad from the kitchen counter, he returns and levels a stare at Drew. "Tell us everything you can about the building and what you saw."

THIRTY-SIX. That's how many steps it takes me to get from one side of the abandoned office to the other. I know this because I've walked it about a hundred times at this point. This office building is one block from the warehouse. We're using it as our headquarters as Cade and Drew scout the area, looking for more wards and getting as much information as they can before we make a move.

With each pass, I stop to peek out the boarded up window. There is a small sliver between boards that gives me just enough space to see the outside world. This area used to be a fairly nice area to live in. I didn't come through here often, but I know it was pretty solidly middle class. After the school was bought and turned into this … whatever it is … the area has slowly gone downhill.

Now, most, if not all, of the homes are abandoned. The stores and office buildings have been left to rot to time. Trash blows through the empty streets, with an occasional stray dog or cat sniffing through the remains. It's as if Sam and Noah have run off everyone who lived within a certain radius of the warehouse. This part of town has become the area everyone avoids. Even the police rarely patrol the streets, and the rumor is if they get a call from this area, it's a 50/50 chance if they respond.

Each glance out the window increases the dread curling in my gut. Nausea has taken a firm hold on me, my stomach constantly tumbling and threatening to empty itself. I can't help but hold my breath each time I approach.

"It's been an hour," I say as I turn from the window, fists balled against my tummy.

Kai stops me, grabbing my face in both of his hands. "Stop pacing. Stop looking out the window. Cade is fine. He's going to be a while. We both know there is no way you are going to sit this one out, so he's going to make sure we know everything there is to know about this place before we make our move. Try to relax."

"Relax? Really?" The idea is absurd.

"I knew it was too much to ask for, but it was worth a shot." He gives me a lopsided grin. "Want me to find a way to distract you?" His grin turns edgier, a hint of fang peeking through.

I gently grab his hands and move them from my face. He sighs as I step around him and continue my pacing, but he lets me. This is one moment a distraction won't work. My mate is captured. My soul-bonded is out there, where he's at risk of being captured as well. Relaxing is not an option. Distraction won't work. Not this time.

"Want to hear a story?" Kai asks, leaning next to the door with his arms crossed over his chest, and one leg crossed over the other.

"Not particularly," I mutter, turning around to make another pass.

"Once upon a time," he begins, ignoring me. "There was a wee young vampire prince, only a teenager in human standards. He had the biggest crush on a girl at school."

My ears perk up. A story of young Kai? And a crush? He immediately has my attention, although I keep with my pacing and pretend like I don't care.

"The big formal dance was just a week away, and he desperately wanted to ask this girl to be his date. But, he was awkward and shy. And just the thought of talking to her made him want to shit in his pants."

Awkward and shy Malakai? I would never believe it unless I saw it with my own eyes. There is no way this swaggering, self-centered, playboy could ever be shy. Or awkward.

"He woke up one morning and was determined to ask her. That day, after their last class, he pulled up his big boy panties and approached her. His mouth was dry, his hands were sweating. He was quite possibly going to either puke or shit from nerves. But he smiled at her, and she smiled back."

His voice was soothing. It didn't distract me, but it did slow my pacing down. I could listen to him talk forever.

"At that moment, he knew. She was the love of his life. Her smile was like the sun breaking through the clouds after a storm. It gave him the confidence he needed to ask her to be his date. Luckily, she ignored the cracking of his voice and said yes."

Love of his life? I almost snort.

"The night of the dance, the young vampire dressed in his finest clothes, which by the way, were *very* fine. It all went well. They went to dinner, as was customary, but seeing as both of them were vampires, neither ate. At the dance, they hung out with friends and laughed. The vampire prince was absolutely in love. He couldn't wait for the first slow dance."

My pacing stopped. Something is about to happen, and I desperately want to know what it is.

"The music changed, and the first slow song of the evening started. He was so nervous, but so excited to dance with his love. He had to wipe his hands on his pants before he touched her. How embarrassing would it have been to have sweaty palms? But the moment he held her in his arms, it was like the world fell away.

She felt amazing. It was the first time the vampire prince had ever been so close to a girl. Halfway through the dance, though, it all changed. See, he was a boy, ultimately. And just like all boys, he was a horny motherfucker. He couldn't help it when he got excited. He knew the moment she noticed. She stiffened in his arms and pulled away. When the dance ended, she couldn't get away from him fast enough. The look on her face, disgusted and totally freaked out, is a look the young vampire prince will never forget."

I slap a hand over my mouth to keep my laugh in. It doesn't work, though. The giggles creep past my fingers, and soon I have tears streaming down my face. "You popped a boner?"

"Oh, yeah. A massive hard on. I was mortified. And apparently she was, too." He grins and shoves his hands in his pockets.

"Aw, poor, young vampire prince," I croon as I approach him. "What happened to the love of his life?"

"She never spoke to him again. He was heartbroken. He thought for sure he would never love again." He shook his head with a small smile. "But he was wrong. He was very, very wrong." Kai reaches out an arm and snags my wrist, pulling me against him. "He just had to wait a hundred years."

"Kai," I say quietly, staring into his gray eyes.

He kisses me. It's a sweet kiss. One that makes me fall in love with him all over again. When he pulls away, he's more serious than I have ever seen him. "I love you, Ellis."

I swallow the lump in my throat and lay my head on his chest. "I love you, too," I whisper.

We stand like that for I don't know how long. I listen to his heart thump under my ear, the rhythm matching mine. His arms hold me tightly, and I soak in the moment of quiet. He brought me a measure of peace in this time of anxiety. A reminder I needed. I have three Shields. And Kai is right before me. Safe. And doing everything he can to keep me sane. I let his strength and surety bolster me, and give myself a moment to forget it all, except for him.

21. MALAKAI

For just a moment, Ellis's anxiety and fear fall away. And in their place ... peace. Something I've never felt from her. I hold her tighter, grateful I was able to give her this small gift. It won't last. Reality will creep in any moment now, but at least for a second she was able to let it all go.

"Thank you," she whispers against my shirt, squeezing me like she's scared of losing me.

I squeeze her back. "Don't ever thank me for taking care of you. That's what I'm here for." My phone buzzes in my pocket, disrupting the moment. Pulling it out, I glance at the screen. "It's Cade." Ellis's peace shatters like broken glass as I answer. "Yeah?"

"So, I can get past this ward. It will take some time, it's fucking intense. But I haven't been able to see anything that will help us. There are no guards outside that I can see. I have no clue the layout of this place, and I know it's been renovated so I can't even trust any blueprints I find online."

"What are you saying?" I push away from the wall and put some distance between myself and Ellis. I'm getting the impression Cade is going to say something she won't like, and I don't want her to overhear it.

"I need more time. There is no way in hell I'd risk Ellis's life barging in there blind. With Drew's help, I'm positive we can get the information we need either by spying or capturing a guard, but I don't know how long all of this will take."

"And..." I prod. Not liking where I think he's going to take this.

"Take Ellis back to the cabin," he says slowly. "I don't like her being this close to Sam and this place. I'd feel more comfortable knowing she was safe behind the wards."

I snort. "You really think I can talk her into that? She'll fight me."

He sighs. "Yeah, I know. But, you guys can't stay there for however long this takes. I'm thinking days here, Kai. I want a solid plan before we bring her in here." He stops and takes a deep breath before saying, "If you have to, use your compulsion."

My stomach drops to my feet. "Fucking hell, Cade." I rub my hand down my face and shake my head, even though he can't see me do it. "You really want me to do that to her?"

"No, I don't. But if she won't listen to you, then yes. Please, Kai. I need her safe before I go any further."

My gaze lands on Ellis. She's pacing again, her concern washing over me. She obviously realizes Cade isn't in immediate danger or she'd be freaking out. But, she'll for sure freak out when I tell her we're leaving him and Sterling behind. "Gods dammit. She'll never forgive me if I have to compel her, and you know very well she won't willingly leave without you and Sterling."

"She'll forgive you. Once we're all safe, she'll calm down and realize it was the right choice."

"I hope you're right. And Cade? Be careful. She's not the only one who needs you to return safely." It's the closest I've ever come to saying out loud what he means to me.

His breath hitches on the other end of the line, then he says, "I'll be careful," before hanging up.

Taking a bracing breath, I slide the phone back into my pocket. This isn't going to go well.

Ellis stops pacing and turns to me. Apprehension pushes

against my mental shields and she wraps her arms around her stomach. "What's going on? He's okay?"

"He's fine," I say reassuringly, placing my hands on her shoulders. "He needs more time."

"What do you mean, more time? How much more?"

"A couple days, at least." I search her gaze to make sure she handles this news okay, but I could have said it with my eyes closed. Panic and apprehension hit me so hard I almost stumble backward.

"What?" she screeches. "A couple of days?"

"He said he can get past the barrier, but he has no clue what's going on inside. Before we go in, he wants to make sure we know everything we can so we can keep you safe."

She stares at me with wide eyes filled with fear. Her heart pounds madly in her chest, of course making mine match. It's unsettling when I'm trying to remain calm, but she is so overwhelmed it bleeds over into me.

"Cade wants us to go back to the cabin while we wait." I hold my breath, waiting for her to explode.

"No! Absolutely not." A curl escapes her bun and falls forward as she vehemently shakes her head. "I will not leave him and Sterling behind. We're not leaving until I have all three of my Shields with me."

Yep. Knew that was coming. "What difference does it make waiting here or waiting at the cabin? At least you'll be behind the wards at the cabin."

"Because if I'm here, I'm closer to them. We can help if they get in trouble. If we're at the cabin, we're hours away. That's time that anything could happen to them." Those big amber eyes are like a dagger to my chest. "Please, Kai. I can't leave them."

Son of a bitch, I hate this. "I understand, baby girl, but Cade asked me to take you back. It will help him focus if he knows you aren't in any danger." I run my palms down her arms and grasp her hands. "If he's worried about you, he's more likely to make a mistake."

"So what's going to happen when we actually go in there to get Sterling? I'm not staying behind, and if I'm there, he'll be worried. So what's the difference?" She pulls away and sets her hands on her hips. With her chin raised and eyes swirling with inner fire, she looks like the harpy she is.

"Ellis, please." I rub my face, dreading the next thing I have to say. "I'll use my compulsion on you if I have to. Don't make me do that."

She rears back with a gasp. "You wouldn't dare!"

I raise one brow and let the leash on my thrall loosen to the point I know my eyes are slightly glowing.

"I'm not leaving willingly. So if you're going to make me, then you're going to have to use your compulsion." She crosses her arms and dares me with her gaze.

"Gods dammit," I mutter, gritting my teeth and letting go of the grasp I have on my thrall. The glow from my eyes is reflected back at me from Ellis's, and I take a step forward, making sure she's caught in my gaze. When her amber eyes are sufficiently glazed over, I say, "You will come with me back to the cabin." I almost end it at that, but then think better of it. "Right now," I add. I have no doubt she'd find a way around it if I didn't add that last bit.

When her mind clears, she shakes her head like she's shaking herself out of a daze. She stares at me so intently, and with so much emotion I have to clutch at my chest and bend over. Rage. Hate. Disgust. Disbelief. It all swirls and collides, battering me until I'm panting.

"I can't believe you did that," she whispers harshly.

When I get myself under control, I glance up and double over again. Tears glisten on her lashes and they're there because of me. "Fuuck," I breathe, rubbing my chest and adding to her emotions with my own. I hurt her. My beloved. The one person I'm supposed to protect and care for above everyone else, and I hurt her. My self-loathing far outweighs any emotions she feels toward me at the moment. Shoving everything way down deep to deal with later, I stand up and harden myself. I need to safely get us out of here and back to the cabin. Then I can try and fix this. "Let's go."

She jerks her arm away when I try to take her hand and glares at me. I sigh, but head for the door. Outside, the moon provides enough light for her to see by. The streetlamps are all broken in this part of town, and without the moon, it would be complete darkness. I parked the Charger in an alley behind the office building, and covered it with a tarp I keep in the trunk, hoping to keep people from noticing it.

Ellis waits as I tug the tarp off, a thundercloud behind me that actually makes my shoulder blades itch as my instincts tell me there's an enemy behind me. I wouldn't be surprised if she shoved a knife into my back. I'd deserve it. When the tarp is off, she climbs in the front seat, slamming the door behind her. I wince as I shove the tarp into the trunk, not bothering to fold it, before climbing in the driver's seat.

The silence is heavy as we head back to the cabin. Ellis stares out the window and refuses to look at me. Her emotions are still pummeling me. So many that it's hard to sift through them. All I know is that she's hurting and she's mad. And I'm the reason for it. I open my mouth to say something, but end up closing it. There is nothing I can say to her right now that wouldn't just make things worse.

When we get back to the cabin, Ellis throws herself out of the car before I come to a complete stop. Again, she slams the door behind her, and my anger sparks to life. I can't help it. With her rage fueling my own, it's out of my control. I know I should keep my mouth shut. I know if I say something right now, it will only make her madder, which in turn will flood over to me and make me madder. But, do I listen to myself? Hell no.

"Really, Ellis? Is that necessary?" I shut my own door, much calmer than she did, and follow her up the front steps.

"Fuck off, Malakai." She throws me the bird over her shoulder, and shuts the front door in my face.

I stand there for a second with my mouth hanging open in disbelief. *What the fuck?* All rational thought evaporates, and I grind my teeth together as the rage steadily burns higher. The monster inside of me isn't used to being treated like that, and he is not happy. I slowly blink and when I open my eyes, I know they've turned red.

I push through the door and my gaze lands on Ellis with one foot on the bottom step. "That was the wrong thing to do, little bird," I growl low in my throat. "You pissed off the monster."

She whirls around with her hand on her throat. Her eyes are wide, but I quickly realize it's not with fear. She is furious. "*You're* pissed off?" Her voice raises an octave, and her words tremble with barely restrained rage. "You have no right to be pissed off. So go fuck yourself, Malakai."

I laugh darkly, unable to contain myself. Her words are true but she's so angry and it's feeding into my own anger, there is no way to stop this. The monster is out of his cage. There's no putting him back now. I grab her wrist before she can take one more step and she freezes.

"Get. Off. Me," she growls. "You fucking compelled me, asshole. You went against my wishes and made me do something I didn't want to do! I can't believe you did that!"

I tighten my fingers around her wrist and tug her closer so she's pressed against my chest. "You refused to listen to me," I growl back. "If you would have done what I asked, I wouldn't have had to compel you. Maybe this will teach you a lesson to listen to me in the future." As soon as the words are out, I wince inwardly. That was the wrong thing to say.

Ellis's eyes narrow and it's the only warning I have before she slams her head forward and smashes it into my mouth. My fang pierces my lower lip and pain explodes in my skull. "Fuck!" I yell, rearing back. My hand grips her wrist even tighter now, the monster not wanting to let her go after that. I lick the blood from my lip and watch as her eyes drop to my mouth. A new emotion bubbles in my gut as her eyes dilate and her chest rises sharply on an inhale.

"I hate you." The venom in her words is tempered by the breathy quality of her voice and the way she pulls her lower lip between her teeth.

A slow grin spreads across my face, causing more blood to well. "Do you, now?" I sniff, making the movement more exaggerated than necessary, reminding her of the predator I am. I know she's aroused right now. Even without the blown pupils and flushed cheeks, her scent would tell me the truth.

She bares her teeth, and if I weren't so pissed and horny, I'd think it was adorable. "Bite me, Malakai."

My fangs descend further and I grin. "With pleasure, little bird."

She yanks her arm away, and I let her go. "Don't even think about it." She points a shaky finger at my chest, to my heart pumping at the same exact rapid rhythm as her own. "You're a disgusting bastard. If you think you're going to fuck me now, you are sorely mistaken."

I step closer to her, my chest brushing against hers. Looking down at her, I grip her chin with my fingers and she gasps. "We'll see about that." I lean down and run my nose up the side of her neck, inhaling her scent that shoots desire straight to my cock. When I lift my head, her lips are parted and her eyes are fluttering. "Run, little bird."

22. Sterling

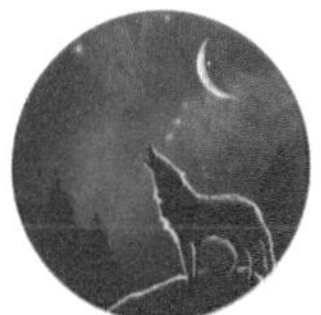

Blood pools in my mouth as I bite my tongue so hard I'm pretty sure I bit all the way through it. But I refuse to make a sound. I won't give Sam that satisfaction. My breath hisses from between my clenched teeth as fire spreads across my upper back. Not literal fire, but pretty damn close. The scent of burning skin fills my nose. A disgusting combination of something sweet and nauseating. My mouth waters as bile climbs up my throat.

After his first attempts of whipping me with some kind of ancient torture device failed, Sam has decided whipping me with a hot iron rod is the way to get information out of me instead. He should know better. I'd never give him anything to use against my mate. He can do whatever he wants to me, but I will *never* betray Ellis.

Sam grunts and his next hit lands along my left hip. The pain flares, but I suppress it. I can handle this. I've been through worse. Knowing my mate is out there and I haven't been able to claim her, knowing I hurt her, it's worse torture than anything Sam can do to me.

"I will get you to talk, shifter." He's breathing heavily. It must be hard work to torture someone. "Maybe this will do the trick."

This time, Sam places the iron rod across my back and leaves it there. Burning—so hot it's almost cold—sears through my skin. I grit my teeth until I'm scared they'll crack and breathe through the excruciating pain. The tendons and muscles of my neck go taut. When Sam finally pulls the iron away, black edges my vision. I let my head drop, too exhausted to hold it up anymore.

Sam curses, and a needle is shoved into my neck. The prick of pain is nothing compared to what I just went through. Burning fills my veins as whatever was in the needle spreads through my body.

"Take him back. Bring out the next one."

I succumb to the darkness when strong hands grip my arms and yank me away.

23. Ellis

Those three words, growled low in Malakia's chest, chase me up the steps as I run as fast as I can. My emotions are all over the place. I'm furious, aroused, thrilled, terrified—not of Kai, but for Cade and Sterling. It all swirls together to create some kind of volatile mixture that makes me liable to explode. My fingers tingle, and I fight the urge to let Cade's magic loose. I don't want to deal with the feverish after effects. Not to mention, I have no clue what I'm doing with it, and I'd be more likely to hurt Kai than anything. Not that he wouldn't deserve it.

I make it to the top step and run into the bedroom, shutting the door behind me. I quickly lock it, although I'm not sure what good that will do me. If a feral vampire wants to get in, he'll find a way to get in. Sure enough, the door bursts open and I whirl around with my heart in my throat.

Kai stands in the doorway, eyes red and fangs gleaming in the moonlight coming in through the windows. A thrill of anticipation washes through me, setting every nerve ending alight. His smile grows as he picks up on my emotions, and I curse. There is no way I can hide what I'm feeling. I can tell him 'no' to my heart's content, but he'll know better. My body, my emotions, will tell him what I really want.

He takes a step forward, and I take one backward. "You can't escape me, little bird," he drawls. "But the more you try, the more I enjoy it."

My back hits the wall, and Kai pounces. Faster than I can track, he has my arms pinned above my head in one hand, his body pressed tightly to mine. I gasp as his other hand wraps around my throat, his thumb pressing lightly on my pulse point.

"You disgust me," I breathe through gritted teeth. "You're a sick bastard."

His smile grows, the promise of pain glinting in his ruby eyes. "Keep telling yourself that. Your body says otherwise."

He drops his head to my neck, and he inhales as the tip of his tongue licks up the side of my throat. Even though he didn't touch my mark, my body reacts. My hips buck off the wall, searching for contact. Heat spreads through my chest and travels straight to my core. I barely bite back a moan that threatens to escape. He chuckles darkly at my reaction.

"Get off me," I growl. "I don't want your disgus ..." My words trail off in a breathy exhale as his hand slides under my shirt and up my ribs.

He palms my breast through my bra. "What was that, little bird?" His thumb and finger pinching my nipple emphasizes his question, and I'm not able to keep the whimper from climbing up my throat.

His ruby eyes darken, and anger courses through me like fire. Fuck him. Fuck his empath abilities. Fuck his sexy fucking body and dangerous vibes. I jerk, trying to shove him off me. With my hands still pinned above my head, I don't get very far. All I succeed in doing is rubbing myself against the hard planes of his body. And damn it all to hell. It feels so good.

Kai growls, his eyes narrowing. "Still fighting, little bird? When will you learn?" Releasing my hands, he grabs the neck of my shirt with both his hands and tears it straight down the middle. His smile grows as I gasp, and he doesn't give me a chance to yell at him. He grasps the waistband of my legging and repeats the process, tearing through them and my panties at the same time.

Stunned at this display of dominance, legs shaking from desire, I stand there while I try to find my words. He takes the opportunity to roughly spin me around and shove me against the wall. With his body pressed tight to mine, I can't move without rubbing myself against him.

"You're lucky I like this bra," he whispers in my ear as he unclasps said garment and slides it down my arms. His hand slips between my body and the wall, sliding down my stomach. "Spread your legs for me, little bird." He doesn't give me a chance to comply—or curse him out—before he kicks my foot with his, spreading my legs for him.

His hand slips lower, and I hold my breath, desperately wanting his touch. I hate how much I want him in this moment. Why can't I just stay angry? Why can't I smack him and walk away? Silently, one half of my mind begs him to hurry up and touch me, while the other screams profanities that would make him proud.

When his fingers finally slip through my folds, I sigh heavily. The touch is a tease, barely a caress. It's not near enough. Somehow, I manage to keep myself from moving my hips searching for more pressure. He slides one finger inside, the heel of his palm pressing on my clit. This time, I rock my hips, desperate for more. I can hear how wet I am as he slides his finger in and out.

"You're so wet for me, little bird." His breath fans across the back of my neck, making goosebumps rise on my skin.

"Fuck you," I say breathily.

He chuckles darkly. "Oh, there will be fucking, little bird. Don't you worry." He grabs my hips and yanks me backward. "Hands on the wall."

I grit my teeth and shake my head. "No."

He tenses behind me, his body going rigid and deadly still. A thrill washes through me. I think I just made the monster even more angry. What will he do to punish me?

Kai growls and grabs my wrists, placing my hands on the wall. "Keep. Them. There." He shoves my head down with a hand on the back of my neck before trailing his fingers down my spine with a feather soft touch. The contrast of the dominance with the sweet gesture only makes me crave him more.

In this position, bent over with my hands on the wall, I can see my feet spread on the beige carpet, leggings in shreds around my ankles, with Kai's black boots between them. The sound of his belt unclasping, followed by his zipper, sends a rush of anticipation through me. Slickness coats the insides of my thighs, and I clench my inner walls, trying to ease the ache that has built there.

As if he can read my mind, and in a way he can, he rubs his cock against me, coating himself in my arousal. I bite my lip to keep from making a noise, or begging him for more. He teases me like this until my legs are shaking and I'm not sure how I'm going to keep standing. When he positions himself at my entrance, it takes all my willpower to keep myself from pushing back onto him.

Kai's fingers grip my hips painfully, sending delicious tendrils of pleasure through me. So slowly, he pushes inside. My inner walls stretch to accommodate him, and I can't keep myself from moaning. His piercings hit differently at this angle, and I can feel them sliding against me. I don't know how he controls himself. He's breathing hard, and his body is trembling over mine as he keeps his movements slow and controlled. Once he's seated to the hilt, he stills.

"I'm going to teach you a lesson, little bird."

That's all the warning I get. Kai pulls out and slams back into me. My arms tremble with the force as I get shoved toward the wall. He keeps up this punishing rhythm, and holy shit. I've never been fucked so hard before. My eyes roll back in my head and the sounds falling from my lips piss me off. I want to hate this. I want to stay angry. But Kai is giving me everything my body wants.

Behind me, his grip on my hips never wavers. He's breathing as heavily as I am, and sweat drips off of him onto my back. I can barely hold myself up as my legs and arms tremble. The pleasure spreading through my body is making me weak. Kai wraps one arm around my middle to support me, at the same time he lowers over my back and runs his fangs along my mark.

Tingles spread from my back and through my limbs. I angle my head, giving him the answer he wants. His fangs sink in and lightning flashes in my veins. My orgasm crashes through me with so much force, only Kai's arm around my middle keeps me upright.

He doesn't stop, even after the orgasm ebbs. His hips pound impossibly harder, and he keeps drinking from my neck. When his fingers slide through my center and press down on my clit, I scream. The pleasure makes my body jerk in his arms and my vision blackens. He growls as his cock thickens inside me and he slams home once, twice, three times before his body shudders around mine.

I have never come so hard in my life. My breath is harsh and uneven, and sweat plasters my hair to my neck and forehead. Kai gently retracts his fangs and licks the wound closed. I shudder as every never ending in my body is oversensitive. He slowly pulls out, and keeps his hold on me as I stumble slightly.

I want to turn around and bury myself against his chest. I want his arms to come around me, and hold me tightly to him. But, then I remember what got us in this position in the first place. *He fucking compelled me.* My anger pushes through the post-orgasmic euphoria.

"Fuck. You." I mumble and shove him off me. I trip as my legs tangle in my torn leggings, and I shove them off before stalking to the bathroom. Slamming the door behind me, I squeeze my eyes shut. How can I feel so many different emotions at one time? That was the best sex of my life. But, I'm so mad at him for compelling me. I want to go back out there and let him manhandle me again, but at the same time, I want to gouge his fucking eyes out.

Releasing a breath, I turn the shower on and step inside. Maybe this will help clear my head.

———

WHEN I OPEN the bathroom door, Kai is sitting on the edge of the bed with his elbows resting on his knees and his head hanging down. He glances up, his eyes gray once again, and in them, I see his regret and self-loathing. He knows what he did. And he knows how much I hate it. I can't help but compare his compulsion to Sam's treatment of me. Both of them took away my choice and forced me to do something I didn't want to do.

I grab at my chest as the pain of that realization hits. The betrayal slicing through me like a hot knife, leaving me gasping for breath. I fall against the door frame and sink to the ground as tears burn the back of my throat.

Kai exhales a shaky breath, and I hear him stand from the bed. He kneels next to me, and tentatively places his hand on my shoulder. "Ellis," he whispers.

Lifting my head, I look at him through watery eyes as tears blur my vision. My lips tremble and I press them together to keep the sob from escaping. Kai squeezes his eyes shut, like the sight of my pain hurts him. When he opens them again, he gently slides his arms under my legs and around my back. Lifting me effortlessly, he walks to the bed and sits, positioning himself so he's leaning against the headboard with me cradled in his lap.

My arms circle his neck on instinct and I bury my face in his shoulder, inhaling his spice and cherries scent. It settles inside me, making my heart calm in my chest. My beloved. A single tear escapes and soaks into his shirt. The safety and comfort of being in his arms is unlike anything I've ever experienced. It calms the raging torrent of anger and betrayal.

"Ellis," he breathes again. "I'm so, so sorry."

"You guys have always made sure my voice is heard," I say shakily. "From the very first moment, I was able to make choices for myself and you honored them. Tonight was like ... was like being with Sam again." He tenses under me, his breath catching in his chest. "Not the sex," I clarify, because I know that's where his mind went. "But just the feeling of not being able to make my own choice. Being forced to follow a command I didn't want to follow. You've only ever used your compulsion on me to help me, not to force me into something."

He exhales, his breath ruffling the hair on top of my head. "I hated doing it, Ellis. I'll never be able to tell you how much I hated it. And I'll forever be sorry for it. But ... I don't regret it. I'll do whatever I have to do to keep you safe. Even if you hate me for it."

"I don't hate you," I mumble and snuggle closer to him. "I hate what you did, but I understand why you did it. As my Shield, it's your job to protect me, and I have to let you do that. I trust you with my life, so I have to trust your decisions are the best ones."

"Not just as your Shield, Ellis," he murmurs. "As your beloved, I want nothing more than to make sure you're safe and happy. That is all I will ever want."

I swallow the lump in my throat his words created, even as a sense of contentment settles within me. My fingers thread through the hair at the nape of his neck, and I idly play with the strands while we fall into a comfortable silence.

"Ellis?" Kai asks timidly after a few moments.

"Hmm?"

"About earlier," he pauses, and his chest rises with a breath. "Did I ... did I hurt you at all? You told me to stop, but your emotions said something else entirely."

My heart squeezes at the worry lacing his words. "You didn't hurt me," I say quietly. "You would have known if I didn't want it. As pissed as I was, I still wanted you. I'll always want you." My lips curve into a smile as I say, "Honestly, it was the best sex I've ever had. So fucking hot."

His chest rumbles under my ear as he laughs, before he sobers again. "Sometimes, when the monster comes out, I can't stop it. Even though I know what I should do, it's too hard to control him." He rubs his hand up and down my back, and I settle closer to him. "I'm having a hard time keeping your emotions outside my mental shields. They slip through no matter how hard I try to keep them out. And the stronger they are, the more they affect me. Your anger tonight fueled my own, and before I knew it, the monster was out and ready to play."

I sit up so I can look at him. I want to make sure he believes me. "I'm not scared of it. I'm not scared of any part of you." When he swallows and tries to look away, I place my hand on his cheek to keep him looking at me. "Kai, I love you. I love all of you. And I trust that you'll never hurt me. The monster ... it's part of you. And I know it won't hurt me either." In fact, any time the monster has come out to play, it's done nothing but give me the best orgasms of my life.

Kai buries his face in my neck and shudders. He says nothing, but his hold on me tightens, and I know those were words he needed to hear.

I run my fingers through his hair, nails gently scraping his scalp, as he soaks in my affection. Sometimes I forget that these badass, powerful creatures have their own insecurities and weaknesses. And I love being the one who can give them the reminder that they are more than enough.

"I love you, Kai," I whisper, kissing the top of his head.

He squeezes me tighter. "Thank you," he whispers back.

24. Ellis

The next three days pass incredibly slowly. Kai does everything he can to keep my mind occupied and off of Cade and Sterling. He tells me stories from when he grew up. We watch movies, play cards, and cuddle. The cuddling is my favorite. Being able to spend quiet time with him, with lazy touches and whispered conversations, is a balm to my aching soul. These moments never last long, though. My fears inevitably creep in and destroy whatever peace I find in his arms.

Sex is the best way to keep my mind occupied. So we have *a lot* of sex. There isn't a room or surface of this cabin where we haven't fucked. I'm also able to lose myself in the book Cade bought for me. Unfortunately, it doesn't take me long to finish it.

I sigh as I set the book on the coffee table, then flop back onto the cushions.

"You okay?" Kai asks quietly.

"I finished the book," I reply. "And now I need to know what happens. She's in the demon world now, with a crazy demon who I may be in love with, but I can't go out and buy the next book."

Kai stares at me with one brow raised. "In love with a crazy demon, huh?"

I scowl at him and cross my arms over my chest. "It's no

different than being in love with a vampire, is it? You're practically a demon."

Kai rears back and gasps. "Excuse me? I am not a demon. Vampires and demons are two very different creatures. I take offense to that. But in all seriousness, can you get the next book as an eBook?"

"Probably, but my account was managed by my da—by Thomas. I'm sure that's no longer an option."

"Use mine." Kai snags my phone and fiddles with it before handing it back to me. "There. You're all set."

I grin as I search for the title and download it. "Thank you!"

He leans in for a kiss, but I'm too absorbed in starting the book, so he huffs and makes his way to the kitchen. I tune out the sounds of him doing who the hell knows what, and fall into the pages. I'm not too far into chapter two when footsteps on the porch bring Kai to the front door. I sit up, heart hammering in my chest as he slowly opens it. I can't see past him, and he only opens it far enough for him to see out.

"Cade." He steps outside, letting the door swing wide, and I'm on my feet faster than I've ever moved.

I run through the room and launch myself over the threshold, practically knocking Kai over in my hurry. And there he is. My mage. My soul-bonded. A sob tears from my throat and I throw myself at him, desperate to feel him again, to know he's okay. My heart stops when he grunts and stumbles.

"Are you okay?" I pull back to look him over. I don't see any blood, but his face is sallow and dark blue circles line under his eyes.

"I'm fine," he tries to assure me, even as he grasps the railing for support. "Just exhausted."

Kai jumps in and wraps Cade's arm around his neck, helping him into the cabin and onto the couch. "Can I get you anything?"

"Water would be great." Cade sits back heavily, his head falling to the back of the couch.

I sit next to him and grasp his hand. "Are you sure you're

okay?" Searching his face, all I see are signs of exhaustion. Nothing that would indicate more serious injuries. Still, I can't get my worry under control.

"I just need rest. I used a lot of magic and it drained me." He takes the bottle of water from Kai and drinks half of it. With a heavy sigh, he lays down on the couch and holds his arm out for me. "Lay with me?"

I snuggle against him and his body relaxes. Almost instantly, he's asleep. His heart beating steadily under my hand is reassuring, and I'm finally able to breathe a sigh of relief. "He's okay," I whisper and close my eyes, tucking myself closer to him.

———

"WHAT ARE YOU DOING?" I ask quietly as I step into the kitchen.

Kai turns to me with a sheepish smile on his face. "Trying to make you guys some food." He rubs the back of his neck, and I grin.

"You're too cute." I stand on my tip toes and give him a quick kiss. "What were you making?" I glance around the kitchen and find puddles of water on the counter and floor, and splotches of red sauce everywhere but where it should be.

"Spaghetti. I thought it would be easy. You just have to boil water and put the pasta in. Then heat the sauce." He shrugs and ducks his head. "Turns out, it's harder than I anticipated."

My heart flip flops in my chest watching Kai act shy and unsure. "I mean, it is pretty easy, but you should have started even simpler." I grab a paper towel and wipe up the sauce. "A sandwich would have been perfect. All you have to do is put meat on some bread. Can't really go wrong there."

"I'm not so sure about that," he mutters under his breath. "I wanted to do something nice for you guys."

I turn to face him. "It wouldn't matter what you made us, we would appreciate it because you took the time to do it." He looks around the kitchen with a frown, and I tug him toward the counter. "Okay, come on. Let me teach you how to make spaghetti."

My fear has ebbed a bit with Cade's return. I'm still a nervous wreck about Sterling, and I know his situation is even worse, but having two of my guys with me helps to give me the strength I need to keep going. As soon as Cade wakes up and eats, we'll be able to talk about what we need to do to save my mate.

I walk Kai through the steps to making spaghetti. The domesticity of our actions is almost painful, because I know it won't last. As soon as Cade wakes up, reality will return and the threat hanging over my head will once again weigh me down. What will it be like when all of this is over? I can't even imagine the future because I'm scared it will jinx me. There is too much at stake, and I can't let myself picture any happiness with my Shields. The pain of losing that future is too much.

"What are you making?"

Cade's voice makes my heart stop. I turn around and take in his appearance. His skin is closer to his normal shade, and while there are still dark circles under his eyes, it's not as bad. He's also standing straight and not leaning on anything. The last bit of worry I had for him disappears.

Kai flings a piece of spaghetti at Cade and it lands with a soft, wet slap across his nose and cheek. "Spaghetti!"

Cade stares at Kai for a moment, blinking, before he pulls the pasta strand from his face. "And did you make it, or Ellis? If I eat this will I die?"

"I helped him," I say, walking over to him and popping my mouth open. He drops the pasta on my tongue. "See?" He smiles and wraps his arms around me. I sigh as I collapse against him. "You're okay?" I ask, unable to stop myself from making sure.

"I'm feeling much better. After I eat some food, I'll be back to normal." He squeezes me tighter. "Thank you for listening to Kai and coming back here." Kai snorts, and Cade pulls away to look at me with a raised brow. "You didn't listen to him?"

My cheeks heat and I duck my head, looking at his chest instead. "Not exactly."

"Ahh, so he had to compel you, huh? And he's still alive?" Cade smirks at me and I narrow my eyes at him.

"Barely." Kai comes up behind me and pulls Cade into his arms, sandwiching me between them. "I'm glad you're back safe," he mumbles.

I can't see them with my face smushed against Cade's chest, but his heart thumps harder under my cheek, and his chest raises as he sucks in a breath. Wiggling myself so I can look up at them fails. Kai presses closer to Cade and squeezes me tighter between them. I let my imagination run wild as two hard lengths press against me, one in front and one in back. *Guess there are worse places to be stuck.*

A loud grumble—louder for me with my ear closer to Cade's stomach—breaks them apart. Kai chuckles. "Let's get you some food."

I let Kai serve us the spaghetti. He looks so proud while he's doing it, and I realize for him, it's a way of providing for us that he's not typically able to do. Cade and Sterling have always made sure I have food, but for Kai, it's the opposite. It's me making sure he's fed. I make a mental note that once all of this is over, to help Kai learn to cook. Maybe we can take cooking classes somewhere as a date option.

My spaghetti disappears from my plate at an alarming rate. I'm so desperate to hear what Cade has to say, I just want to get this whole eating thing out of the way. Cade eats almost as fast as I do, but he ends up getting thirds. Kai watches us with amusement, well mostly me. Cade twirls his around his fork like a gentleman, while I slurp mine like a toddler. I can't help it, though. Gracie and I used to eat our spaghetti like this on purpose to annoy our mom.

When Cade's finally had enough, we relocate to the living room. Cade sits on the couch and reaches for the book he bought me sitting on the coffee table. "Have you started this yet?" he asks, leafing through it.

"Finished it," I say, plopping down next to him. "Kai hooked me up so I can read the rest on my phone."

He smirks at me, setting the book down. "Did you take any notes?"

"Maybe," I reply coyly.

The levity in the room drops away as Cade sighs and sits back. "So," he begins, threading his fingers through mine. "I wasn't able to get in the building, but Drew did. He returned home to rest, but he's going to map out the layout for us, as well as note the guard rotation for the inside."

"Why do I feel like there is a 'but' coming," Kai mutters, running his hand through his hair.

"Because there is," Cade sighs. "I got through the ward around the property, and luckily it was the only one. The guard rotation is pretty simple, and the doors to get into the property are not warded, just locked, which is easy enough to get through."

"Where's the 'but?'" I ask, trying to not hold my breath.

"But," he looks at me, his violet eyes appearing heavy. "I can't do it by myself. Getting myself and Drew through the ward is what drained me. After, I had to let him go on inside by himself. When it was time to get back through the wards, I could barely manage it."

"So, we need another mage that we trust to help us get inside the wards and back out." Kai's brows draw down as he thinks through this. "Someone we trust with Ellis's life."

"There aren't many I'd trust," Cade says. "So many of the powerful mages work for Kennedy. I wouldn't trust a single one of them."

"Is there someone who works for him who is being forced, like you? Maybe they would be willing to help," I offer.

Cade shakes his head. "None of them would risk it. There's too much at stake for them—their family, their lives."

Silence falls heavily through the room as we all contemplate this situation. Not going in isn't an option. I'm getting Sterling back, no matter what. In this situation, I'm probably not very useful. I don't know many magicals. All the ones I do know are from Thomas's company. Connor is the only mage I know outside of the Kennedy Corporation.

I gasp. "Connor!"

Kai and Cade look at me expectantly.

"Connor is a mage," I explain. "He owns the gym Allie and I trained at."

"Is he the one who trained you?" Kai asks, leaning forward in his chair.

"Yes. I trust him. He doesn't have anything to do with Thomas. And he's strong." My words fly out of my mouth with eagerness. Connor would be perfect for this.

"But would he be willing to help?" Cade asks.

I nod enthusiastically, my bun sliding around on top of my head. "I think he would. He cared enough to train Allie and me. And last I heard, they were going on dates. And he's always mentioned how he hates how humans get shit on in our world and how he wishes there was something he could do to help." When my words finally quiet, I'm panting slightly.

"Breathe, Ellis," Cade says with a smile. "If you trust him, I think it's worth meeting with him. I'm not committing to anything until we've met and talked things through."

"Agreed," Kai says.

I grab my phone from the table. "I'll call Allie."

25. Sterling

My heads lolls to the side as the guards drag me to the torture room. Matted silver hair falls into my eyes, blocking my view. Not that I need to see where I'm going. I don't have the energy to attempt to lift my head, and even if I did, it would hurt too much. The raw burns on my back send pain through me. Pain unlike anything I've ever felt. My skin is hot, sweat coats my body, and every single move I make aches. Even blinking my eyes hurts. Pretty sure I have an infection. And if I do, it must be a nasty one if my shifter blood isn't healing it.

"On the table," Sam says.

I've come to dread hearing his voice. Sam means pain. But, if I'm the one on the receiving end of his torture, I'll take it. It means Ellis is still safe. I'd gladly take her place.

The guards shove me onto the metal table with no thought of gentleness. I hiss through my teeth as the blisters on my back make contact with the cool surface. I still haven't given Sam the satisfaction of making a single noise during any of his torture sessions. But a sliver of apprehension washes through me this time. This is the first time he's had me on my back. At least the other times I knew what to expect. A whipping of some sort. Now, I have no idea.

His magic swirls around him, green bands of shimmering light that he fastens around my wrist and ankles. *Holy fuck*. They burn. It's not anywhere near as painful as the real burns on my back. But, is this what Ellis went through with him? That thought hurts more than anything he's done to me. Imagining my mate in Sam's hands, the pain and fear I know she'd go through, is fuel enough to keep me strong.

"It's a new day," Sam says with a cruel smile. "Shall we try something new?" He snags a slim silver blade from a tray next to the table and examines it. "I figured as long as I have you in my possession, I might as well make use of you, since you refuse to give me the information I want. For now."

He places the blade against my skin, right in the middle of my bicep, and slices through my muscle. At first, I feel nothing. Then the wicked sting of a blade slicing flesh washes through me. I grit my teeth. Honestly, it's not near as bad as the burning iron. Blood wells, ruby bright, and slides down my arm.

"Hmm," Sam muses. "Nothing? Let's keep going. Shall we?"

He gives me six more cuts, avoiding any major artery and nothing deep enough to bleed too much. One on my shoulder, two along my ribs, one below my belly button, one on the outside of my knee, and one on the inside of my thigh.

By the sixth gash, fresh sweat has broken out on my skin. The salt stinging something fierce as it meets the cuts. But I still haven't made a single noise. He'll have to try harder.

"Still holding out?" Sam asks, pulling the blade away. A vein pulses in his neck, he's starting to get angry. That's never a good thing. "Why won't you just tell me what I want to know? Where. Is. She."

Stupidly, I grin at him. Peeling my tongue off the roof of my mouth, I say. "Try harder." I have to force each word out, and they rasp against my unused and parched throat.

Sam's eyes flare with unchecked anger and red suffuses his neck and cheeks. That did it. I really pissed him off. The next few slices of the blade are deep. Probably too deep. But I still say nothing. Even when he places the edge of the blade at the top of my scar, the point digging in enough to draw blood.

"Maybe I should finish what was started here?" He breathes. His chest is rising and falling rapidly in his anger.

My heart stutters as utter terror careens through me. Losing my sight has been one of my biggest fears since I got that scar. I fight to reach my wolf, even though I know it's pointless. My limbs tremble in the magic restraints.

Sam grins, and pulls the blade away. "Oh, now I see. I think I'll wait for that one. Once Ellis is in my possession, I can use that fear against her."

Fuck. I have to get myself together, but my brain is going foggy. I can hear the splatter of my blood as it drips onto the floor. There is real risk I'll bleed to death. But, I think I'd welcome it. Then Sam can't use me against her.

"Johnson! Get in here!" Sam yells over his shoulder. A door opens, and a middle aged mage steps into the room. "Collect some blood."

Johnson approaches, and with a sympathetic look, he gathers three vials of my blood. Must be someone forced to work for Sam. I wonder if I could convince him to help me somehow, but I'm distracted from my plans with Sam's next words.

"Maybe watching his mate's sister get tortured will make him talk. Bring Grace in."

26. CADE

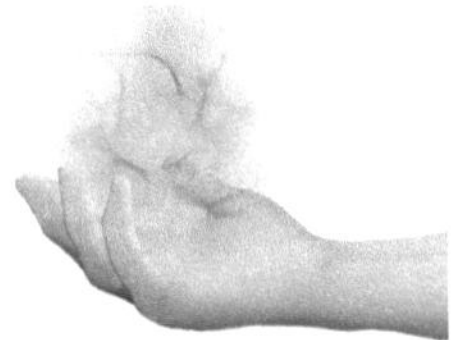

I HATE TAKING ELLIS OUT FROM BEHIND THE WARDS, but I know I can't keep her locked up until this is done. I really wish I could, though. Also, all of this mixing up daytime and nighttime shit is starting to get old. We need to stick to one schedule. Ellis is yawning in the backseat, despite the large coffee with an extra shot of espresso she downed ten minutes ago. I think Kai is asleep, it's hard to tell. His eyes are closed, but that could just be because of the sunlight. I'm doing okay this morning, but I think that's because I slept so much the day before, recovering from using so much magic.

"Can we stop for another coffee?" Ellis asks blearily.

"Did you already finish that one?" I shoot a glance in the review mirror. Her head is tipped back on the seat, and her eyes are closed. But she holds up her empty coffee cup and shakes it at me. "Is it an emergency?" I ask.

"That depends on how much you want to deal with a cranky Ellis," Kai chimes in.

Not asleep then. And definitely not afraid for his safety.

Ellis sits up and smacks his shoulder. "Fuck off, dick."

Kai looks at me with one raised brow. "I'd say it's an emergency."

I hold my snort in, mainly because I don't want to die. Ellis is cranky when she's tired, and I'm not willing to risk it. The rest of the drive to the city is, thankfully, quiet. I'm just driving in the city limits when Kai suddenly sits up straight in his seat.

"Pull in here. Now." He says pointing to a parking lot to the right.

"What the fuck!" I turn the wheel sharply and the tires squeal as the car veers to the right. I'm dimly aware of Ellis rubbing the back of her head and complaining, but my attention is glued to our surroundings, searching for any sign of danger. Purple sparks light up at my fingertips, ready to protect my soul-bonded. "What is it? Kai?"

"Huh?" He's distracted as he looks out his window, and when I see what he's looking at I curse.

"Really, Kai? What the hell?" I throw the Charger into park, and Kai hops out immediately.

"What's going on?" Ellis asks, eyes wide and face pale.

"Oh, nothing. Just Kai getting a new car, apparently. " I hop out and open Ellis's door, grabbing her hand and following Kai.

"A new car? Right now?" She glances at her phone to check the time. "We have thirty-minutes. This will take too long."

"It won't take half that time. Kai's too good at this, and with his name, we'll be done with plenty of time to get to the gym."

My point is proven when we catch up with Kai and he's already working the salesman. He's not even using his compulsion. Just his name and his charm, and he has these people in his pocket. Ten minutes later, the keys are handed over, and Kai is the owner of a brand new car.

Before he walks away, he lowers his head to stare into the salesman's eyes. "You won't remember who you sold this car to." His voice is tranquil but authoritative, and the salesman's eyes glaze over as Kai's compulsion takes hold. When the man nods, Kai smiles and pats him on the cheek. "Good deal. Thanks for the new ride." He turns to us with a grin, holding up the keys and jingling them.

"What did you get?" I ask, heading back to the Charger to get all of our stuff out of it to put into the new car.

"A Hummer," he says, slipping his sunglasses back on.

"You just bought a fucking Hummer in ten minutes?" Ellis's eyes are wide, her voice raised an octave.

"Yep. No more worrying about taking the Charger up that damn mountain. Plus, it's electric. You know me. Whatever I can do for the environment."

"Right," she drawls. "A total conservationist. Why the thrall, though?"

"All of our vehicles, or what's left of them, are too recognizable," he explains. "This way we can try to keep this car as underwraps as possible. If I hadn't wiped his memory of this, it would be all over the tabloids. 'Vampire Prince buys new Hummer EV. Saving the world one car at time.'"

I snort. "You think so highly of yourself. Here." I shove a bunch of his shit into his hands, and grab the rest. "Where's this Hummer?"

He leads us to a dark gray SUV and we all climb in. Literally for Ellis. The damn car is so high off the ground she almost needs a boost to get in.

"I feel like I'm in a spaceship," she mutters once we're on the road. "Who needs a screen that big for their car?"

I chuckle. "Not going to lie, I'm kind of jealous. This is a nice ride."

"Please," Kai says. "You end up driving my car more than me anyway. For fuck's sake, you're driving it before I get to!"

"Not my fault you're a baby and can't handle the sunlight."

Kai grumbles. "I'd hit you, but I don't want to risk you wrecking."

The rest of the drive to the gym, Kai fumbles around with the settings on the giant ass screen mounted on the middle of the dashboard, while Ellis watches in amazement.

"Hey, Ellis," I say, a thought suddenly hitting me. "Can you drive?"

"No. Fucking Thomas never let me. Another way to control me. I had to walk everywhere, or beg a ride off one of the house staffers."

I catch her gaze in the rearview mirror as I pull into the small parking lot behind the gym. "When this is all over, I'll teach you."

Her eyes light up with so much excitement, it breaks my heart. The prospect of learning to drive shouldn't be that exciting, but for someone who lived under the thumb of a so-called parent, every little experience is a novelty.

"Really?" she asks, hand on her chest.

"Of course. You should be able to drive yourself wherever you want, when you want, without relying on anyone else."

She squeals and claps her hands. "Thank you!"

I grin. This *almost* carefree version of Ellis is one I definitely love seeing. I only wish it could last. But I have a feeling things are going to get much worse before they get better.

We hop out of the Hummer and find Allie waiting by a back door, bouncing back and forth on her toes, bottom lip pulled between her teeth. The light in her eyes is excited, though. Probably to see Ellis. Even as this thought crosses my mind, Ellis dashes across the parking lot to crash into her.

"Fuck, Ellis." I mutter, and hurry after her. This girl has no sense of self-preservation, despite everything she's been through and everything going on.

"I missed you!" Ellis squeezes Allie so hard I'm afraid the girl might pop, but she's squeezing Ellis just as hard.

"I missed you, too! And I have so much to tell you." Allie pulls back and whispers, "We went out again last night. It was ..." she trails off and bites her lip again, a faint blush creeping up her neck.

Ellis gasps. "Did you have sex?"

Allie cringes and flaps her hands, making a shushing motion. "Quiet!" she hisses.

"I really hate to break up girl talk," Kai says, "But, we should get inside and out of the public's eyes."

Allie ushers us inside the door and into a back storage room in the gym. I let my magic sweep the area to make sure there are no threats or hidden traps. Sensing my magic, a mage steps into the backroom from another door. He's built, with brown hair pulled into a bun on the back of his head. His mouth splits into a smile when his gaze lands on Ellis.

"Connor!" She rushes toward him, but stops abruptly when a growl climbs up Kai's throat. "You'll have to forgive them," she says with a slight shake of her head. "They're a little possessive right now."

"I understand." He nods his head in our direction, then motions us to follow him. "We can talk in my office. It's warded, so no one can listen in."

Kai tugs Ellis to him. I hear him whisper an apology, and she stands on her tiptoes to kiss his cheek. I'm glad she's being patient with him. This is hard on all of us, but for Kai with his predator instinct and his beloved in danger, it's even harder.

In Connor's office, I scan the surroundings. "Do you mind if I check things out?"

He shakes his head. "Go ahead."

While Connor sits in the rolling chair behind his desk, I use my magic to double check everything again. He has an impressive ward surrounding this space, and it gives me hope if he decides to help us. I can sense his strength, and he's pretty damn powerful. How he's kept out of Kennedy's line of sight is beyond me. I nod the all-clear, and Ellis sits in the only other chair in the office. Kai and I take up position behind her, while Allie perches on the desk, legs swinging.

"So," Connor says, leaning back in his chair, arms crossed and biceps popping. "Allie said you guys wanted to talk to me."

"Before we begin," I say, "You need to know Kai and I will do absolutely anything to keep Ellis safe. No matter what it is. You know Kai is an empath, and he's going to be using that on you during this conversation. We have to make sure we can trust you."

Luckily, Kai's abilities are sort of like a lie detector, and it will help us determine if Connor is trustworthy.

He nods his head. "I understand," he says again.

I tap Ellis on the shoulder, letting her know she's good to go.

"Has Allie filled you in on anything? Anything that's been happening to me?" Ellis asks.

"No, she's been super quiet about you. Even when I ask her where you've been. Besides the contest—which I've heard has been canceled—I know nothing."

Ellis takes a deep breath, preparing to share her story. We talked about this last night, and decided to keep her Harpy abilities quiet, but everything else is fair game. "So, during this contest, we," she waves her hand toward Kai and me, "discovered Thomas Kennedy isn't really my dad. The alpha of the Iron Shadows pack, Noah Martin, is."

Connor whistles through his teeth. "I'm guessing that's why the contest was canceled?"

"Yes," she continues. "And in the process of us getting the proof of my parentage, we found something really awful. Noah and Sam Morris are working together to do some kind of testing or experiments on magicals and non-magicals. And there have been a lot of deaths in the process." She takes a breath and rubs her eyes. "My name is on the list of subjects they want to experiment on. My sister's name is, too."

Allie gasps and clasps her hand over her mouth, eyes wide and full of shock. Connor sits forward in his chair and rests his forearms on the desk. "I'm assuming this is being done illegally?"

"As far as we can tell," I say. "I'm sure they have some authorities in their pockets to keep the place funded and up and running smoothly."

"So what do you need from me?" Connor asks.

"When we discovered all of this," Ellis says, "Sterling decided to go check things out. He got caught in some kind of ward and they captured him." Her voice trembles as she tells this part of the story. Kai places a hand on her shoulder.

I take over to let Ellis breathe. "I was able to get through the wards to check the place out. We have a crow shifter who's been helping us, and he got in to scope the inside. But, getting past the wards two times took all of my magic."

"So you want my help to get through the wards." Connor says, staring at me with an expression I can't decipher.

"Yes. We need to get Sterling out. And we need to find a way to end these experiments."

"What exactly are they doing? What's their goal?" Connor asks.

I shake my head. "Not positive. But we know he mentioned weapons, and reinforcing a room for testing. It all sounds appalling, and from what I've read so far, at least twenty non-magicals, and seven magicals have been killed in the process."

Ellis turns around in the seat to look at me with a question burning in her eyes. I didn't tell her I spent a night reading through those files Sterling sent me. Even the ones that depicted all the horrendous things Sam did to my soul-bonded. It was fuel for my fire before we went to scout the warehouse. Those details will be forever burned into my mind. And I can't wait until I can get my hands on that bastard, if only so I can hold him down while Ellis ends his life in the most painful way possible.

I give her a reassuring smile, before turning my attention back to Connor. "Ellis mentioned you don't agree with the way non-magicals are treated. Is that true?"

Connor sighs, and sits back in his chair, his gaze trained on Allie. "I don't agree. Anyone with a conscience wouldn't agree. It's why I trained these two and gave them free access to my gym." His eyes slide to me, hard and unyielding. "But I don't see how we can make any difference."

"Maybe not in the grand scheme of things," Ellis says quietly. "But we can help a little, by stopping this experimentation. Since this contest started, well before actually, I have been attacked multiple times. Sam is trying his hardest to get his hands on me, and I just want it to stop." She shudders, and Kai's hand on her shoulder tightens.

"Why does Sam want you so bad?" Connor asks.

She looks down at her hands in her lap. "I don't know."

His eyes narrow, like he knows she's lying, but he doesn't question it. "What all would this entail?"

"Well, it will obviously be dangerous," I say. "The first phase of our plan is to get Sterling out. Once he's safe, we'll regroup and make a plan for destroying this warehouse and taking Sam and Noah out of the picture. Hopefully, killing the leaders will quell the followers. If it doesn't, we'll have to deal with it."

"You said you have the layout and guard rotations of this warehouse?"

"We do." I nod. "Any extra bit will help us. I can get us through the wards, but I wouldn't have anything left to defend Ellis. That's not a risk I'm willing to take. If we can't find another mage we trust, there is no way we can get Sterling out."

Ellis stifles as gasp, but it's loud enough to draw Connor's attention. I don't know what kind of emotions Ellis is putting off, but Kai kneels next to her and turns her head to face him.

"Breathe, Ellis," he says quietly. "You know we're not going to leave him in there. We will find a way to save him."

Her lower lip wobbles as she looks at him. "Promise?" she whispers.

"I promise, baby girl." He kisses her forehead and stands back up.

"I feel like there are some details I'm missing," Connor says, staring at us. "But as long as I get all the necessary information, I'm in."

"Really?" Ellis scoots to the edge of her chair, hands clasped tightly together. "You'll really help us?"

His eyes soften as he looks at her, and my hackles raise on instinct. No one else looks at my soul-bonded like that except Kai and Sterling. Kai stiffens and takes a step forward.

"Of course I'll help you," Connor says, oblivious to mine and

Kai's sudden focus on him. "I've been trying to help you girls for a long time now. If someone is trying to hurt you, I'll do what I can to help keep you safe."

Fuck. We're not enough for her. I grind my teeth as the thought floats through my mind. Kai and I aren't enough to keep her safe. We had to ask someone else to help us. Someone else who makes me want to punch him when he looks at her like that.

Connor drags his gaze from my soul-bonded, to look at me. "So, when does this all go down?"

27. Ellis

"You need to try to get some sleep, love."

"I can't sit still. If I sit still, my brain starts working." Although, it works even when I'm pacing. But my limbs feel like electricity is being pumped through them. I have to move. The nervous energy in me makes me feel twitchy.

I got Cade back, but Sterling is still captured. Who knows what's happening to him. Although, I can guess, and I don't like the images that pop into my head. Tomorrow morning, Drew, Allie, and Connor are meeting us here, at the cabin, to go over plans. Our first goal is to rescue Sterling and bring him back here, where I'm assuming he'll need time to heal. After that, we'll make plans to take out Sam and Noah.

"Ellis, love," Cade's voice is low and quiet, making my skin shiver. "Come here."

I stop in my tracks and my gaze travels to Cade without my permission. He's sitting on the edge of the bed, wearing nothing but a pair of black joggers. His hair is still damp from his shower, laying unstyled across his forehead. Those violet eyes draw me in, and I'm moving before I realize I took the first step. He stands and effortlessly lifts me off my feet. I wrap my legs around him and he spins us, dropping me in the middle of the mattress.

I squeak as I fall, landing in a heap. Swiping the hair from my eyes, I find Cade crawling toward me, a predatory look in his eye. Butterflies take flight in my stomach as anticipation settles within me. Being the solitary focus of these guys is addicting. The rush I get when I realize just how much they care for me, is better than any high I could get from a drug.

Cade's hand is warm when he cups my cheek. Leaning down, he captures my mouth in a soul-claiming kiss. There is nothing rushed or frenzied about this one. He takes his time, tasting me, memorizing the way I feel, leisurely exploring. His hand slides down to my back and he pulls me closer so I can feel his heart thumping behind his ribs.

A sound escapes my throat, and he presses me tighter to him. His erection is hard against my thigh and I want to get my hands on it. My mouth around it. But he won't let me. He keeps me against him, so all I can do is soak in this kiss and thread my fingers through his damp hair.

I break away, chest heaving and head swimming from lack of oxygen. "Cade," I breathe.

He ignores me, and moves to my neck and throat. Leaving a trail of hot, wet kisses over my skin. I arch my back as he gently nips at my collar bone and he groans when my thigh rubs against him. Fire is building inside me, searing me from the inside out. My body is craving him in every possible way.

"Arms up," he demands in a low, throaty growl that makes me shiver.

I comply, and he slides my tank over my head, tossing it to the floor over his shoulder. His eyes darken when he realizes I'm not wearing a bra, and sucks a nipple into his mouth, making my back arch off the bed. I tangle my hands in his hair again and hold him to me, not wanting him to stop. When his hand skims down my stomach and slides under the waistband of the gym shorts I'm wearing, anticipation pools in my core, making my inner walls clench.

Cade releases my nipple and stares at me with swirling purple eyes. "I love when you're all flushed and flustered. The noises you make. The way your body reacts to mine."

Each word is a whispered caress against my skin as he worships me with his mouth and tongue. His hand slips lower and runs through my center, drawing forth one of those noises he claims to love. Lifting my hips, I silently beg him for more, and his dark laughter is a promise of what's to come.

When he pushes one finger inside, I let go of his hair to grasp the sheets in my balled fists. My eyelids flutter shut, and I let my head fall back onto the bed. Each thrust of his fingers is but a whisper of the pleasure I know he can give me, and the anticipation only stokes the flames even higher.

Cade adds a second finger, and captures my mouth in another deep and sensual kiss. The slow, drugging kiss and equally lazy movements of his fingers is driving me wild. I need more. This teasing has gone on long enough and I'm more than ready for him.

"Cade," I rasp, breaking away from his kiss. "Please, I want you."

His smile is sweet, but with a hint of darkness, as he pulls his hand away and licks my juices off his fingers. My chest heaves, and he yanks my shorts and undies down and throws them with my tanktop. He takes a moment to admire me, and his violet eyes are almost black as he slowly tugs his pants down. Swallowing thickly, I return the favor and let my gaze travel over his body. He grins and climbs over me, settling atop me and kissing me again.

These kisses. They are going to destroy me. Each one is like he's trying to devour my soul, and I will gladly let him have it. It's almost painful. Like my heart knows this happiness can't possibly last. My chest is heavy and tears burn the backs of my eyes, but I don't let them fall. I push the dark thoughts away and force myself to stay in the present. It's not too hard, with Cade's hard body heating my own. Each place our skin touches sends lightning skittering over my skin.

His fingers gently grasp my thighs and he spreads my legs wide, settling his hips between them. "Look at me, Ellis."

My gaze latches onto his, and I bite back a moan as he slides his cock through my wetness. Once, twice, three times. *Oh, fuck.* My toes are already curling, and pressure is already building inside me.

His chest is rising and falling rapidly, his breaths stuttering in and out as quickly as mine. "Watch, Ellis. Watch me disappear inside you."

My gaze drops to where his cock is pressing against my entrance. I have to fight the urge to let my eyes close, instead watching as he slowly pushes inside, stretching and filling me.

"The perfect fucking fit," he groans. Grabbing my legs, he sets my ankles on his shoulders, changing the angle.

Before he can start moving, the bathroom door opens and Kai steps out, hair still dripping onto his shoulders. He grins. "Don't stop on my account," he says, repeating the phrase that has become one of my favorites. The towel falls from his hips, and both Cade and I get distracted by his naked body, with drops of water from his hair sliding down his chest.

I clench around Cade, and the sensation kicks him into gear. He moves within me, building the fire that he started with his drugging kisses. Even in this, Cade is slow and deliberate. No rough thrusting or frenzied slamming of his hips. I lift my arms over my head and grab the sheets, arching my back as a soft moan slips past my lips. Cade bends down to drag his teeth over my nipple and my hips buck against his.

Glancing at Kai, I find him standing by the bed, stroking himself as he watches. It messes with my head. Cade practically making love to me, and Kai watching. Usually, when it's the three of us, it's rough and fast, this is not, and it makes my heart flutter in my chest.

Kai climbs on the bed and kneels next to us. He threads his fingers through Cade's hair and pulls him in for a kiss. I expect the brutal dominance Kai usually shows, but it's not. Is sweet, and deep. Everything about this is different. It's intense and passionate. All-consuming.

Until Kai turns his dark gaze on me and gives me a wicked, fang-filled grin. "Don't come, baby girl. Not until I say you can." Then he turns that wicked grin on Cade. "You, however ..." He trails his hand down Cade's back and over his ass, giving him a little squeeze. "You can come whenever." With that, he runs his finger through Cade's backside, and Cade's pace falters.

"Fuck, Kai," he groans. "You're gonna make me come."

"That's the idea," Kai practically purrs, then licks up the side of his throat.

I don't know what Kai does, but I can imagine it. Whatever it is, Cade grabs my thighs tightly and his cock thickens. He rocks his hips against mine and tenses as he comes. When he releases my legs, he falls forward, hands on either side of my head, and rests his forehead against mine.

Breathing heavily, he slowly pulls out, lowering my legs, and I clench around him again, not ready for him to leave. "But—" I don't get to finish my thought.

Kai takes Cade's place. "Don't worry, baby girl. We'll make sure you're taken care of."

With my wetness and Cade's release, Kai is able to slip right in. I moan as his piercings slide along my inner walls. *Oh, fuck.* I'm so fucking ready to come. My body is shaking with need. The pressure is building higher and higher, and I'm positive I'm going to combust.

Kai watches me with a look that says he's about to eat me. Being the sole focus of his gaze is unnerving sometimes. His intensity settles inside me, and draws me even closer to the edge.

"Kai, please. I need to come," I beg. My heart is racing, my muscles are tense, my lungs straining for oxygen. Every nerve ending is on fire.

Kai smirks at me and glances at Cade. My gaze follows his, and I find Cade hard again, his hand working his thick length.

Kai grabs the back of Cade's neck, never breaking his

punishing rhythm. "Come for us, baby girl," he mutters at the same time he sinks his fangs into Cade's neck.

Cade comes again with a groan, warm stickiness landing on my belly. It sends me over the edge. I fall into my orgasm with a scream. My body shakes and trembles as my release shudders through me. Wave after wave of pleasure, until my body finally stills. I can't move. I can't open my eyes. I just lay on the bed and try to catch my breath.

Around me, the guys are moving. The bed dips, footsteps sound, water runs. I'm too blissed out to focus on any one sensation. A cool cloth wipes across my stomach, cleaning up Cade's release. Arms slide under me and tuck me against a warm chest. It must be Cade. Kai's skin is cooler. The bed dips again, and another arm wraps around me, cooler to the touch.

With my body exhausted, and my mind too foggy to worry, it's easy to slip into sleep with my guys surrounding me.

———

"ELLIS," Kai groans. "Stop, they'll be here any minute."

I grin, but he can't see it. "So?"

"So? You're putting my hair in pigtails!"

Cade chuckles, leaning forward to get a better look. "You look adorable," he says with big eyes and pouty smile, before his act slips and he laughs.

I keep working. It's not just pigtails. I'm braiding it before it goes into the pigtail. Running my fingers through his silky black hair is calming. I love the way it feels, and the way the curls at the ends wrap around my fingers.

Kai tries to pull his head away, but I grab a fistfull of the black strands and yank him back. "Stop moving," I hiss. "You're going to mess me up."

Before he can respond, there is a knock on the door. Kai tenses, and I can't tell if it's in preparation of danger or in preparation of people seeing him like this. Cade opens the door for everyone.

Allie grins when her gaze lands on Kai sitting on the floor between my legs. Connor raises one brow. Both of them luckily keep their mouths shut. Drew, on the other hand, catcalls and winks at Kai. "Looking good, bro," he says with a laugh.

A low growl rumbles up Kai's throat, but I yank his hair again until he stops. "Play nice," I whisper.

"Does anyone want anything to eat or drink?" Cade asks once everyone is settled around the living room.

"We're good, thanks," Connor says, for him and Allie.

Drew shakes his head. "Nah, let's just get this over with."

I wrap a rubberband around the first pigtail, and move onto the second.

"Drew, you have the layout of the building?" Cade asks, sitting next to me, causing the cushion to dip and tilting me sideways.

"I do." He leans to the side to pull a folded stack of papers from his back pocket. Unfolding them, he spreads them on the coffee table, and we all lean forward to get a better look. "This is what I could get of the main floor. It's the path I took to the basement." His finger traces over the sketched map as he talks. "There are no guards directly by the doors, but they are stationed further down the hallways, usually at an intersection. I'm assuming this gives them the time they need to alert others of intruders, and the distance to use ranged attacks—weapons and magic—to defend."

"Drew got in through a window we were able to get open," Cade chimes in. "The building is an old elementary school, and from the looks of the maps, the first level is still untouched. So, the window he went through was a classroom window."

"Why is it so unguarded?" Connor asks.

"I have two theories to that," Drew says. "One, they think the outer ward is enough to keep people out. Two, they want people to get inside."

"Why would they want people to get inside?" I ask, finishing Kai's last pigtail.

"More subjects to test on," Cade says quietly. "And now, with Sterling being captured, I'm willing to bet Sam is assuming you're going to try and rescue him."

"So this is a trap?" Fear flutters in my belly. Maybe it's best if I *do* stay behind. Not that I'd ever admit that outloud.

"It's only a trap if we don't expect it," Kai says, running his hands over his hair with a shake of his head.

"What about the lower level?" Cade asks.

Drew slides the first paper to the side, and flattens out the second. "The basement has been completely remodeled. The classrooms have been divided into three or four sections. Each section is basically a cell." He points to a spot on the map that has a question mark. "There is a room at the end of the hallway that I'm assuming they use for their 'experiments', but I wasn't able to get close enough. The guard presence increases the closer you get to it."

My heart thunders in my chest, and I grab the back of Kai's shirt subconsciously. "Did you see Sterling?" My question is a hoarse whisper.

Drew gives me a sad smile and shakes his head. "The doors were all closed and I couldn't see inside them."

"So we don't know which cell Sterling is in?" Cade asks.

"We do," Drew says. "There is a guard outside his cell, and I overheard a conversation confirming it. He's in this one." He points to a random room, no different than any of the others.

Cade slides off the couch to sit closer to the coffee table. Connor and Drew join him, and Kai scoots next to Cade. I'm left on the couch by myself with only my emotions for company. Emotions Kai is either blocking or is too distracted to notice. We're going to walk into a trap. My Shields are going to put themselves at risk for me. Sterling is already hurt, I have no doubt about it. Cade and Kai may end up getting killed. I can't handle this.

My chest is tightening, and each breath is getting harder and shallower. I squeeze my eyes shut, so I can't watch the blackness creep in. The scent of rose wraps around me and the couch dips slightly. Small hands grasp mine, and I open my eyes to see Allie giving me an encouraging smile.

"It's all going to work out, El."

My lips tremble as I whisper, "What if it doesn't?"

"It will." She places a hand on her chest. "I have a feeling."

A feeling. Allie's sixth sense has never led her wrong yet. But there's so much that can go wrong here. There's so much at stake. Still, her words bring me some peace. I lay my head on her shoulder, and let her scent of roses calm me further.

28. STERLING

WHAT THE FUCK?

Her sister is dead. I was there that night. This has to be some kind of trick. A way to get me to talk. But, I never saw her body. I was in the kitchen, protecting Ellis.

It can't be true. Can it?

I fight back the darkness that is threatening to pull me under. Too much blood. I've lost too much blood. I can still hear it splattering on the floor. My healing hasn't kicked in. Or my body is so overwhelmed, there's too much to heal, it's just given up.

My eyes focus when the door opens, and the guards drag a girl in. She's in a ratty hospital gown, riddled with holes. It's so covered in blood, I can't tell the original color of the fabric. Her arms and legs are bone thin, like she's being starved, and her skin is a sickly shade of yellow. But, it's the hair that makes my heart stop in my chest. The wild brown curls are matted and crusted with blood, but it only takes one glance to tell this girl is clearly related to my mate.

Grace.

Her gaze meets mine, her eyes a light brown, not amber, but her facial features are the same. *Oh, shit.* Ellis's sister is alive. This entire time, she has been alive. Tortured and abused, but alive.

The need to escape, to get this information to Ellis, burns to life inside me.

"Grace," Sam coos, brushing a matted curl from her forehead. "I'd like to introduce you to Sterling. You're sister's mate."

Grace's eyes widen. It makes my stomach roil. She looks so much like a skeleton. Her cheeks and eyes are so sunken in, that it's like she's looking out at me from blackened pits. She mouths her sister's name, no sound emitting from her throat, tears building along her lashes.

Sam turns to me, grinning widely. "If I can't get you to talk using your own pain, maybe your mate's sister's pain will do the trick."

His magic wraps around her wrist, ankles, and throat, and she winces. A tear slips down her sunken cheek. She meets my gaze, and even with fear in her eyes, she shakes her head and mouths three words.

"Don't. Give. In."

It's hard. It's so fucking hard to keep my mouth shut as Grace screams. Tears roll freely down her cheeks, and her entire body trembles. Sam is ruthless. Cuts and burns. Broken bones. Bile climbs up my throat and chokes me. I shut my eyes, unable to watch as Grace is tortured. But her screams echo in my head until her voice is so hoarse, no further noise escapes her open mouth.

I want to cave. I want to tell him to stop. But I can't. I can't let him know where Ellis is. I pray she'll forgive me for this. I pray she won't hold this against me. But my mate's safety will always come first. Even if this tears me up. Even if this leaves a scar so deep, I'll never heal from it.

Sam only stops when Grace passes out. He uses his magic to heal all of her injuries. A fresh slate for the next torture session. That's when I notice the tears on my own cheeks.

Forgive me, Grace. Forgive me, Ellis.

I close my eyes as the guards come to haul Grace back to her room. I welcome the darkness. And I hope it stays this time.

29. Ellis

I'm going to puke. My anxiety is so high my entire body is vibrating. Each breath I take is shallow, and I'm breathing out more than I'm breathing in. I'm a live-wire, and it won't take much to set me off.

Back in the abandoned office building, feet away from the warehouse, we're going over the details one last time. I can't focus on what Cade is saying, though. There's a buzzing in my ears and it's the only thing I can hear—besides my heartbeat pounding against my ribcage.

This is it. This is the moment that can forever alter my life. I slowly back away from the group until my back hits the wall. I close my eyes and press my fingertips to the plaster, using a grounding technique I learned in therapy years ago. It doesn't work. Tears burn the back of my eyelids, and I squeeze them shut tighter. A gasping sob crawls up my throat, and I can't keep it contained.

I catch a whiff of cherries and spice a second before Kai rests his forehead against mine. "We're going to get him back. I won't settle for any other alternative." He grabs my hands and places them on his chest, where his heart is beating as erratically as mine.

"I'm so scared," I whisper, leaning into him.

"I know, baby girl. But you need to trust us. We know what we're doing, and we won't let anything happen to you."

Shaking my head, I open my eyes and look into his gray orbs. "I'm not scared for me. What if something happens to one of you?" My voice catches, and I have to swallow back the despair that threatens to drown me.

"You can't worry about 'what ifs'. It will consume you. Live in each moment, and know that whatever happens, you'll be okay. We will always make sure you are okay." He wipes a tear away with his thumb and kisses me gently. "Do you want me to use my thrall to help you calm down? I need to stay focused in there."

For some reason, his asking me calms my nerves. I guess it's just the proof I need to know I will always be taken care of. "Not yet. I think I'm okay for now. But if I start to panic, just do it."

He nods and searches my eyes. "I love you, Ellis."

My lips wobble and I have to press them together. The words I want to say get stuck behind the tears. But Kai smiles and nods, picking up on my emotions. I don't need to tell him I love him. He knows without words.

Cade approaches, and Kai steps to the side. He doesn't say anything, because he knows nothing will truly make me feel better until I have all three of my guys back at the cabin with me. Instead, he frames my face in his hands and kisses me. I melt under his touch and let it soothe the jagged pieces of me that fear and anxiety have chipped away at. When he steps away, he squeezes my hands.

"Is everyone ready?" Kai asks, glancing at Drew and Connor.

Allie stayed back at the cabin with her medical supplies ready just in case. I don't want to think about the reason why we would need her instead of Cade's healing abilities.

With everyone's confirmation, we file out of the abandoned office with me sandwiched between Cade and Kai. Drew strips out of his clothes and shifts, taking to the skies to ensure the coast is clear. At his signal, we approach the ward.

It's invisible—to me at least. I squeeze Kai's hand as Cade and

Connor step away. This is the first part of our plan. Connor raises his hands and red light flares around him as he closes his eyes and focuses on the ward. Violet shimmers up Cade's arms and he waits for Connor's nod to add his magic to the ward.

I have no clue what they do, I can't see anything happen. But sweat beads on Connor's brow, and Cade's face is twisted in concentration. When they finally let their magic fade and step away, both are breathing heavily.

"We're good," Connor rasps quietly.

Before Cade can take a step forward, Kai grabs his forearm and forces Cade to look at him. "You good? Do you have enough left to be safe in there?"

Cade nods. "Yeah. Connor did most of the work."

Kai pulls him in for a quick kiss. "Be careful."

"You too."

A crow waits on the ledge of a window, and we make our way to it. They picked this window because it's close to an intersection with the basement stairs. The hope is to surprise the guards before they can signal for help. Cade carefully slides the glass up, and I hold my breath. We wait in tense silence as Drew flies in and scouts the room and hallway beyond. He comes back and lands on the ledge. Three clicks of his beak. Three mages in the hallway.

My hands shake as I climb through the window after Cade and Connor. Kai gives me a boost before he follows. I can't see anything inside the room except the glow of Cade and Connor's magics. Carefully, and quietly, I make my way to them with Kai's hand on my low back. Connor looks back at us, making sure we're ready, and I repress a shiver. With his red magic swirling in his eyes, he looks like a demon. Purple and red wreathed hands stretch out, and they rush forward around the doorframe, with Kai following at supernatural speed.

I wait in the darkness, hold my breath again, and strain to hear every sound. Not a whole lot makes it way to me. Faint mutters and thumps. I jump when Drew lands on my shoulder, talons digging in through my leather jacket. That's my signal. I hurry around the door into the hallway and my gaze scans the scene for Kai and Cade first.

Kai is at the end of the hallway, standing in the intersection with blood dripping down his chin. Three bodies lay at his feet, but only one is missing its throat. Cade is by the door I just exited, and Connor is halfway down the hallway. All three are unharmed. I take a deep breath before grabbing Cade's hand and following him to the door that will lead to the basement. And Sterling.

Drew flies off my shoulder and through the door. He waits at the bottom for Kai to quietly crack the last door for him to slip through. Kai keeps it propped open, waiting for Drew to return. When he does, he clicks his beak five times. Five guards to deal with.

My heart takes off at a gallop. We're so close. I reach inside myself, to see if I can sense the bond between me and Sterling, but there's nothing there. It reminds me of when he almost died. Just vast nothingness where the bond should be. I clutch at my chest and try not think about what that could mean.

Drew settles on my shoulder again, and Cade and Connor slip into the hallway, magic wreathing their bodies. Immediately, shouts erupt and I hear the crash of magic as it slams into walls. Kai grabs my hand and drags me the other direction down the hallway, toward Sterling's cell. I count the doors as we go, trying to distract myself from the battle being waged behind us. Two against five. *Please, please let them be okay.*

A single guard stands outside of Sterling's room. Blue lights twine around his arms as we approach. Kai rushes forward, dodging the blasts of magic with his inhuman speed and reflexes. He's on the mage faster than I can blink, but the mage is prepared. He has some sort of shield around him and Kai can't get to his neck with his fangs. I watch with my heart in my throat as they fall into a fist fight, with the occasional burst of blue magic.

Glancing behind me, I see Connor and Cade have taken out three of the five guards. But the last two are proving more difficult. Connor is limping, and blood dips down Cade's eye from a cut in his forehead. An urgency has built in my chest. The closer I get to Sterling, the more the need to get to him grows.

Inching forward, I keep a close eye on Kai and his opponent. When I reach Sterling's door, I push it open and slip inside, closing it behind me. All the breath in my lungs leaves me at the sight.

Sterling is laying on the ground curled in a ball facing away from me. He's naked and bloodied. Burns criss-cross his back and blood pools underneath him. His silver hair is matted and stained red.

The ground slides out from under me and I hit the floor hard. Drew flaps his wings to maintain his balance. I can't help but imagine curly blond hair, soaked in blood, with a gaping wound on her neck. My realities collide, and I feel myself spiraling down a dark hole I know won't be able to climb out of alone. A peck on my ear pulls me from my panic, and I take a deep breath. The copper scent of Sterling's blood fills the room. With my entire body shaking, I crawl to him. His blood is cool under my palms and I have to push away the memory of me doing exactly this with my mom.

"Sterling?" I whisper, my voice shaking as hard as my body. "Sterling?"

No response. I hold my breath and reach my hand out to rest on his shoulder, careful to avoid any of his injuries. His skin is hot, hotter than even a shifter's skin should be. I don't want to roll him over. His back is blistered and raw, so I crawl around him. With a shaky hand, I brush his hair from his face. Cupping his cheek, I try again. "Sterling. I'm here." I lean down and press a gentle kiss to his cheek. "We're all here, and we're going to get you out."

His eyes flutter and my heart leaps in my chest. I catch a sliver of his icy blue eyes before he tenses and closes them again. "El..." His voice is hoarse and he trails off before he can finish saying my name.

"Shh. It's okay. Everything is going to be okay now." I keep brushing his hair back, because I don't know what else to do. What is taking them so long? Has something happened? I distract myself by talking to Sterling. "When we get you all healed up, you better fucking bond with me. I won't take no for an answer."

"You ... need to ... go." Each word is labored and he has to stop for breath between each one.

"I can't go without you. Kai will be here in a minute and we'll get you out."

"Leave ... me ... please." He groans and his entire body shudders. "I'm ... dying."

I'm dying. No. No, he can't be dying. We got to him in time. I won't accept any other outcome. The fear that spreads through my body lights me up inside. The blood in my veins boils, burning every bit of fear and anxiety to ash, leaving nothing in its wake but determination.

A golden light flickers over Sterling's body and Drew squawks, flapping his wings to get away from me. I raise my hands and find them wreathed in golden flames. A smile grows across my face and the door to Sterling's cell opens.

30. Malakai

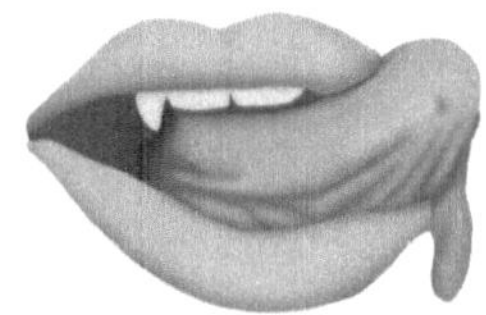

I watch Ellis slip into Sterling's cell and I take a breath. She should be safe in there from any random attack. I need to get this guy down, but he has some sort of shield protecting him. I can't get my fangs anywhere near his neck.

Dodging another blow laced with magic, I get in a good shot with my elbow. Bone crunches and blood sprays from the mages now broken nose. He stumbles back a step and gives me the moment I need to grab his head in both of my heads. With a grunt, I twist until his neck snaps. I let his body fall to the ground, and I turn in the direction of Cade and Connor. They are down to the last mage, but he's powerful. Between both of them, they are struggling to get a hit in on him.

Sprinting down the hallway, I use my vampire speed to blur past them and barrel into the mage. I take him to the ground, with my hands around his head, prepared to snap his neck like the last guy. He's fast though. Faster than a mage should be. He kicks me off him and I fly through the air, hitting the wall hard enough to make my vision blur. *What the fuck?* A typical mage shouldn't have that kind of speed or strength.

He levels a hand at me, blue light flaring in his palm.

"Get down!" Cade yells.

I duck, right as violet light streaks above my head. It would have been a perfect shot, but the mage jumps to the side, avoiding the hit entirely. However, Cade's attack gives me the space to duck into an open room. Chest heaving, I take a moment to catch my breath, and try to figure out what the hell is going on. The only thing I can think of is this must be some part of Sam's project. Maybe enhancing supernatural strengths? Whatever it is, this guy is definitely part of some kind of experiment.

I pull my phone from my pocket, keeping my attention on the doorway, and call Cade.

"You okay?" he asks when he picks up.

"What the fuck is that thing? He's not a normal mage."

Cade laughs, but it's lacking in humor. "Yeah, tell me about it. He almost got both Connor and me. We need a plan."

"What if you two distract him. There is no way he can defend himself against two magical attacks and me. Right?"

"Fuck. I hope not." Cade relays this information to Connor, who is apparently in the same room as him "Okay. We'll wait for your signal. Keep low and to the right. We'll aim our attacks high and to the left."

"Alright. Let's do this."

I slide my phone back in my pocket and creep to the edge of the door. With my hearing, I can tell the mage is shifting back and forth on his feet. I wonder why he hasn't made a move to attack us? He has to know where we are. As I peer around the doorframe, the mage is staring down the hall, and his eyes ... I shudder when I get a good look at them. They are eerily blank. The blue of his magic sizzles through his irises like lightning, but there is no thought, no life, behind them. This guy is like a fucking robot.

I catch Cade peering around a door further down the hall behind me, and I nod my head. Red and violet light spears straight for the mage as both he and Connor jump out from the room. I dart into the hallway, keeping low, and rush the mage. He's distracted keeping Cade and Connor at bay, so I drop to my knees and slide behind him, twisting at the last second. I pop up and grab his head, twisting until I hear his bones snap. I drop him like a sack of stones.

"Is he dead?" Connor asks?

I stare at him for a moment longer, just to make sure. With that dead look in his eyes, I wouldn't be surprised to see him rise from the ground. "I think so."

"Ellis?" Cade asks.

"In Sterling's cell."

We run down the hall, and I push open the door, stopping in my tracks.

She's kneeling next to him. Golden flames billowing from her body. Her hair floats around her head, the atmosphere in the room reminding me of the way the air feels right before a lightning strike. And her beautiful amber eyes are streaked with gold light.

She's a fucking goddess.

Her beauty freezes me. The power that radiates from her makes my blood sing. My fangs ache as desire sweeps through me. I want to shove her against the wall and fuck her sensless. Cade shoves me to the side and I snap out of the hold she has on me. My gaze drops to Sterling and my heart sinks to my stomach. *No.*

Cade falls to his knees and hovers his hands over Sterling's still body. His magic flares then stutters outs. He turns to me with concern creasing his brows. "We need to get him out of here. Now. I can't risk healing him where we can be caught. But every second is going to count."

I can read between those lines, and I wish I couldn't. Grimacing, I bend down to pick him up. There isn't a part of him that hasn't been beaten, cut, or burned. This is going to hurt him. Before I can scoop him into my arms, Ellis growls. Her flames flare brighter and she fixes me with her golden stare.

I raise my hands and back away. "Whoa. It's okay, Ellis. It's me." I keep my voice calm and soothing. No thrall, though. For all I know, when she's like this it will only make things worse. 'I'm not going to hurt him. We need to get him out of here so Cade can heal him.”

Her body is tense, her gaze unwavering from me. With her top lip peeled back in a silent snarl, I expect to see fangs descending. Maybe one day she’ll get them. How hot would that be? *Not the fucking time, asshole.*

“Baby girl,” I whisper.

At the use of my nickname for her, she blinks and recognition flares in her eyes. “Kai.” She glances behind me. “Cade.” Tears pool in her eyes, and it’s like they calm the fire inside her. The flames wink out in the blink of an eye. She sags to the ground and Cade rushes to her and wraps an arm around her waist.

“Okay,” he says. “Get Sterling, and let’s get out of here.”

I scoop Sterling into my arms as carefully as I can. Still, he moans slightly as the burns on his back touch my leather jacket. “I’m sorry, bro. I’m so fucking sorry.”

With Sterling in my arms and Cade holding Ellis’s hand, we follow Drew as he flies through the building. We make it up the steps and onto the first floor before trouble finds us. Ellis stumbles as her gaze lands on Sam standing in the middle of the hallway.

He grins at her. “Ellis, doll. I’ve missed you so much.”

A soft whimper escapes her, and if it weren’t for me carrying Sterling, I’d destroy the fucking bastard on the spot. Cade tucks Ellis behind him, and Connor steps around us, getting between Cade and Sam.

Sam ignores Connor, his gaze glued to my beloved. “I’ve missed that warm, tight, pu—”

Cade blasts a beam of magic around Connor. Sam ducks, and when he stands back up, his grin is gone.

“I’ve let you have your fun with my fiancé. But your time is up. I’ll be taking her back now.” He extends a hand in Cade’s direction, but he doesn’t get a chance to fire off his magic.

Drew swoops down from above, beak aiming for one of Sam’s eyes. In his moment of distraction fending off the crow, Connor attacks. Cade doesn't wait to see how this game will play out. He drags Ellis into a room and I follow. The sounds of battle from the hallway chase us as we run to the window and Cade shoves it open. He climbs out first, then helps Ellis. I glance behind me as Connor rushes into the room.

"Go! Hurry!"

Connor practically shoves me toward the window, and I pass Sterling off to Cade before climbing out. We run to the ward, and stop, waiting for Connor to get us through. I watch behind us, waiting for a sign of pursuit, but there is none. Motion catches my attention, and a black crow flies from a different window and takes off toward the direction of the Hummer.

Ellis's anxiety fuels my own. My foot taps the ground as I watch for Sam or another doped up mage. Ellis's pulse rattles in her wrist where my thumb rests against the thin skin there. My own heart echoes hers. It's almost painful how fast and hard it's beating.

"Go," Connor rasps, waving us forward.

I take one last glance behind us before dashing through the ward. Sam is standing in the window, slumped over, a hand pressing against a bleeding wound. With my supernatural sight, I can see the fury in his eyes. But he doesn't chase us. Something about that raises my hackles. It's like he knows he'll have another chance.

"Hurry up," I say, dragging Ellis toward the alley where the Hummer is parked. "Let's get Sterling back to the cabin."

31. Ellis

In the back of the hummer with Sterling's head on my lap and his legs on Connor's, I try my hardest to control my breathing. Kai is driving us back to the cabin, and the last thing I want is for my emotions to spill over to him while he's driving. It's hard though.

I can't stop looking at Sterling. His matted silver hair stained red. The cuts, bruises, and burns. His chest rises and falls so shallowly, there are times I think he stops breathing entirely. The heat radiating off of him soaks through my clothing, and I know every second that ticks by is one second closer to him not surviving.

My chest hurts. Every beat of my heart spreads paralyzing terror through my body. What if I lose him? What if we never get to really know each other? Despair climbs up my throat and I clutch my chest, unable to hold back the gasping sound that escapes. Cade turns back to look at me, but I hunch over Sterling's body, like I can keep his soul inside by sheer force of will.

"Hold on, Sterling," I whisper. "Please, hold on."

Drew flaps his wings on the floor by my feet. I meet his beady black gaze, and I swear I see sadness reflected in their dark depths.

I'm not the only one at risk of losing someone important to them. Sterling has friends and family who need him. He can't die.

When Kai turns off the road, the Hummer bounces and jolts as he drives up the mountain. It's not as bad as in the Charger, but it's still a rough ride. Sterling doesn't even make a sound. I press my hand to his chest and hold my breath. His heartbeat is so faint and uneven, skipping beats entirely.

"Hurry, Kai," I croak, even though I know he's driving as fast as he possibly can.

When we finally reach the cabin, Kai is out of the driver's seat faster than I can blink. My door opens and he hauls Sterling into his arms. I jump out and head for the door, where Allie is already standing with it wide open. The warm lights from the inside spill out onto the porch, and the soft glow is reflected in the grass from the windows.

"On the couch," Cade commands.

Kai lays Sterling on the couch, and I try to go to him, but Kai stops me. "Let Cade do his thing."

With Kai's arms around me, I watch, breath held, as Cade kneels on the floor and places his hands on Sterling's chest. Violet light spreads through his body, growing brighter and brighter each second. I blink against the brilliance. Sterling's body isn't even visible anymore in the glow. Cade's breathing grows more labored but he keeps pumping his magic into Sterling.

Cade wobbles, and Kai jumps in to hold him up. "Cade, stop."

He shakes his head. "Not enough." His words are a wet rasp in his chest, and the violet light grows even brighter. Cade grunts.

"Cade, that's enough," Kai says urgently.

"A little ... more."

Cade's light flares one more time before flickering, then disappearing entirely. His body slumps to the side and Kai catches him. I rush forward to Sterling and place my hand on his chest. His heart thumps steady and strong, but his skin is still too hot under my touch.

"He's still feverish," I say, looking at Kai.

Cade is unconscious in his arms, and hopelessness grows inside me. "Allie, can you do anything to help with the fever?" He hefts Cade higher, and stands. "I'm going to take Cade to the bed, then I'll come back for Sterling."

"I'll give him something for infection, and some advil." Allie digs through her bag, but looks up before pulling anything out. "I'll do it in the bedroom, where there's more room."

I nod distantly, and brush silver hair from his forehead, the heat searing my skin. "It's going to be okay, Sterling," I whisper in his ear. "I won't settle for anything less."

Kai's heavy footsteps sound on the stairs as he comes back down. I look up at him, and his shoulders sag when he meets my gaze. He says nothing, but he squeezes my shoulder before scooping Sterling into his arms. Allie and I follow him. Each step I take is like trudging through quicksand. I'm exhausted, terrified, desperate. So many different emotions, I don't know which one to focus on or how to fight them all.

In the bedroom, Kai lays Sterling next to Cade on the bed, and the sight of two of my Shields laying motionless side by side sends anxious energy through me. My fingertips tingle and I look down to see golden flames sparking to life.

"Kai," I whisper, his name tumbling from my trembling lips.

He turns to me, and his eyes widen. "Allie, can you take care of Sterling?" She must agree, I don't hear anything, but Kai approaches me and frames my face in both of his hands. "Ellis, you have to trust everything will work out. Cade healed him. Allie will make sure the infection doesn't spread. Everything will be okay. And when Cade wakes up, he can do more." He pulls me to his chest and wraps his arms around me, careless of the flames that are threatening to engulf me.

"Kai, can you help me for a second?" Allie asks.

We break apart, and I see Allie is placing an IV in Sterling's arm. Kai helps Allie hold the IV bag up while she secures it to the tall stand lamp by the bed, the only elevated place it will reach.

"That will have to do," she mutters, eyeing the half-assed IV pole. "This will help fight off whatever is causing the infection, hopefully. I have no idea why he still has one even after Cade's healing, or why his shifter nature hasn't kicked in." Her brow furrows as she studies Sterling.

"Who knows what Sam did to him or gave him." Kai stares at both of his friends for a second longer before turning to me again. "Why don't you go shower, Ellis. I'll make sure there's food for you when you get out."

Walking away from the bed is almost impossible. I don't want to leave them for even a second. But, I know Kai is right. I need to shower and eat, even if I don't feel like it. Arguing won't help the situation, and it will only stress Kai out more. I'm thankful he's here to take care of all of us. Without him, I'd fall to pieces.

"Thank you, Kai." I give him a quick kiss, and head to shower.

I intend for it to be quick, but the hot water feels amazing on my skin, especially as a fever takes hold and makes my body shake with chills. If this is the price to pay for using my magic, I will never use it again after all this shit is over. It's not worth it.

When I finally step out of the bathroom, I find Kai waiting with medicine for my fever and a bowl of soup.

"I figured the fever would be hitting soon." He looks at me shivering, and his lips thin as he presses them together.

I know they all hate this and not being able to do anything about it. But Kai offering me medicine before I even asked for it makes me want to cry. Even dealing with Cade and Sterling, he's making sure I'm taken care of.

I quickly eat the soup, while Kai goes back downstairs to ask Connor to lay a few more wards around the cabin. When I'm done, I set the bowl aside and climb into the bed. Someone, I'm guessing Kai, undressed both Cade and Sterling and covered them with a blanket. Sterling's injuries were healed with Cade's magic. Besides the fever, he looks like he's just sleeping. Albeit with bloody, matted hair. The need to wash it hits me suddenly, so I climb back out of bed and grab a towel, a cup of water, shampoo, and a brush. It's not ideal, but it's the best I can do.

When Kai enters the room, he sighs when he sees me shivering and wincing as I run the brush through Sterling's hair, trying to wash out the blood. "Ellis," he says gently, and grabs the brush from my trembling fingers. "You need to rest."

"But, his ha—"

"His hair isn't hurting him," he says, and carefully pushes me into the bed between my guys. "Besides, he wouldn't want you fussing over his hair when you need to rest."

Damnit. He's right. And he knew saying that would be the one thing to convince me to lay down. Curling under the blanket, I carefully cuddle up to Sterling. The heat from his fever washes against my own. I almost laugh. Two peas in a pod. Reaching back with one arm, I grab Cade's hand and thread our fingers together. With my vampire watching over us, I fall into a restless sleep.

THE RED CARPET under my feet squishes with each step. Red carpet? I glance at the rug in confusion. It's supposed to be cream with flowers. Why is it red? I take another step and watch the crimson ooze between my toes. It's thick and sticky, and cool against my skin.

My gaze follows the rug, climbing the stairs. More red is puddled on the treads. I step in each one, fascinated by the contrast of the bright color against my tan skin. At the top of the stairs, two bodies lay sprawled on the wooden floor, a floor now soaked in the same red liquid.

I recognize the blond hair splayed out around the first body's head. The curls are the same as mine. Now, they're stained crimson.

"Mom?" It's so quiet in our house. My voice echoes, reverberating off of the wooden floors and walls. "What are you doing?"

I kneel next to her, the red soaking into my pants. It's so cold. I brush my mom's hair from her face. The sight is so unexpected and so gruesome. A scream tears from my throat.

I scream, and scream, but my mom doesn't open her eyes. I'm scared to look at the other body, but I force myself to take in the brown curly hair, the blood that's pooled around the body, and the unnatural angle of the limbs.

"Gracie?" I whisper.

Her head turns. Slowly and jerkily, like it's being pulled by a puppeteer. When she's facing me, her eyes open and there's nothing in her gaze but death. A grisly smile tugs at her lips, and I scream again.

Scrambling backward on my butt, I drag myself through the puddles of blood as Gracie pulls herself toward me with skeletal arms. Her head hangs at an unnatural angel, but her gaze pierces mine. Milky white eyes and a bloody smile bringing bile to the back of my throat.

"Help." The raspy whisper doesn't match the gruesome smile.

I swallow back the urge to vomit and continue scooting backward until my back hits the wall. Skeletal arms shake and rattle. One arm falls off, dropping from the shoulder socket and clattering to the wooden floor. The body falls, but the other arm keeps trying to pull her closer to me.

"Help."

"ELLIS, WAKE UP."

I jerk awake, gasping for breath. I slap my hand over my mouth and swallow repeatedly until the rolling of my stomach stops. Cade rubs my lower back through all of it, murmuring incoherent words that soothe the shaking of my limbs.

"Another dream?" he asks quietly.

I nod, afraid to open my mouth. Taking a deep breath makes me wince. I still ache. Cade's hand slides higher on my back, and I cry out, twisting away from his touch, as fire-like pain spreads from my spine outward.

"Shit, Ellis. What's wrong?" He sits up quickly, hands hovering over me like he's afraid to touch me.

"My back," I moan.

"Can I lift up your shirt?"

When I nod, he gently grabs the hem of Kai's shirt I threw on after my shower, and lifts it up. Cool air hits my fevered skin, making me shiver. The fabric sliding over my upper back makes me whimper. It's like millions of needles are being pricked into my flesh each time the fabric brushes it.

"There's nothing there," Cade mutters. Frustration laces his words, and he gently lowers the shirt. He places a hand on my forehead, and his magic sweeps through me like a warm breeze. "Have you taken anything for the fever?"

"I did before I fell asleep. I don't know how long ago that was. What time is it anyway?"

"I have no clue. I woke up right before you did."

I glance at him. The dark circles under his eyes are almost gone, but I know he'll need to eat to fully restore his magic. "Where's my phone?" I ask, glancing around the room. I spot it on the dresser and make to get up, but Cade puts a hand on my thigh.

"I can get it. Stay here." He climbs out of bed to get my phone, then sits on the edge. Instead of giving me my cell, he texts Kai himself. "Lay back down, love." He stands with a heavy sigh and raises his arms over his head to stretch.

I don't even have it in me to admire his naked body. My eyes are heavy and sandpapery. Each blink burns and a faint throbbing in the back of my skull matches my heartbeat. I feel like shit.

Cade pulls on a pair of sweats that were laying across the chair, and walks to Sterling's side of the bed. He kneels down and places a hand on his forehead. Violet light flares and sweeps through Sterling's body. His brow furrows and he pulls his lower lip between his teeth. "I don't get it," he mutters.

The chill that sweeps through me has nothing to do with my fever. "What's wrong?"

He shakes his head and sits back on his heels, eyes crinkled with confusion. Before I can ask him again, Kai pushes through the door.

"Hey, how're you feeling?" he asks, sitting on the edge of the bed.

"Shitty."

He gives me a small smile and holds out a couple of pills. "Take these. Are you hungry?"

"No." I swallow the pills with the water he also brought. "Cade won't tell me what's wrong with Sterling."

"There's something wrong?" Kai asks, turning his attention to the shifter's still body.

Cade releases a heavy breath. "I don't know," he admits grudgingly. "It's weird. I've healed him many times over the years, and I can always get a sense of his wolf lurking in the background. Now, it's like he's there but he's locked behind a door I can't get through. I really think that's what's causing his fever. He needs his wolf."

"What the hell does that even mean?" Kai asks. "How is his wolf locked away?"

"Sam."

I whip my head around at the broken, labored whisper. "Sterling," I say on a shaky breath.

His eyes are half opened, a hint of glacier blue peeking through. His throat works on a swallow and he grimaces.

I grab the cup of water from Kai. "Do you want some water?"

He nods shallowly and Cade helps to lift his head as I tip the cup against his parched lips. He sighs as the water slides down his throat. I pass the cup back to Kai, then brush my fingers over his stubbled cheek.

"What does Sam have to do with your wolf?" I ask quietly.

His arm trembles as he brings his hand up to brace my own on his cheek. "You're so hot, Kitten," he mumbles.

"Now's not the time for flirting," I say with an exasperated breath. "Why is your wolf locked away?"

One corner of his mouth pulls into a small smile. "Not flirting." Each word sounds labored, and he has to pause for breath. "Feverish. But you are hot."

I huff a sigh, and pull my hand away, only so I can tuck his hair behind his ear. "I'm fine. But, we're not talking about me right now. Answer my question."

"Bossy," he mutters, eyes falling shut. "Sam gave me some kind of injection." He talks slowly, pulling each word through layers of exhaustion and fever.

"An injection?" Cade repeats.

Sterling nods. "Everytime he sent me back to the cell. It made it impossible to reach my wolf."

Cade frowns and thinks through what Sterling said. "So, it sounds like we just have to wait for whatever that injection was to wear off. Then your wolf should be able to take care of the fever."

Sterling mumbles something that sounds like an agreement. His eyes peel open again and land on me. "Kitten, we need to talk."

My heart almost bursts from my chest at the use of his nickname for me. "We can talk later," I say. "You need to rest."

"So do you," Kai says, gently pushing on my shoulder to get me to lie down.

I glare at him, but I let him cover me up. Turning to Sterling, I cuddle against him. He grunts as he slides his arm around my lower back and tugs me closer. Tears burn the back of my eyes. I have wanted this for so long now, I just wasn't ready to admit it to myself. I place my hand on his chest, right over his heart beating steadily behind his ribcage.

My eyelids fall closed, and I'm distantly aware of Kai kissing my forehead and tucking me and Sterling under the blanket. Then sleep claims me.

32. Ellis

The tickle of something in my hair wakes me. On instinct, I scoot closer to the body next to me and inhale. Pine and night air fill my nose and I jolt all the way awake. It's not Kai or Cade sleeping next to me, it's Sterling. And by the fingers twirling through my curls, he's awake. He's awake and not pulling away. *Is this progress?*

"Sterling?" I ask tentatively, afraid he'll bolt.

"Hmm?"

I shift so I can look at him, but still keep my head on his shoulder. "How are you feeling?"

His arm tightens around me as he says, "Better. When I woke up my wolf was back." He sighs heavily, as if being able to sense his wolf again takes away some of his stress. "How are you feeling?" He places his free hand on my forehead. "You're still hot."

My lips twitch. "Thank you."

A small laugh rumbles in his chest under my palm. "Don't be a smart ass. How are you feeling?" he asks again.

Emotion bubbles up inside of me. This entire interaction seems so ... normal. Like something I would have with Cade or

Kai. I'm scared of the hope that flutters to life in my belly. I'm not sure how I would handle his rejection again, especially after this.

I shrug my shoulder. "I feel okay. Just a little cold and achy." It's not the worst I've felt during one of these weird fevers, but it does seem to have lasted the longest.

"Are you feeling up to talking?" His heart pounds under my palm, harder than it was just a few moments ago.

"Yes." I sit up, holding back my wince as my sore muscles protest the movement. I scoot to the head of the bed and lean against it carefully. It doesn't hurt my back, so I relax and tug the blanket up. The chills are still making me cold.

Sterling pushes himself to a sitting position so he's facing me, and he pulls the other half the blanket over his naked lap. I catch myself frowning, and quickly wipe it away. Now is not the time for that.

"Ellis—"

I shake my head. "No," I say. "Let me go first. Please?"

He studies me for a minute with his icy blue eyes, before running a hand through his hair, wincing as it gets caught in a bloody mat. He sighs and nods.

I take a breath, clearing my head and trying to think through what I want to say. I have no clue how to make him believe me. What words do I need to convince him? I look into his eyes, and just go with what's in my heart. "I know you think I changed my mind after meeting your family. And in a way I did." He stiffens and I quickly shake my head. "Not for the reasons you're thinking. I mean, yes, I want to help your family and your pack, but that's not the reason I changed my mind.

"It was something your mom said. She said 'Fate will always find a way.' And it really made me think. You didn't choose to be there that night." I swallow thickly and blink back the tears that build on my lashes. I don't think I'll ever be able to talk about that night without crying. "But fate put you in that position to meet me. Your mate. And it wasn't the right time. I would have never gone with you. I was only sixteen and my life would have just crumbled down around me."

Sterling reaches out as if to wipe away the tear that escaped, but he stops himself.

"Then, fate put you back into my life ten years later. I know if I walk away from you right now, sometime down the road, fate would try again. I don't think she'll give up."

"But I don't want you to choose me because fate says so," he says fiercely. "I want you to choose me because you *want* me. And how the hell could you possibly want me after what I did? Ellis, I'll never forgive myself for not telling you, and for letting things go that far. You deserve so much better than that. *Than me.*"

I shake my head. "No. Don't say that. It's not true. Besides, I've thought a lot about that. You made a mistake in not telling me, and yeah, it hurt. A lot. But, people make mistakes." I look at my hands in my lap and fiddle with the blanket. "And, I kind of forced you to sleep with me."

Sterling jerks, his eyes widening. "Like hell you did."

"It's true. I wouldn't take no for an answer. I kept at you until you caved."

"I didn't have to cave, Ellis. That was my choice."

I shake my head again. "I don't think it was. Not really. The mate bond is ... a lot. You were fighting against so much. The bond, your wolf, your own desire. I know it had to have worn you down. I'm impressed you held out as long as you did."

"Ellis, that's not—"

"If I hadn't pushed you that night, it wouldn't have happened. That's on me, Sterling." My words are firm, leaving no room for him to argue. I take a deep breath and say quietly, "And I'm sorry. I put a lot of pressure on you, and I made everything worse."

"You have nothing to apologize for." His eyes are gentle, and I want to dive into them and never re-surface.

"Either way, I am sorry. And I say all of that because I'm trying to make you understand that I *do* want you." My throat clogs with tears and I have to swallow before I can continue. His form blurs in front of me as tears build on my lashes and spill over down my cheeks. "I want you so fucking bad it hurts. Cade and Kai are just two parts of me. There's a third part that's been missing. It's like a gaping wound that will never heal." I wipe away my tears, and embarrassingly, the snot as well. My chest heaves with my sobs, and each one sends pain through my feverish body. "I don't know how else to tell you. What else I need to do to make you understand. And I'm so scared you're going to walk away and ..." I trail off as words become too hard to get out around my gasping breaths.

"Ellis," Sterling breathes. The bed dips under his weight as he scoots closer to me.

When his arms come around me, and he scoops me into his lap, the little control I had over my emotions evaporates. I bury my face against his chest and let the tears fall. All of the fear, hurt, and hope comes pouring out of me. I'm helpless to stop it, so I just let him hold me as I purge my body of everything that's been building up inside.

Drawn by the surge of emotions I'm throwing out into the universe, Kai opens the door and slips inside. "Everything okay?"

I nod and huff a snotty laugh. "Yeah?" I still don't have an answer from Sterling, so I'm not sure if everything is okay.

"How's your fever?"

Sterling brushes his hand across my forehead. "Still hot." Before I can make a smart ass remark, he says, "Fever hot."

Kai pulls some meds from his pocket like he's decided to walk around with them just in case. "Here, take these." He grabs a paper cup from the bathroom and fills it for me. "I'll give you guys some privacy. Let me know if you need anything."

"Actually," Sterling says, "I have something that all of you need to hear." He shifts me on his lap so he can look at me better. "And you need to hear this before you make any decisions on the bond."

Dread fills me like ice being poured in my veins. How much

more can I handle? Not a lot, at this point. Kai hollers for Cade, and he hops up on the dresser while we wait. Once Cade is seated on the edge of the bed, Sterling gives me one last squeeze, like he's scared it will be the last one, and sets me back against the headboard. I draw my knees to my chest, hoping I can make myself small enough to avoid whatever words I know are going to hurt.

"Fuck, there is no easy way for me say this." Sterling runs his hand through his hair and curses when his fingers get stuck again. He looks at me, and I shrink further into myself at the deep well of sadness in his eyes. "Sam was trying to get me to tell him where you were, along with collecting my blood for who the fuck knows what reason. I never told him. My first instinct was to keep you safe, no matter what he did to me."

I bite my lower lip to keep from saying something. I can't imagine what he went through, and all because he refused to tell Sam where I was. Tears well in my eyes again, but I blink them away.

"When torturing me didn't work, he changed tactics. Ellis, he has your sister. She's alive."

He has your sister. She's alive.

I've been on a boat a few times in my life. One time, the weather turned too quickly for us to make it back to shore before the storm hit. The feeling of the boat rising high on a wave before plunging down the other side is exactly what I'm feeling now. My stomach drops so fast it makes my head spin. The room wobbles alarmingly and I grab the blanket in my fists like it will keep me upright.

"What?" The word scrapes up my throat, and I blink at Sterling. "That's not ... she can't be ..."

I don't realize I'm not breathing until Kai hops from the dresser and crouches on the bed in front of me. His eyes take on an eerie glow as he uses his compulsion. "Breathe, Ellis."

I gasp, a shuddering breath that hurts my chest and throat. "I don't understand," I rasp.

"How is that possible?" Cade asks, scooting to sit next to me against the headboard. He takes my hand in his, his finger warm and comforting. "There were two bodies found, right?"

Sterling shrugs. "At this point, I wouldn't be surprised to learn the reports had been falsified. Noah was there that night. He's obviously invested in whatever is happening at the warehouse."

"It actually all makes sense now," Kai says. He scoots back to be able to see all of us better. "I never understood why Noah would let Ellis live that night. But, he had Grace to keep him occupied, and the knowledge that Ellis was still alive and could be used when needed."

"How do we know it's really her?" Cade asks.

"She looks just like Ellis," Sterling says quietly, tracing my features as he talks. "The same brown curls, the same facial structure. It was like seeing Ellis there." He swallows and looks down at his hands in his lap. "Sam used her to try to get me to talk." He glances back up, eyes shining with unshed tears. "She mouthed the words 'Don't give in,' before Sam ... before he ..."

I cover my mouth with a shaky hand. "What did he do to her?" I whisper. It doesn't take a lot for my imagination to conjure the possibilities. I went through my own torture at Sam's hands.

Sterling's eyes soften. "Not the same. But, Ellis, I'm sorry. I let it happen. He wanted me to give in. He hoped watching my mate's sister being—" he cuts off and swallows. "I didn't give in, Ellis. I couldn't. I let him hurt your sister, and I did nothing to stop it. My only thought was to protect you."

The pain in his voice is what draws me from the fog of disbelief. I blink away the tears, and focus on my mate. If I had Kai's empath abilities, I know what I would feel from him. Guilt. Regret. Sorrow. And the most prominent, fear. He's scared I'm going to change my mind after hearing he didn't stop Sam.

"Sterling," I whisper. My limbs tremble as I crawl toward him.

"This doesn't change anything. You did what you had to, and I don't blame you for it."

"How can you possibly say that?"

"Because I would have done the same thing." It hurts to admit that, but it's true. "Your safety will always be my priority, just like mine is for you. I get it." And I do. Cade is the same with his family. The four of us, we are the most important people in each other's lives now. And I'm okay with that.

His eyes are wide, and I'm not sure he's breathing as he reaches a hand out to brush his fingers along my cheek. They tremble slightly. "You haven't changed your mind?"

Despite what I just learned, despite everything that has yet to come, I find myself smiling. "I haven't changed my mind," I whisper.

His chest hitches on a breath, and he drags me to his chest. "We'll get her out," he promises. "We'll get her out, Ellis."

"I DON'T UNDERSTAND why she's still feverish," Cade says quietly.

I know they're trying to keep their voices low so they don't wake me, but they woke me up twenty minutes ago with their hushed conversation. The fever has not gone away, yet. It's not as bad as it could be, but it still sucks. All I want to do is sleep, but even that is difficult with my shivering and aching muscles.

"How long has it been?" Sterling asks. He's sitting next to me in the bed. As far as I'm aware, he hasn't moved from this spot.

"Almost twenty-four hours." Kai's tone is somber, missing his usual laughter. It's almost enough to make me blow my cover in an attempt to comfort him. "And I know you're awake, Ellis."

Rats. I open my gritty eyes and stare at him. "How'd you know?"

He huffs. "Your emotions are all over the place. Your heart rate is increasing. Your breathing is uneven. Shall I go on?"

"Fuck off," I mutter as I snuggle back under the blankets.

"Are you hungry?" Cade's fingers brush over my forehead. "You've hardly eaten."

I don't feel like answering him. All of my energy has been sucked away by this fever, along with the discovery of my sister still being alive. The effort it would take to answer him, let alone actually eat, is not worth it. I close my eyes and try to fall back asleep, but their conversation keeps me awake.

"Sterling, do you think you can get in contact with that old shifter?" Kai asks. "Maybe she'll have answers."

"It's worth a shot," he agrees. The bed shifts as Sterling climbs out, and I want to grab him to keep him next to me, but again, that would take too much effort.

"Ellis," Cade says softly. "Will you at least drink something?"

I don't answer. Finding the words and dragging them up my throat is like staring at a vast desert expanse and hoping to find a specific grain of sand—daunting and impossible. The very thought weighs my limbs down until it's impossible to move.

"Allie is still here," Cade continues. "She's really worried about you. We're all worried about you. If you don't start eating and drinking, Allie will have to give you an IV."

I try to grunt my acknowledgement of their concern, but I don't think I succeed. I'm not trying to worry them, but I just can't bring myself to do *anything*.

"Drew is going to pick up Agatha and bring her here," Sterling says as he comes back to the room. The bed dips as he settles to my left again. I try to reach for him on instinct, but my arms don't seem to want to move. "It's okay," he whispers, tucking my hair behind my ear. "We're going to make sure you're okay."

33. STERLING

Ellis's words have been on repeat since our conversation. She wants me. She's choosing me and the bond. Despite everything that's happened and everything I've done, I'm going to get the chance to be with my mate. If only this fever would break.

Since I woke up over a day ago, I've only left her side long enough to shower and only because Cade convinced me to. Honestly, getting all that blood out of my hair and combing out the tangles made me feel ten times better.

Propped on my elbow, I trace my mates features with my eyes. I've spent countless times watching her from afar, making sure she was safe. I've always thought she was gorgeous, but up close her beauty steals my breath. I only wish her amber eyes were open so I could see them sparkle when she looks at me.

My phone dings, and I check the screen. It's a message from Drew saying he's at the base of the mountain with Agatha. They'll be here in twenty minutes. I quickly shoot off a text to Cade and Kai letting them know. I'm grateful they've given me some time alone with Ellis, even though she's mostly been sleeping. Just laying next to her eases some of the tightness in my chest and keeps my wolf somewhat calm.

Kai pokes his head in the room and I glance at him. "Still no change?" he asks. His usual grin is gone, replaced by a frown that pulls his brows down over his gray eyes.

I shake my head and his frown deepens. All three of us are anxious balls of energy, and I imagine Kai is even worse, filtering mine and Cade's worry as well. "Agatha will be here soon."

"What if she doesn't have the answers we need?" His question is so quiet, I wouldn't have heard it if it weren't for my supernatural hearing.

I don't have an answer for him, though. Because in my mind, that isn't an option. I just got my mate. I'm not losing her now.

There is a knock on the front door downstairs, and my heart picks up. I should get up and greet Agatha. As an elder shifter, she deserves that at the very least, but I stay where I am and let Cade help the old woman up the steps.

I haven't seen Agatha in years. The last time was right before I left pack lands for good. Subconsciously, I rub my scar. If it weren't for her, I'd probably have lost my eye that night. She's aged quite a bit. Even back then, deep wrinkles carved lines through her face. Now, her wrinkles have wrinkles. Long white hair, tied back with a red ribbon, hangs to her waist in loose tangles. Her frame is hunched over, and her gnarled hands grasp a cane for support. Cade leads her to a chair we pulled over to the bed, and each step looks labored. This woman has to be the oldest shifter alive.

"Agatha," I say from my spot on the bed, bowing my head in respect.

"It's good to see you again, Sterling." Her voice is hoarse and raspy, but still strong. Pale green eyes study me for a minute before dropping to Ellis. "So," she says, steepling her fingers in front of her mouth. "This is the one you had Drew ask me about? The woman who has apparently bonded to three different men?"

"It is." I wait for Cade and Kai to settle in the room. Kai on the dresser, and Cade next to me on the bed. "We went to the library and found the book you mentioned to Drew. She's a harpy." I don't mince my words. There is no point in beating around the bush, and the sooner we get to the root of the problem, the sooner my mate will be back to herself.

Agatha's eyes pop wide, deepening the creases in her forehead. "A harpy," she breathes. "It's been a long time since a harpy has walked in this world."

Kai leans forward from his perch. "Do you know anything about them? We learned a bit from the book, but we still have so many questions."

Agatha nods distractedly. Her gaze travels over Ellis's body. "You three are her Shields."

"We are," I say, and it doesn't escape my notice the pride in my voice, or the way Cade and Kai's shoulders straighten. It's a title all three of us proudly accept and do everything in our power to ensure her safety.

"Shields give the harpy their magic. Ellis should be able to use all three of your powers. In addition, she'll have some of her own. With each bonding, Ellis's power will grow."

"We've noticed that," Cade says, running his hand through his hair. "But, each time she uses any magic, she ends up with a fever. Typically, it only lasts a few hours. This one has lasted over a day."

Agatha runs a calculating gaze over the three of us. "She has accepted all three bonds?" Her eyes land on Ellis's neck, and the very obvious bite mark from Kai, before rising to meet mine. Knowing swirls in the pale green depths.

Heat climbs up my chest, and I rub the back of my neck. "Well, she just accepted our bond last night."

Agatha's eyes drop back to Ellis's neck. When she looks at me again, one white eyebrow is cocked in question.

"I haven't marked her yet," I ground out. "She's had a fever. It hardly seems appropriate."

Agatha hums in her throat. "Then the bond isn't official. Until she has secured all three bonds, her magic will take a toll on her body. All magic comes at a cost."

"That's it?" Cade asks with a frown. "With the acceptance of all three bonds, the fevers will stop?"

"And she'll come into her power in full," Agatha confirms.

"You mean she's not at full power yet?" Kai asks, eyes wide on his beloved. "Holy shit." A slow grin spreads across his face.

"But ... how can I mark her when she's sick?" I look at Ellis, with her skin pale and eyes bruised with fatigue.

"I can give you the recipe for a tea that will hold the fever at bay long enough for you to mark her." Agatha's arms tremble as she pushes herself to her feet. Cade jumps up and rushes to her side. "When she's feeling better, I'd love to meet her."

"I'm sure she'd love to meet you, too," I say and follow her and Cade down the stairs.

Allie is pacing in the living room, hands clenched in front of her. "Is she going to be okay?"

"She'll be fine," Cade reassures her with a small smile. "What ingredients do we need?"

Agatha lists off five ingredients and Cade writes them down. "Give it to Drew," Agatha says. "He'll be able to get you everything you need." With Agatha's hand on my arm, I lead her to the front door. "I'm keeping an eye on your mom, Sterling."

My breath catches in my throat, and it hurts to swallow past the lump. "Is she doing okay?" I'm scared to hear the answer.

"Okay enough." Agatha studies me with her all-seeing gaze. "With your mate, you could take back control of the pack."

I sigh as the weight of all of our problems settle on my shoulders once again. "There is so much we need to do. And Cole ..." I trail off, unable to continue with that train of thought.

"Don't worry about your brother," she says, patting my arm. "He'll come around. But, the pack needs you. Don't forget that."

I hand her off to Drew who is waiting on the porch, and thank her for all of her help. Cade gives Drew the list of ingredients and we head back inside. To our harpy.

———

NERVOUS ENERGY FIRES through my body making me fidgety. I'm never fidgety and I hate the way it feels. We forced a nasty mixture of tea down Ellis's throat an hour ago. Her fever broke and she woke feeling more like herself. At least that's what she said. Currently, she's in the shower and I'm waiting like a nervous teenager about to have sex for the first time.

I explained to her what Agatha said, about me having to mark her for the bond to be complete and for her to come into her powers fully. Even with her previous words echoing in my head, I held my breath, waiting for her to change her mind. She didn't. So now I'm waiting for her to shower, so we can finally accept this bond between us.

When the bathroom door opens and she steps out wrapped in a towel, my mouth goes dry. This is the moment I have been waiting for for ten years. I can't believe it's actually happening.

Her small smile drops and she climbs onto the bed. Placing her hand on my cheek, she says, "What's wrong?" Her amber eyes search mine, and I want to let them swallow me.

I don't realize I'm crying until her thumb wipes away a tear. "This is something I never thought would happen. For years, I've dreamt of this moment, but never once thought it would come to pass. I don't deserve this. I don't deserve *you*."

She shakes her head. "That's not true, Sterling. You deserve all of it."

I'm not prepared for her climbing onto my lap and claiming my mouth, but I quickly wrap my arms around her and pull her closer. She tastes like the minty toothpaste in the bathroom, and she smells like heaven. Lavender and vanilla wrap around me and my wolf growls at the scent of his mate.

Ellis pulls away, breathing slightly uneven. "Mark me, Sterling. Make me yours."

The words make me shudder and anticipation grows in my chest. I slowly lower her backward to the bed and pull the towel away, exposing her beautiful body. My fingers shake as I trace the curve of her jaw and the line of her collar bone. Her nipples pebble and she arches her back with a breathy sigh.

Bending my head down, I run my tongue over one peak while I roll the other between my thumb and pointer. Her fingers tangle in my hair, holding me in place. She feels amazing under me, and I want to memorize every inch of her. I want to take my time, and make her writhe underneath me. I want her to beg and scream my name. But I'm craving her too much, I don't think I have the willpower to draw this out.

I use my knee to spread her legs and kiss my way down her belly. Her fingers catch in the knots in my hair, and the stinging of my scalp only adds to all the sensations building inside me. The first lick makes us both moan. She tastes better than I ever could have imagined. I'll never get enough of it for as long as I live. Her hips buck as she searches for more, so I add two fingers and smile against her when she cries out.

"Sterling," she pants. "I don't want to wait anymore, please."

I make her wait for another minute while I taste her. It's not enough, but I can't deny my mate what she wants. Crawling up her body, I wipe my mouth on my shoulder and meet her gaze. Her pupils are blown, and heat courses through me at the look of pure desire on her face. I kick off my sweats and kiss her deeply.

Pulling away, I catch her gaze again. "Are you sure, Ellis?" I have to ask it one last time.

She wraps her legs around me, her wet heat rubbing against my aching cock. "I'm positive. I want you, Sterling. I want it all."

I'm pretty sure my scarred and cracked heart healed a little bit with those words. I'm barely breathing when I line myself up with her entrance. It's not the first time, but it feels like it is. It's the first time I've allowed myself to really sink into the emotions. I'm not hiding anything this time. There is no guilt weighing me down. There is only love and affection and hope swirling inside of me now. Her eyes fall closed as I slowly slide inside. Each inch is pure bliss as she surrounds me.

"Kitten," I breathe against her shoulder. "So fucking perfect."

My hips move on instinct. The need to claim her rising higher and higher. My wolf is pacing inside me, desperate to make sure it happens this time.

Each noise that falls from her lips make my thrusts harder and faster. And when she tilts her head to the side, gaze meeting mine, I lose all control. My wolf rises to the surface and I lick the side of her throat, opposite the side of Kai's mark.

"You're mine, Ellis. Mine to protect. Mine to love. Mine. Always." I punctuate each word with a thrust of my hips. Her fingers dig into my back, nails scraping as she leaves her own mark on my skin.

Letting my wolf to the surface, I graze my teeth along her neck before biting down. She cries out, my name falling from her lips. I bite down harder until I break the skin and her blood wells. My wolf greedily laps it up, tasting the very essence of our mate. I feel the bond shimmering inside my chest as it falls into place where it was always meant to be.

Ellis cries out again and her inner walls flutter around me. It sends pleasure along every nerve ending in my body, and my own orgasm hits me so hard I see stars.

When both of our breathing has finally calmed, I lift my head to look at her. A smile graces her lips, and her eyes are heavy with post-orgasmic bliss. My beautiful mate. Holy. Fuck. It finally happened. I have my mate. She accepted the bond, and it's there, in my chest. Shining like a golden thread woven between us. Wrapping her tight in my arms, I roll us over so her head is resting on my chest, and I soak in the feeling of her skin on mine.

34. STERLING

Her finger is cool as it traces my scar. "Where did you get this?" she asks lazily, her words soft and slow.

I don't usually like talking about that night, but with her there is no hesitation. I want her to know everything about me. "The night I was kicked out of the pack. My wolf fought it. He knew our rightful place was as alpha, and he didn't want to let it go. He forced the change on me, which was taken as a threatening move. Noah's nephew, Alex, shifted and our wolves fought. His claw sliced my face, and it was the only way I was able to get control of my wolf again. Agatha saved my eye. She could have been killed for it, but no one, not even Noah, is willing to go against her."

Ellis leans up on her elbow and gently kisses the bit of scar running through my eyebrow. "I'm so sorry. I can't imagine what it must have been like losing your family and your pack at the same time."

"It wasn't easy, but having Cade and Kai helped. Without them, I don't know what would have happened to me."

She lays her head back on my chest and her finger idly traces patterns on my skin. "When all of this is over, when we take care of Sam and Noah, will you take back your position as alpha?"

"That depends," I say, rubbing my palm up and down her back. Her skin is like velvet to the touch. "It's a big responsibility. I would never do it if it wasn't something you agreed to. And I don't want you agreeing to it just because you think it's what I want."

She huffs a laugh, her breath tickling across my chest. "You know me too well," she says quietly. "What *do* you want?"

I sigh and wrap a curl around my finger. "I don't know," I say truthfully. "I'm not sure I want to go back to a pack that essentially turned its back on me. I know there wasn't much they could do, but it still doesn't make the betrayal hurt less." She drops a kiss to my chest and presses herself tighter to my side. "I've lived my life thinking there was no way I could go back. I'd accepted the fact. I don't mind the life I've built with Cade and Kai ... minus the work for Kai's dad. And now with you, the possibilities of what our lives could be, are endless. At least, once we get everything taken care of. Whatever decision I make, will be one discussed with everyone. We're all in this together now."

"I'll be happy with any decision you make. As long as I'm with all three of you, I'll be happy." Her words are getting slower, and her fingers no longer trace idle patterns on my chest.

"Go to sleep, Kitten," I say, kissing the top of her head. "It's been a long couple of days."

She snuggles against me, warm and inviting, and I close my eyes. The thread of gold between us shining brightly.

———

I'M DYING. It's so hot. The feather blanket over me is heavy and sweltering. My body temperature always runs higher being a shifter, so I never use feather blankets. What the hell possessed me to use one last night?

Last night. I smile. I finally claimed my mate. I sense her behind me. Her skin warm against my own. If I wasn't so hot, I'd lay here forever. Stretching, I roll over and yawn. Something soft falls into my mouth and I splutter, trying to spit out whatever it is. But as soon as I get it out, another one falls in.

"What the fuck," I mutter around a mouthful of soft fluff. Opening my eyes, I see only white. The blanket is pulled over my head. Dragging it down over my face, my eyes slowly grow wider and wider. "What. The. Fuck."

Slowly, I climb out of bed, careful not to wake Ellis. I stare at my mate, mouth hanging open in disbelief. Wings. Snow white wings threaded with gold, sprout from her back. They're huge. One has fallen to the floor while the other, the one that had been covering me, spreads across the bed, the ends trailing along the wooden floor on the other side of the bed.

I quickly text the guys, and wait. Gaze trailing over Ellis, taking in every detail. Their steps falter when they enter the room.

"What the fuck?" Kai breathes, echoing my own thoughts just a few minutes ago. "Wings? When did that happen?"

I shrug, never taking my eyes off Ellis. "I woke up and there they were."

"She is going to freak out," Kai says.

That's an understatement. I finally manage to pull my gaze from her and look at Cade. I can only assume his expression mirrors my own. Utter shock, disbelief, and awe line his features. His violet eyes glow with something I can't name.

"What do we do?" Kai asks.

"What can we do?" Cade finally says. "We will need to keep her calm when she wakes up."

Like his words were magic, Ellis stirs. The three of us freeze, unsure how to proceed. She tries to roll over, but the massive wing prevents her. A confused mumble climbs up her throat and her eyes open. Slowly, they grow in size until white shows all the way around her irises.

"What is that?" Her voice is shaky and unsure. She sits up, faster than any of us anticipated, and her wings slash through the room. "What is that?" Her voice rises an octave.

Jumping to her feet, she turns around, trying to get a look at her back. Kai and I duck, but Cade is too slow. Her wings knock him to the floor, and he lands with a muffled curse on his ass. When she turns back to face us, her skin is pale and her amber eyes are terrified.

"What is that!" she screams. Her body shakes as tremors take over.

Kai finds his voice first. "Wings. You have ... wings."

She chokes on the breath she takes. "Wings?" she screeches. "Why do I have wings? Make them go away. Make them go away!" Tears pool in her eyes and she flaps her hands like she's trying to rid herself of something sticky.

Her tears hit me like a knife to my chest and I jump into action. "Breathe, Kitten. It's okay. It's going to be okay." I grab her shoulders, but my gaze falls behind them. To the wings.

"Okay? How is it going to be okay? I have wings!" The tears stream down her face now, and she's shaking so hard the feathers flutter behind her. The golden veins threading through them shimmer with the movement.

"You are so fucking beautiful," Kai breathes.

Her gaze snaps to him. I can see the words building, the disbelief that he can think she's beautiful, but she must see something in his expression. She looks to Cade, still sitting on the floor, then me. All of us staring at her with identical expressions of awe and adoration.

Her tears slow as she looks at us. Her breathing evens out. The tremble to her lips stops. "Wings?" she whispers.

"Beautiful wings," I say. Reaching behind her, I run my finger over the downy soft feathers and she shivers. "Can you feel that?"

She nods and wipes her cheeks, her wings shifting with the movement.

"Are they heavy?" Kai asks, stepping forward.

"No. I can't even feel them," she says between little hiccups. Tears well in her eyes again. "I can't walk around with wings." Her voice is so small and terrified.

Cade gets to his feet and stands on my other side. With her

three Shields before her, I see something shift in her gaze. A realization that she's not alone.

"We'll figure it out," I say quietly. "We'll always be here to help you figure things out. I promise. You're not alone anymore, Ellis. We've got you."

End.
For Now.

Acknowledgments

As always, thank you to my husband for the amazing amounts of support. If it weren't for him, these books would never see the light of day.

To my friends who constantly show me understanding when I disappear to write, edit, format, etc. Thank you and I love you!

To my Midnight Tide Publishing family who makes this entire process fun and exciting.

And finally... to you. As I always say, if it weren't for you, I wouldn't be writing. So keep reading, and I'll keep giving you the stories and spice you want!

About the Author

Whitney L. Spradling is a full time Occupational Therapist and autism mama, who has had a dream to write and publish a novel since she was a little girl. She lives outside of Cincinnati with her husband, son, and two cats. When she is not writing she can be found in her craft room making custom tumblers, or curled up with a good book and a cup of coffee (or glass of wine).

The Hunters of Ironport is a series set in the same universe as Witches of Moondale (just a town over), and thus will have crossover characters from time to time. That being said, it can be read separately if you so choose. For more information on how Hunters of Ironport and Witches of Moondale fit together please visit the author's website.

***

Frost Claim by Elle Beaumont and Candace Robinson

Sometimes, the beauty does claim a beast.

Aeryx is a warrior in Morozko's army, yearning to destroy those who brought ruin to his home. But when duty brings him to the human world, he encounters a problem. An intoxicating problem he wants nothing to do with.

A problem he can't resist.

Noel has rebelled for most of her life, and college is doing nothing to change that fact. Until one sorority night, when she witnesses the unthinkable and stumbles upon a monster from another realm. A monster who makes her question everything.

Including her desire for the beast.

Perfect for fans of Elizabeth Briggs, C.N. Crawford, Laura Thalassa, and Beauty and the Beast. Frost Claim is inspired by Krampus and book one in this fantasy romance series with enemies to lovers, plenty of banter, heavy steam, and sexy demons you won't be able to resist.